SPE… …EADERS

THE … …DATION
(registe… …er 264873)

was established in 1972 to provide funds for research, diagnosis and treatment of eye diseases. Examples of major projects funded by the Ulverscroft Foundation are:

- The Children's Eye Unit at Moorfields Eye Hospital, London
- The Ulverscroft Children's Eye Unit at Great Ormond Street Hospital for Sick Children
- Funding research into eye diseases and treatment at the Department of Ophthalmology, University of Leicester
- The Ulverscroft Vision Research Group, Institute of Child Health
- Twin operating theatres at the Western Ophthalmic Hospital, London
- The Chair of Ophthalmology at the Royal Australian College of Ophthalmologists

You can help further the work of the Foundation by making a donation or leaving a legacy. Every contribution is gratefully received. If you would like to help support the Foundation or require further information, please contact:

THE ULVERSCROFT FOUNDATION
The Green, Bradgate Road, Anstey
Leicester LE7 7FU, England
Tel: (0116) 236 4325

website: www.ulverscroft-foundation.org.uk

THE THEFT OF THE IRON DOGS

While hot on the heels of serial coupon-racketeer Gordon Ginner, Chief Inspector Macdonald of Scotland Yard receives word of an intriguing incident up in Lancashire — the summer cottage of local farmer Giles Hoggett has been broken into, with an assortment of seemingly random items missing which include a complete reel of salmon line, a large sack, and two iron dogs from his fireplace.

What first appears as a simple break-in quickly spirals into a mystery of contested land grabs for fishing between farmers, made all the more enticing to Macdonald when a body is then found in the river — the body of Gordon Ginner.

E.C.R. LORAC

THE THEFT OF THE IRON DOGS

Complete and Unabridged

BRITISH LIBRARY CRIME CLASSICS
Leicester

First published in Great Britain in 1946

This edition first published in Great Britain in 2023

First Ulverscroft Edition
published 2024
by arrangement with
Edwards Fuglewicz Literary Agency

*A catalogue record for this book is available
from the British Library.*

ISBN 978–1–4448–5288–2

Published by
Ulverscroft Limited
Anstey, Leicestershire

Printed and bound in Great Britain by
TJ Books Ltd., Padstow, Cornwall

This book is printed on acid-free paper

Introduction

The Theft of the Iron Dogs strikes me as a pleasing and intriguing title for a crime novel. The author, E.C.R. Lorac, published more than seventy books, but this has long been one of the most highly regarded mysteries. The novel was first published by Collins Crime Club in 1946 but its title proved to be rather too mysterious for Lorac's American publishers, who brought it out the following year. They opted for the commonplace, renaming the novel *Murderer's Mistake*.

A particular strength of the novel is the period atmosphere. The story opens in September, and the early paragraphs begin with a description of harvesting time in the dairy farming district, where 'the war effort had not been concerned with the nervous energy required by resistance to bombs or doodles or rockets; it had been the strain of sustained physical effort'.

We are introduced to a farmer (and former book dealer) called Giles Hoggett, of Wenningby, and one rainy day he decides to go fishing. He takes a look at a summer cottage, only to find that two iron dogs are missing from the fireplace, as well as a complete reel of salmon line, a strong chain and hook, a clothes-line, a raincoat and cap — and a large sack. Giles' wife is amused: 'I told you if you read so many detective stories you'd be getting the subject on the brain. I quite agree you could make a good story out of 'The Burglary at Wenningby Barns,' — so the best thing you can do is come home and write it, while you're in the mood. Crime pays much better than cows.'

Giles consults John Staple, who met Chief Inspector Macdonald the previous year in connection with the events described in *Fell Murder* (which, like *Crook o' Lune*, has been published as a British Library Crime Classic) and decides to consult the Scotland Yard man. When he receives Giles' letter, Macdonald has 'a momentary vision of Crook o' Lune, shining in the September sunshine, and Ingleborough behind him, with Penyghent and Whernside'. He has already fallen in love with the area; he loves walking and is also interested in fishing and the farmers' way of life. Lorac's own love of Lunesdale will be evident to anyone who reads this novel. She doesn't sentimentalise, but her ability to evoke the landscape and — crucially — the people who make their livelihood from it is a key strength of her writing. It is significant that the central crime comes to light because the person responsible, 'was lacking in in a sense of detail and of real understanding of the inhabitants.' At the end of the story, we learn precisely why the theft of the iron dogs was such an important clue.

Macdonald needs no second invitation to make a few discreet enquires, arriving in Lunesdale, only for it to turn out that he and Giles actually had a brief previous acquaintance on the rugby pitch. A friendship begins to blossom between the detective and the Hoggetts.

By the time she came to write this book, Carol Rivett (Edith Caroline Rivett, whose principal pen-names were E.C.R. Lorac and Carol Carnac) was well-established as a detective novelist, with two long series being published by Collins Crime Club. During the war, she had moved to Aughton in Lunesdale to be close to her sister Maud Howson and her husband John. John was a former headmaster, while Maud had been educated at university at a time when that was relatively uncommon for women. In 1962, Maud wrote an interesting and rather poignant account (which can be found online) of her family's voyage from Australia to England in the sailing ship *Illawarra* in 1900, at a time when she, Carol, and their sister Gladys were young, and their father was dying of tuberculosis.

The Theft of the Iron Dogs is dedicated to Maud and John and they were the real-life models for Kate and Giles Hoggett. John had a brother called Giles. Lena Whiteley, who knew both Maud and Carol, remembers Maud as a keen plantswoman, as was Carol, and it's no coincidence that in the story, Kate does most of the work in the Hoggett's garden. Maud had a strong social conscience (as did Carol) and had worked in a soup kitchen in the 1930s.

The British Library's Crime Classics series has resulted in the revival of interest in many authors, none more so than Lorac. Her gift for evoking place appeals to many readers, while the variety of her settings and storylines also helps to explain her popularity. It is strange to think that she was, for nearly sixty years after her death in 1958, an author forgotten by all but a handful of detective fiction devotees. The Crime Classics series includes, at present, one novel published under the Carnac name (*Crossed Skis*) as well as a novel never published during the author's lifetime (*Two-Way Murder*). Her Lunesdale novels were among the personal favourites of my parents, who first introduced me to her writing. I have no doubt they would have been delighted to see this book back in print, and so am I.

MARTIN EDWARDS
www.martinedwardsbooks.com

A Note from British Library Publishing

The original novels and short stories reprinted in the British Library Crime Classics series were written and published in a period ranging, for the most part, from the 1890s to the 1960s. There are many elements of these stories which continue to entertain modern readers; however, in some cases there are also uses of language, instances of stereotyping and some attitudes expressed by narrators or characters which may not be endorsed by the publishing standards of today. It is not possible to separate these stories from the history of their writing. We acknowledge therefore that some elements in the works selected for reprinting may continue to make uncomfortable reading for some of our audience. With this series British Library Publishing aims to offer a new readership a chance to read some of the rare books of the British Library's collections in an affordable paperback format, to enjoy their merits and to look back into the world of the twentieth century as portrayed by its writers.

The following text is reproduced from original publications with the inclusion of minor edits made for consistency of style and sense. We welcome feedback from our readers, which can be sent to the following address:

British Library Publishing
The British Library
96 Euston Road
London, NW1 2DB
United Kingdom

To
MAUD and JOHN
jointly
not forgetting
BLUE-BELLE, LADY CLARE and SUSIE
and with gratitude to all those in Lunesdale who helped directly or indirectly with information and advice.

1

I

It had been grand harvest weather in Lunesdale. Even the most reticent among the farmers had been heard to say: 'Aye. We mustn't grumble.' The glowing golden days of late August and early September had meant hard work for every soul in the valley; but before the middle of September all the oats had been carted, and a quantity of it threshed as well.

Harvest, like haymaking, was a communal effort in those parts. The Lunesdale farms were small, compared with those of East Anglia or the Midlands, and before the war there had been very little ploughing. It had been a dairy farming district, with permanent pasture on the uplands, and meadow land in the rich river dales. In the north-west of England the war effort had not been concerned with the nervous energy required by resistance to bombs or doodles or rockets: it had been the strain of sustained physical effort. There was hardly a pause between the long days of haycarting and the equally strenuous ones of harvest. Everybody had helped everybody. When Mr. Hayman of Lower Stacks had cut his oats (and his was the earliest for cutting) he and his men helped Mr. Lamb, of High Fell, then Mr. Lamb lent a hand to Mr. Blackthorn, of Great Gill. They all worked like one family until the stubble stretched unbroken in the cornfields on the north banks of the River Lune, and then they got busy on threshing and ploughing.

It was about the middle of September that the fine weather broke. After two days in which the barometer behaved erratically and the wind wailed in fitful gusts, the rain came — and when it rains in Lunesdale it rains thoroughly. At first it was a soft grey mistiness, permeating everything and making the fields and woods sodden. Then, with a steady west wind, the rain came down in floods and the river rose swiftly. The older farmers were the first to bring up their beasts from the rich river pastures. They drove them into paddocks and pastures high above the flood plain, and the air was full of complaining calls as ewes and lambs and bullocks and heifers registered their complaints against this departure from the normal. The pasture up above was definitely inferior to that by the river, and the beasts said so in no half-hearted way.

Mr. Giles Hoggett of Netherbeck Farm, Wenningby, had no complaint to make about the weather. When Mr. Hoggett had looked outside first thing that morning he was conscious of a warm feeling of satisfaction when he saw the grey sheets of driving rain and the wide white expanse of river in the valley below. The river was rising well, but not yet in full flood; its serpentine curves were losing their contours, but the water had not yet spread right across the flood plain as it would do later.

These conditions meant one thing to Mr. Hoggett — fish. By fish he meant trout, though an occasional eel was not to be despised these days. It was a long time since Giles Hoggett had had a real good day for fishing; he had been busy on the land all the summer, and he had done all of his share in hay field and harvest field. Mid-September was not an ideal time of year for fishing, but sometimes, after a prolonged spell of fine weather, if the river rose suddenly, trout sometimes lost their heads, to use Mr. Hoggett's description. As the becks filled and poured into the main stream with any amount of edible matter in their torrents, the trout would snap madly at this bounteous manna — and that was Mr. Hoggett's chance. Worm was the bait for these conditions; no use to be a fly-purist on a day like this. Good, fat, juicy worms; Mr. Hoggett had laid in a supply overnight.

At breakfast-time, Mr. Hoggett was rather silent. His wife, Katherine, looked gloomily at the weather. She was thinking of her garden, and her husband knew it. The summer bedding was looking draggled, and it was time to think about 'putting the garden to bed' — clearing, digging and storing. Mr. Hoggett felt a little bit guilty. When he was younger — before he took to farming — he had worked a lot in the garden. Now his wife did nearly all the work.

Giles risked a glance at Katherine's profile. Her expression denoted no satisfaction at all with the weather, or even with her husband. Giles Hoggett decided to take the bull by the horns.

'No chance to get on the garden to-day,' he said judicially. 'I might do worse than get a few fish.'

Katherine looked round at him.

'I thought you said you were going to clear up the near barn and do that limewashing,' she said. 'It looks more like a lunatic asylum than anything else — and you've got most of the honey to extract, and I want the bench in the potting shed mended.'

Mr. Hoggett finished his coffee. 'I'll see to it, Kate — but it'll be a good day for fishing, and I want to see that the cottage in the dales is all right. I'm not sure about the roof, and I believe the ditches want clearing.'

He got up from the table firmly and left Katherine looking gloomily out of the window.

II

Half an hour later Giles Hoggett set out towards the river. The rain was pouring down so hard that visibility was reduced to a few yards; it was a grey, dour world, and Giles Hoggett looked part of the landscape. Any kind-hearted and prosperous motorist, seeing the laden figure in ancient colourless raincoat, deplorable sodden hat, and shapeless waders, might well have stopped his car and offered a coin to the drenched, sorry-looking derelict. Certainly none would have gone so far as to offer him a lift. Not the most imaginative could have guessed that Mr. Hoggett was a modest land-owner, a man who had known the delights of rugger playing as a forward, who had once paddled peacefully on the Granta or sat in a backwater imbibing Paley's Evidences and the philosophic systems of Kant and Hegel.

Whether his youthful erudition in philosophy had really penetrated his subconscious or not, Giles Hoggett in his early fifties was now more of a philosopher than he had ever been in his academic days — but his philosophy was now implicit rather than explicit. It expressed itself in his serene dealings with his cows and heifers, in his understanding of the needs of calves, in his appreciation of muck and his enjoyment of ducks and their behaviour. As he walked joyfully towards the river, his philosophy blossomed like the rose into utter contentment with the leaden skies, the streaming rain, the weight of old waders and the comfort of his appalling hat which sent a steady stream of rain water just clear of his chilly nose. To say that he was thinking, in any active sense, was inaccurate, but he was very much aware. Cerebration of a bookish sort was growing less and less needful to him, but his mind was in tune with his environment — and what more can philosophy do for any man?

The road he followed was midway up the scarp on the north bank of the river. He passed two other farmhouses and was then about to turn down the steep brow which led to the valley bottom and the river. At the junction of the ways he saw another figure ascending the brow. Early though Mr. Hoggett was, a fellow land-owner had been earlier, it seemed. This was Mr. Shand, whose land bordered Mr. Hoggett's, but the former was owner of a much greater acreage, and was a gentleman of some importance — though being a comparative newcomer to the district, his importance was only considered in inverse ratio to the duration of his ownership in Wenningby. Mr. Shand wore a very fine and capacious raincoat, a new sou'wester and good looking waders. His creel had the same prosperous appearance.

Mr. Hoggett greeted him pleasantly.

'Good-morning, Mr. Shand. A bit dampish to-day.'

Mr. Hoggett was not making a deliberate understatement, or even indulging in negative hyperbole. He had unconsciously attuned his speech and tempo to those of the farmers from whom he was proud to have been derived. The teeming sodden day was 'a bit dampish,' that was all.

'Good-day, Mr. Hoggett. River's rising well,' barked the other. 'No use to a fly fisherman though.'

He nodded and pursued his way and Giles Hoggett grinned a little under his sodden hat. Had he put his thoughts into words he might have said the day was a bit too dampish for gentlemanly fishing.

Giles Hoggett tramped happily on down the brow. The gradient was so steep that the roadway, though marked on the Ordnance Survey as a thoroughfare, was impossible for any wheeled traffic except farm carts, and even for these it was a heavy pull.

This was an advantage from Mr. Hoggett's point of view, for his favourite stretch of water lay at the bottom of the brow. Had the gradient been less steep, motor tourists from Lancaster and the Lake District would certainly have taken advantage of access to the River Lune in one of its most beautiful stretches. As it was, there was no metalled road leading to the river for two miles on either side — and motorists as a race do not like hilly walking. Giles Hoggett had sometimes watched with pleasure when some adventurous driver had risked a partial descent of the brow. Their 'outfits' could be rescued by a couple of stout farm horses towing them up in reverse. Apart from that, only a caterpillar tractor could deal with the situation.

Arrived at the bottom, Giles Hoggett turned dutifully towards the cottage. He wasn't really anxious about either its ancient flagged roof or its unkempt ditches, but he had told Katherine he was going to inspect it, and he was a very truthful man.

The cottage stood some hundred yards from the river, a low stone wall separating it from the dales — the rich hayland which had been divided into strips among the inhabitants almost before the dawn of history. Giles Hoggett was proud that he, and his ancestors before him, owned some of the dales; also their possession gave him fishing rights. The cottage was an ancient building, stone-walled with stone-flagged roof, and a stone barn. It had probably stood there for several centuries, and its long roof covered shippon and barn as well as dwelling-house. Since the time of Giles Hoggett's father, the cottage had been used as a holiday dwelling for the Hoggett family, while the hay barn and shippon were let with the dales to Richard Blackthorn, one of the biggest farmers in Wenningby. The fact that the place was so inaccessible had saved its being commandeered by billeting officers in the war, and the Hoggett family had had the undisputed use of it as their playground.

Giles was deeply attached to the place, for it seemed part of his very roots, a place he had always known; it was always the same, peaceful, silent, solitary, and it always seemed to welcome him as if it had been waiting for him. When he was a boy, Giles Hoggett had had a secret dream that he would one day come and live by the river in Wenningby Barns, and wherever he had gone, either to University, or in the Army, he had carried the thought of the cottage with him — something peaceful, safe, and exceedingly desirable.

Giles had not been down to the cottage for some weeks, because harvest work had kept him busy in the fields above (the dales had never been ploughed), and he was glad of a chance to come and see that all was in order.

He entered the garden by a stiff little iron gate set in the low stone wall, and gave a glance to see that the fold yard beyond was draining properly. He next glanced, as a matter of habit, at his wood-pile.

The wood-pile was a matter of some pride to him. In the early days of the war, when 'anything might have happened,' Giles Hoggett thought that the cottage in the dales might be a safe refuge to any of his family or friends who were driven out of their own homes. Perhaps he thought of it, as the High Lama thought of Shangri-La, as a place which might 'faintly hope for neglect' on the part of the enemy. It was so isolated, so small, under the great wooded scarp in the wide peaceful valley. Anyway, Mr. Hoggett decided to provision it to some extent, and since the prime need, in that damp northern climate, would be for fuel, he cut and stacked a very fine pile of logs and kindling. The kindling had mostly been used up, but the logs were still neatly stacked — enough fuel to last a family for weeks.

His first glance at the wood-pile showed Mr. Hoggett that something was amiss. Some of the logs were scattered on the grass, as though somebody had withdrawn one carelessly, and others had toppled down. Mr. Hoggett's reaction was immediate.

'Someone from away has been meddling.'

No one in Wenningby would have disturbed his wood-pile. Somewhat put out, for he resented even the thought of trespassers in the cottage garden, Giles Hoggett walked up to the door of the cottage, and then stood feeling foolish, his jaw dropping a little. He had forgotten the keys. He had been so taken up with the thought of fishing that he had omitted to get the keys from their hook up at the farm. As he stood there, with the rain running off his hat, he paused to think. Now had he seen those keys lately? He thought back, remembering the last time the cottage had been used. Nearly a month back, when George and his family came for a few days, and they had all bathed in the river in the hot August sunshine. He seemed to remember saying to George: 'Don't bother to bring the keys up. Leave them in the usual place and I'll fetch them.'

Had he done so? A rather sheepish grin turned up the corners of Mr. Hoggett's close shut lips. 'A good thing Kate didn't come here first,' he said to himself, and began to search in 'the usual place.' This was behind a loose stone in a crevice in the porch. The keys were there all right, and Mr. Hoggett went inside.

III

Mrs. Hoggett, when she had put the house to rights, realising that the weather would preclude any out-of-door activities to-day, decided to make a virtue of necessity and do a day's mending. She was an industrious woman, but war-time mending had become a weariness and she felt that she hated the sight of Giles' socks and stockings and shirts. He seemed to have a genius for making holes and ever larger holes. She looked at the wireless programmes, hoping for a little entertainment to enliven her labours, but there was nothing she could listen to. Katherine Hoggett had a very selective mind.

Since the wireless was quite unhelpful, she lighted a fire: at least she could toast her toes in comfort while she darned. Giles always forgot the time when he went fishing, and though he had not taken any food with him, it was quite likely that he would not turn up until tea-time.

It was a matter of considerable surprise to her,

therefore, when she heard his footsteps before mid-day, and she looked up to see a dripping apparition standing in the doorway which led to the kitchen.

'Take your coat off,' she said promptly, looking at the runnels of water on the flagstones, and then: 'What's the matter?'

Giles took his coat off, and a moment later came into the sitting-room in his stockinged feet and stood by the fire.

'Someone's been in the cottage, Kate.'

'I'm not surprised. Did you bring the keys up? I thought not. What have they taken this time?'

It was not the first time the cottage had been broken into.

Mr. Hoggett lighted a cigarette and sat down by the fire.

'It's a queer business. I can't make it out,' he said, then added: 'Will you come down there with me?'

'What on earth for? On a day like this too,' she said indignantly. 'You know what's there. If you've missed anything, say so. Did you leave any of your coats down there again?'

'Only my old raincoat. I want you to come down because you know just how things were left. You'll notice at once if anything's amiss. I'm puzzled.'

Katherine studied her husband's face. She knew of his particular attachment to the cottage, but he was behaving a bit oddly; he was generally a very reasonable man.

She looked at the pile of mending and disliked it more than ever. She looked at the window: the rain was still descending in sheets, but there was a luminousness about the fells across the river. The river would be well up by now, and the floods always attracted her. Katherine Hoggett was fifty, and her hair was grey, but she was a sturdy healthy woman, capable of long hours of digging and longer hours of walking. She could tire out women twenty years younger than herself.

She put her darning back into the basket.

'All right. I'll come — but if I do, you can come back to dinner sensibly and go fishing again later if you must.'

He agreed without a murmur, and she went and fetched raincoat and gum-boots, and they set out together in silence.

'Any one might imagine you'd found a corpse in the cottage,' she said.

Mr. Hoggett replied solemnly, 'Oh, no, there's no corpse in the cottage. Honestly there isn't. I shouldn't ask you to come and see it if there were. I just want your opinion, that's all.'

Katherine Hoggett pulled off her streaming raincoat before she entered the cottage — she hated seeing water run over the flagstones — and when she was inside she stood and looked around her, glancing this way and that.

At length she said:

'Someone's had a fire since I was here; the hearth wasn't left like that. I came down here on the morning the Georges were leaving and the hearth was swept perfectly clear and the fire-irons stood up as we always leave them. Someone's tried to tidy the hearth, but they weren't much good at it.'

She advanced over the flagged kitchen floor to the great open chimney and stared at the ashes on the ancient hearth stone, curling up her nostrils a little.

'That's not wood-ash; someone has burnt an old

coat or something like that; and the chain and hook have gone.'

'Yes,' agreed Mr. Hoggett.

He came beside her and knelt down by the hearth, peering up the open chimney. There had always been a chain hanging from a staple inside the chimney with a hook at the end on which the big iron kettle was suspended. The kettle was still there standing on the hearth (and these days it was a very valuable kettle).

'Do you notice anything else?' he inquired anxiously.

'Yes, of course. Your iron dogs have gone.'

Giles Hoggett's 'iron dogs' were two blocks of metal he had acquired to support logs on the hearth. The chimney was so wide it was possible to have a huge log fire on the flat hearth stone, and some sort of props made it easier to support the big logs so that they burnt to best advantage. Giles Hoggett had carried these weighty irons down the brow, and he resented their disappearance.

Katherine turned to her husband.

'What else has gone?' she demanded.

'A complete reel of salmon line — very good line, and some food. You'd better look in the larder.'

Katherine walked into the old dairy which was now used as a larder, and her husband stood by the open hearth, having lighted a cigarette, and cogitated deeply. He ran his fingers through his thick grizzled hair as he stood. Many a book-lover would have recognised that unconscious accompaniment of deep thought on Mr. Hoggett's part, for before he had come back to the north to farm some of his own acres, he had been a bookseller — and a very good bookseller, wise, leisurely, appreciative.

Standing by the empty hearth in Wenningby Barns (for so the cottage was named) clad in ancient tweeds which his wife had given up mending in despair long ago, Giles Hoggett looked exactly as he had so often looked when considering a bookselling problem.

'I want a book whose name I have forgotten by an author I don't know and it's a sort of world history written before H. G. Wells thought of doing it.'

Such was the type of problem Mr. Hoggett used to solve.

'Aye. It'd be Wynwood Reade you're thinking of,' he would reply, after having ruffled his hair up.

So to-day, Giles Hoggett, of Wenningby, smallholder, ran his fingers through his hair. 'The chain and hook, two iron dogs, salmon line and my old raincoat,' he murmured to himself.

Katherine came into the room again: a strong, trim, well balanced figure, practical to the tips of her competent fingers, sensible and self-possessed.

'My clothes-line has gone too, and that big sack you used for bringing logs in — you left it here, didn't you?'

'The sack — aye, I left it here,' said Mr. Hoggett.

'And I think some eggs have gone, but I can't be sure,' she went on. 'I put some down in March but the Georges may have had some.'

'George brought his own eggs,' said Mr. Hoggett. 'There's a tin of beans and another of sardines gone from the iron ration; the tins are outside. He tried to bury them, but he couldn't find a spade. He must have used the coal shovel.'

Katherine laughed. When she laughed it didn't matter that her hair was grey: her face became young again, the merry face of Kate Rivers of twenty-five years ago. Fresh complexioned, grey eyed, strong muscled, Kate Hoggett was a wonderful fifty.

Her husband looked a little indignant.

'I'm not so sure it's a laughing matter,' he said portentously.

'Perhaps it isn't, you poor old misery,' she retorted, 'but if you could only see what you look like in those clothes, streaming with water, talking about burying things with coal shovels, you'd have to laugh too. He can't have buried much with a coal shovel, anyway. All the tools are locked up in the loft — because I locked them there. Have you noticed anything else?'

'My old raincoat's gone, and George's fishing cap, and father's spectacles; also the old creel, and Uncle Henry's trout rod.'

Katherine looked at him suspiciously.

'Don't go making things up,' she warned him. 'I believe the old creel fell to pieces ages ago, and I know we used your father's spectacles for charades last winter and George's fishing cap, too. As for your old coat, I'd been meaning to send it for salvage, only it smelt so awful after you'd used it for mucking out the shippon.'

'It was a very good coat,' said Mr. Hoggett indignantly. 'I was very fond of it.'

'Never mind,' she replied cheerfully. 'You haven't lost anything that matters. If a tramp slept in here and made a fire and had his supper, you've no business to complain. You'd better be more careful about the key in future. It looks as though someone has spotted the place where you hide it.'

'But you don't understand, Kate,' said Mr. Hoggett, speaking very seriously. 'It's not the *value* of the things which have gone that matters.'

'No, I know it's not,' she said serenely. 'It's your detective instinct. I told you if you read so many detective stories you'd be getting the subject on the brain. I quite agree you could make a good story out of 'The Burglary at Wenningby Barns,'—so the best thing you can do is to come home and write it, while you're in the mood. Crime pays much better than cows.'

Giles Hoggett rumpled his hair up again.

'I don't think you realise all the implications,' he said. 'I looked round outside before I went to fetch you. I found traces of wheels, and some very big footprints. Unfortunately the river came up and expunged the evidence before I could take any measurements.'

Mrs. Hoggett sneezed.

'It's cold down here, Giles. If you want to stop here to argue, I'm going to light a fire.'

'Not there, Kate, not there!' exclaimed Mr. Hoggett in scandalised tones. 'You don't know what's been burnt there . . .'

'I do. An old coat. Probably yours. It smelt. Perhaps the tramp was particular. If you won't light a fire, I'm not going to stay here. I'm going up to get dinner. It's Irish stew and dumplings, and they're horrid when they're cold, so don't be too long . . . If you are going to write that story, I think *The Loss of the Iron Dogs* would be a better title than the other.'

'*The Theft of the Iron Dogs*,' murmured Mr. Hoggett experimentally, and produced his last cigarette from an inside pocket.

'Be sure you put that cigarette out before you come away, we don't want a fire here as well as a burglary,' said Mrs. Hoggett, 'and don't forget the keys. Dinner will be on the table in half an hour.'

Mr. Hoggett wasn't listening.

'I believe it's those potters,' he murmured to himself, as his wife pulled on her coat and went out into the rain again.

2

I

Mr. Hoggett got home in time to enjoy the Irish stew and dumplings, with apple cake to follow. He was very silent during the greater part of the meal, but when he drew up to the fire and lighted his cigarette, he unburdened his soul to his wife as she sat and darned his socks and shirts. Mr. Hoggett put forward his evidence very clearly and cogently and proceeded to his quite reasonable deductions. He ended up with a weighty peroration.

'I have always said that I distrusted the potters. Reuben Gold and his wife are anti-social nomads. Whenever there's been a case of thieving hereabouts I have been certain they were at the bottom of it. They had the ducks we lost last December, I never doubted it. They had Allan's geese and Mrs. Clout's sheets which were stolen from her washing-line.'

Mrs. Hoggett intervened here. 'It's no use saying the Golds were the thieves if you have no evidence to support it. You may suspect them — and you told Sergeant Cobley you suspected them at the time, but he was quite right in saying that you had no evidence, and the Golds proved that they were at Preston when our ducks were stolen.'

Mr. Hoggett was silent. He had been very angry about the loss of his ducks, which had been stolen one night just before they were ready for the Christmas market. Reuben Gold and his wife Sarah were itinerant hucksterers: 'tinkers' was the term which would have described them in the south; 'potters' was the northern idiom. They would buy any old junk — rags and bones, odd metal, rabbit skins, crocks, old clothes, broken furniture. They had a decrepit cart and an ancient nag, and they plied their trade from Carnton in the north to Preston in the south. Sometimes they had goods for sale on a hawkers' licence — combs and pins, brushes and brooms, besoms and mats — but as a general rule they sought to buy any old oddments which housewives were willing to dispense with. They would also act as carriers or take messages for anybody who trusted them. All the farmers regarded them with suspicion, and Giles Hoggett would have found plenty of worthy neighbours to support him in his belief that any petty theft in the district could be blamed on to Reuben Gold and his wife, but it was a fact that they had never been convicted of any offence. They always had an alibi when thefts had occurred in the Wenningby district. The local police knew all about the Golds, and Sergeant Cobley had wasted a good deal of his valuable time in the effort to bring offences home to them, but the Sergeant had been quite unsuccessful. Far from earning a feather in his cap on the only occasion when he had charged them in court, the Sergeant had lost a lot of prestige, because his evidence had been incomplete, and the Golds had been clever enough to let him produce his evidence before they proved their own alibi. There had been a new J.P. sitting on the bench on the occasion of this case, and he had lent a sympathetic ear to the potters' whines about police persecution. It had been a poor day for Sergeant Cobley, and he had gone home feeling hot under the collar, swearing he would let the lying varmints alone until he had absolutely foolproof, copper-bottomed evidence to convict them on.

Of course, both Giles Hoggett and his wife knew all about the Sergeant's troubles, and Katherine was quite right in reminding Giles that he only risked a snubbing if he reported nebulous suspicions without conclusive evidence.

Having heard all her husband's recital, she summed up:

'What indisputable facts have you, Giles? Someone has been in the cottage; you are sure of it and I am sure of it. Someone lighted a fire and meddled with your wood-pile; but I doubt if the magistrates would really believe that I could swear to the condition of the hearth. The chain and hook have gone, and the iron dogs, but neither is of any value, and they might argue that some children had been playing tricks. Apart from that, you have no conclusive evidence. The clothes-line and sack may have been moved at any time. I can't swear to the time I last saw them — and neither can you. One tin of beans is very much like another, and I don't believe you could really swear that your salmon line was still in the cottage.'

'I could,' said Mr. Hoggett morosely, and then, because he had a very sensitive conscience, he added: 'At least, I think I could.'

His wife laughed:

'That's just it, Giles. Neither you nor I would be a bit good at swearing to something we weren't sure of. You could say you were morally certain the salmon line had gone, but in court you've got to swear by Almighty God . . .'

'I know that,' said Mr. Hoggett sadly. He was kicking his toes — a sure sign of unease.

'Then there's the bogie tracks, the footprints and that bit of curtain stuff I found in the dales,' he went on.

The 'bogie' was a contraption on wheels which Mr. Hoggett had fabricated in an optimistic moment, saying (in defiance of Katherine's judgment) that the easiest way of getting suitcases up the brow was by harnessing himself to a wheeled vehicle and pulling like a cart horse. The experiment had been tried once only, for despite Mr. Hoggett's determination to act as a horse, the 'bogie' was a complete failure. It had jibbed, it had side-slipped and finally capsized; the suitcases were rescued from the ditch, and the 'bogie' had ambled back to the dales under its own velocity. Since then it had been relegated to a corner of the hay barn at the cottage, save when the children used it to play with. Mr. Hoggett felt that to have entered the bogie as serious evidence while talking to his wife was a tactical error, because Kate felt every symptom of acute appendicitis the moment the contraption was mentioned. She had laughed so much on the only occasion the bogie had seen active service that the mere mention of it gave her the pain which accompanies excessive mirth.

'The bogie tracks,' persisted Mr. Hoggett painstakingly. 'I saw them in the dales, just across the stones crossing the ditch. I hadn't time to measure them, because the flood water rose while I stood there.'

'Canute . . .' murmured Mrs. Hoggett, firmly controlling the mirth which unfairly tried to demoralise her. After all, Giles was in dead earnest, but he must have looked very funny standing in the pouring rain while the tracks of his bogie were 'expunged' as he had said, by the rising flood.

'So you can't enter the tracks as evidence,' she said firmly, 'nor the large footprints. They were probably your own. As for the piece of curtain you brought back, it's true I *did* give those curtains to the potters; it was less trouble than burning them, and they were quite rotten, but I couldn't swear I didn't give some pieces to the children when they were playing Red Indians down there.'

Mr. Hoggett looked hurt.

'You're not being helpful, Kate,' he said, and she replied:

'I know I'm not, but it's much better for me to tell you all the defects in the evidence than for the Sergeant to do it. Anyway I am *not* going to swear to anything at all unless I'm absolutely positive it's an objective fact, observed by me, without any possibility of mistake.'

'Of course,' murmured Mr. Hoggett, and she went on:

'You'd much better get some paper and make a short story of it. You could write jolly good stories if you'd only take the trouble.'

Mr. Hoggett got to his feet. 'It's no time of day to start writing,' he said. 'I'm going to see the beasts are all right. That Friesian heifer has been trying to break out of the pasture into the meadow again.'

'None of your cows has any feeling for discipline,' murmured Katherine.

II

True to his declaration, as always, Mr. Hoggett went to the nearby pasture to inspect his stock. He had now two cows in milk: a blue roan named Blue Belle, with the accent on 'Belle' because Mrs. Hoggett said she was the ugliest cow in the neighbourhood, and Suzette, a mild lustrous-eyed companionable young Friesian, black, save for graceful white lines down her flanks and a white belly. In addition to this modest milking herd was a two-year-old Friesian heifer, Lady Clare, the pride of Mr. Hoggett's pasture. He had bought her as a small calf, impressed by her build and coat, and she had developed into a beauty, with creamy white dewlap and quarters and a broad white star on her forehead.

Lady Clare had been fed and tended by Mr. Hoggett alone since her arrival, and she behaved far more like a domestic pet than any heifer should, running up to her master and curvetting around him every time he put in an appearance. Mr. Hoggett knew quite well that Lady Clare had broken bounds and was having an illegitimate gorge in the rich fog grass in his meadow, where she had no right to be. He found, as he expected, that his three stirks, Nanette, Patchey and Kitty, had managed to follow Lady Clare into the forbidden territory, though the sedate milking cows, and Rosie — a roan cow who was in calf — were standing morosely in the pasture, considering the gap in the hedge made by their slimmer and more athletic juniors.

Mr. Hoggett considered the situation. If he rounded up the truants and opened the gate between the meadow and the pasture to drive them through, the stirks would almost certainly elude him again. If, on the other hand, he opened the gate first and then rounded up the trio, the cows would immediately take advantage of him and hasten into the meadow. He decided to let the situation alone until he had some co-operation. The fact was, as Mrs. Hoggett often told him, his cows did not know what a stick was really for, but she also admitted that her husband had a knack with calves — they always looked sleek contented creatures. Mr. Hoggett satisfied himself with a playful buffet on Lady Clare's flanks, in appreciation of which she nearly knocked him over in an excess of affection — though Giles Hoggett was a big hefty fellow.

When he left them, the whole bunch raised their voices in bellows of protest; they had hoped for apples — or at the worst, a cabbage. Mr. Hoggett was in process of building up his herd, and though he had had to pay on occasion for his lack of experience, he had 'a likely lot' and was steadily acquiring knowledge of the principles of milk production.

Leaving his own acres, Mr. Hoggett turned up towards the main road. He had an idea. Some three miles lower down the valley was the village of Garthmere, where Garthmere Hall stood above the River Lune. The bailiff of the Garthmere estate was one John Staple, a man of sixty, full of ripe knowledge concerning the land and its cultivation, and cognisant, moreover, of everything that happened in Lunesdale. Giles Hoggett decided to consult John Staple concerning his present problem at Wenningby Barns, for not only was Staple knowledgeable about local matters, but he had had experience of detective procedure when a chief inspector of the Criminal Investigation

Department had come to Garthmere the previous year to investigate the death of old Robert Garth.

Staple had formed a real regard for the Scotland Yard man, whom he held to be a man of notable common sense, willing to profit by the experience of others, and not at all a daft southerner. Mr. Hoggett had heard that this same chief inspector had fulfilled a promise made to John Staple and had come up to lend a hand at haymaking. Report had it that the C.I.D. man had shaped well for a novice, and by the end of his week had been fit to trust with most of the jobs at haymaking for the simple reason that he did just what he was told, 'and a power o' folk ha'n't the sense to do that' as old Bob Moffat had said.

The rain was still falling steadily, and by the time Giles Hoggett had breasted the hill to the main road, he could see the river had risen until the flood covered the dales, 'a white unbroken radiance.' It was a beautiful sight, with the grey fells rising to the shoulder of Clougha in the west, and white drifts of mist settled in the hollows. Mr. Hoggett was not consciously aware of any æsthetic admiration: he had seen such floods too often; it was just part of his experience, a phase in the life of Lunesdale which had become his life, too. And the trout would be quite demoralised by now, sated, so that no worm could tempt them.

Longsghyll, John Staple's farm, lay half-way up the scarp. It was well situated, not too high for good pasture, though Giles Hoggett's grass provided 'the early bite' in spring at least ten days earlier than Staple's higher pasture. This, however, was a topic it was as well to avoid. A better opening with the bailiff would be, 'A good air up here, Mr. Staple. Less close than in the valley!'

Giles Hoggett found the Garthmere bailiff in his barn, checking up on the contents of his bins, and seeing that the gear used at harvest was well housed for its winter retirement, cleaned and oiled and in order. Hoggett looked thoughtfully round the barn, as he waited for John Staple to finish putting the hinges of a bin to rights. The disorder of this barn was unlike his own: it was an orderly disorder, from which a planning mind could be deduced. Even Katherine, excessively tidy though she was, would not have called this barn 'a lunatic asylum' as she had called his.

'Kate's quite right. I must see to it,' thought Mr. Hoggett, just as John Staple turned round with an inquiring 'Eh . . . ?' — that aggregate of vowels uttered in such varying tones by all good Lancastrians, and quite inimitable to the southerner.

'Good-day, Mr. Staple. I hoped I might find you at home to-day; dampish for outdoor jobs.'

'Good-day, Mr. Hoggett; you're very welcome.'

John Staple was a sturdy grey-haired fellow, with a fine long head and blue-grey eyes. He spoke with the ease and courtesy of the northerner who yet calls no man 'Sir.'

'That roan cow calved yet?' he inquired.

'Not yet,' replied Mr. Hoggett. 'I'm hoping she'll drop a heifer; she comes of a good milking strain and I reckon she should have a good bag.'

'Aye, I mind you bought her from Aughton,' replied Staple. 'I had a cow from that same herd, a shorthorn. Five gallons she gave. Come inside, Mr. Hoggett. I'm through here, and I've nought to do that can't bide till after milking.'

Seated in the comfortable farm-house kitchen, Giles Hoggett stretched his legs to the fire and began to feel happier. Staple was the man he wanted, no doubt about that.

'You remember the potters, Mr. Staple — Reuben and Sarah Gold?'

'Aye, I mind them, and a good-for-nothing pair they are. If they put their noses inside my fold yard they know what to expect because I've warned them.'

'Aye. I think you're quite right,' said Mr. Hoggett. 'Have you seen them of late?'

'Aye. I saw their outfit on the Borwick road, and I'm told Reuben Gold was seen in Yealand Conyers — but not his old woman.'

'Ah,' said Mr. Hoggett, and his tone spoke volumes. He leaned forward confidentially.

'I hope you've the patience to listen to rather a long story, Mr. Staple. The fact is I'm worried, and I've come to you for advice.'

John Staple chuckled.

'That's putting the cart before the horse, judging by the usual way of it, Mr. Hoggett. I'm told you're a rare good hand at advising on some of these plaguey forms the Government sends us, though if you're wanting a hand when that roan shorthorn calves, you've only to let me know.'

'Thank you very much,' said Giles Hoggett. 'Very good of you to offer, but it's not my beasts this time. It's quite another story. I was down at Wenningby Barns this morning . . .' and Mr. Hoggett told his story.

John Staple was a much more satisfactory audience than Kate Hoggett had been. He was interested from the word go. Staple knew all the habits and conventions of life in Lunesdale. He took it seriously that a man's garden had been entered and his wood-pile meddled with. He entered wholeheartedly into Mr.

Hoggett's resentment concerning 'liberties' with his property, and when it came to the list of missing objects, he saw the point without further leading.

'Eh . . . but that looks like dark doings to me,' he said simply. 'For why should a housebreaker take a sack and cord and salmon line, eh, and weights, too? I don't like the sound of yon o'er much.'

They sat in silence, cogitating. Had a portraitist been there, he would have been interested in the salient points of resemblance between the two men. Hoggett was more erect and slighter in the hips, but both men had the long heads, strongly marked brows and light eyes of the Norse. John Staple had never left his own fell country; Giles Hoggett had spent thirty years in the south midlands, but now, as he grew older, he reverted in appearance to his northern forebears. Sitting by John Staple's fireside, he was just part of the picture.

Staple scratched his short stubby grey head, and broke the silence.

'With the river up, what d'you reckon's the depth of that pool down yonder end of your dales, Mr. Hoggett?'

'Jacob's Buttery?' queried Mr. Hoggett, giving the pool its traditional name. 'I'd say it's never less than ten feet. It may be nearer twenty to-day. The river scours its bed as it rounds the bend and that pool is always deep.'

'Aye. That's the way of it. I've known beasts drown in Jacob's Buttery,' said Staple.

'And Reuben Gold's wife hasn't been with him of late?' inquired Mr. Hoggett.

John Staple did not reply. There was no need to. Both men were following an identical train of thought, in complete sympathy.

'That's the deepest pool for a tidy stretch, either up or down stream,' said John Staple. 'With the fine weather we had for harvest the river was very low these past weeks. Jacob's Buttery is the only pool which would serve that purpose between Garthmere and Wenningby I reckon.'

Giles Hoggett was beginning to feel very much perturbed. Now he had to face the logical results of his own deductions, he felt like John Staple. 'I don't like yon o'er much.'

He tried to minimise his own apprehensions.

'Perhaps I'm making too much of it, Mr. Staple. After all, this is only guess-work.'

'Call it guess-work if you like, Mr. Hoggett. T'isn't guesswork about those iron dogs disappearing, is it? How much did they weigh?'

'Twenty pounds the pair.'

'Aye. And for why should a tramp burden himself with a weight like that, and take an empty sack and line when he could have filled the sack with good tinned victuals? I don't see it, Mr. Hoggett. 'Twas a big sack?'

'Aye, a chaff sack.'

The two were silent again. Both knew all about the capacity of sacks.

At last Mr. Hoggett broke out:

'What ought I to do? If I go to the Sergeant with a tale like this he'd tell me I was imagining things.'

'Aye. Likely he would.'

Then Mr. Hoggett got to the point.

'This Scotland Yard man who came up here for haymaking — wasn't he a capable sort of fellow?'

'Aye. He was that. A sensible, hard-working chap he was, forthright too, no sort of nonsense about him, aye, and he could use his head. A very useful, reasonable man — and kindly, too. Did his job well, as I'd reason to be grateful for. But he's not hereabouts now. He's back in London.'

'I could write to him,' said Mr. Hoggett. 'I tell you what. I'll put the story down on paper and send it to him and let him use his own judgment. If he thinks it's all moonshine, well, no matter. I shall have got it off my chest, and nobody will ever be able to say I didn't do anything about it.'

John Staple scratched his head thoughtfully. He was used to keeping accounts and to filling in forms and making returns, but to put a long story down on paper was the sort of activity for which he had no liking.

'Rather you than me,' he muttered, and then brightened perceptibly.

'See here, Mr. Hoggett,' he said. 'You're like one of us these days, though happen you've not our experience in farming because you took to it late — though you're shaping none so badly — but you're used to a pen and paper. Happen you could put it all down, plain and straightforward, though it'd take me a month o' Sundays and a sorry mess I'd make of it. You do as you say, and tell Mr. Macdonald I advised you to write. He told me if ever I was bothered by aught I could write to him and he'd tell me the rights of it if he could. That was when we were having a crack about wills and such like. He's got a head on him, and he's a plain man, not conceited like because he's a London policeman. He wasn't too proud to ask advice from me. Aye. Reckon you couldn't do better.'

And when Giles Hoggett took his leave he felt like John Staple, 'reckon I couldn't do better.'

III

When her husband produced a packet of foolscap paper and sat down at the table to write that evening, Katherine Hoggett made no comments. She hoped he was doing as she suggested: writing a short story. She knew that he had a gift for narrative, an ability to clothe the bare bones of a story in simple but unusual phrases. Perhaps his countryman's sense and townsman's experience combined to produce a particular awareness, an understanding of rural happenings and persons which endowed his writing with a charm which was hard to analyse. Katherine had often told him he could make a success of his writing if he'd only get down to it and try. He was trying that evening, obviously enough; he didn't even want to listen to 'Farm Record.'

As a general rule it was Giles who got sleepy first; after a long day in the open air he would yawn over his book, then nod, then snore gently, whereupon Katherine woke him up and told him to go to bed. This evening, however, it was Katherine who was reduced to yawns while her husband still wrote industriously. She didn't want to interrupt him by getting up and going to bed, so she sat on, knitting, and wondering if the evenings would really be brightened much if Giles did take to writing seriously.

At length he put his pen down and read through his sheets, and at last Katherine said:

'May I read it, too?'

Mr. Hoggett pondered. He would have liked to be secretive over this letter, because he was certain his wife would put into words all the arguments against his intention which had already occurred to himself.

However, it wasn't worth an argument.

'You can read it, provided you don't criticise until you've finished it,' he said.

He gave her the sheets, and went outside for a last look at Rosie, who was now in the shippon.

When he came back, Mrs. Hoggett said:

'It's a perfectly good description, Giles, but he'll only laugh. You know quite well the Metropolitan Police don't interfere in areas outside their own. The only thing this Macdonald would be likely to do, if he takes your letter seriously, is to send it to our local police — and they'll be awfully snorty with you for writing to Scotland Yard.'

'I know,' said Mr. Hoggett glumly, 'but I've written it and I'm going to send it.'

He produced a large envelope and directed it in his good legible hand:

Chief-Inspector Robert Macdonald,
Criminal Investigation Department,
New Scotland Yard,
London, S.W.1.

Looking at this superscription, Mr. Hoggett felt more and more sceptical about the chances of his letter ever reaching that sensible and considerate man to whom it was directed. Turning the envelope over, he wrote on the flap:

'From Giles Hoggett, Farmer, Netherbeck Farm, Wenningby, Lunesdale.'

He stamped it carefully and then said to Kate:

'I'm going to put it in the post-box now. If I don't I shall lie awake all night arguing with myself as to whether to post it or not.'

'All right,' said Mrs. Hoggett, and proceeded to turn the hearth rug back. 'Lie awake all night . . . I'd like to see you,' she murmured to the dying fire.

3

I

Mr. Hoggett's letter was duly delivered at Scotland Yard, and Chief-Inspector Macdonald found it lying uppermost on his desk when he arrived at his office on Thursday, September 16th. Macdonald had a varied mail. His name was well known, and various eccentric persons took it into their heads to write to him about problems not always connected with the C.I.D. He was accustomed to warnings concerning the end of the world (frequently imminent); he had many letters from persons suffering from persecution complexes of varying kinds; he had many offers of assistance from those whose friends told them they were born detectives; he also had some letters of abuse.

Mr. Hoggett's decent envelope and clerkly hand looked different from most of the shoddy missives which lay below it, but the point which really took Macdonald's attention was the postmark, LANCASTER. It brightened his morning, as though a honey-laden breeze from the fells blew through the room. Macdonald had a momentary vision of Crook o' Lune, shining in the September sunshine, and Ingleborough behind him, with Penyghent and Whernside. He turned the letter over and read the address on the back: 'From Giles Hoggett, Farmer, Netherbeck Farm, Wenningby.'

'Perhaps he wants some help with harvest,' thought Macdonald.

An ignorant Londoner, he was unaware that Lunesdale had had the earliest harvest it had enjoyed for years: the oats were all in, and no wheat or barley was grown in those parts. The bulk of the envelope told him that this was no brief communication. On impulse he shoved it into his pocket.

'I'll read it at lunch,' he said to himself, with a quite illogical feeling that this letter from an unknown farmer in Lunesdale was going to give him pleasure.

Macdonald's morning was spent in sifting reports concerning a missing man. This latter, by name Gordon Ginner, had left his lodgings in a midland town a month ago and had disappeared into the blue. The inquiry about him had been set on foot by a middle-aged widow who was affianced to the missing man. She had gone to the local police in a great state of alarm saying that she was certain he had been murdered, and producing a long vague story about 'enemies.' The Midshire police had not been much impressed. Frankly they thought Mr. Ginner had done a bolt to escape from the importunate widow. However, as the days went on and no news came in concerning the missing man, it seemed reasonable to look into the circumstances.

The fact which quickened the interest of the police was the discovery of a letter which seemed connected with a theft of clothing coupons which had occurred recently. Since this letter had been posted in London, the Metropolitan Police were informed, and the activities of Mr. Ginner considered from a London angle. It was soon found that he had rooms in Pimlico, but he had not visited them for some weeks. Letters found here indicated even more plainly that Mr. Gordon Ginner may well have thought it wise to 'beat it.' Undoubtedly he was connected in some illicit dealings with the wholesale wool market. Macdonald was occupied in making out a précis from the various reports which had come in. It was a dull, plodding job, analysing the essential points concerned with the comings and goings of a very commonplace rogue — one of the Smart Alec type who make a good deal of money until their doings are brought to the notice of the police.

When it was time for him to get a meal, Macdonald strolled northwards to a restaurant in Covent Garden. Here, seated in a quiet corner, he drew Mr. Hoggett's letter from his pocket and read it through; then he re-read it.

Mrs. Hoggett was perfectly correct in saying that Giles could write when he tried; his letter was not only an excellently clear description of what Mr. Hoggett had noticed that wet morning at Wenningby Barns; the narrative had a quality which made Macdonald feel that he knew Mr. Hoggett, that he had seen Wenningby Barns, that the wheel-marks of the 'bogie' were reasonably to be connected with the loss of the iron dogs, the chain and hook, the salmon line and sack, the tin of beans and sardines, and Mrs. Hoggett's clothes-line. Macdonald was even pleased to note that George had brought his own eggs with him.

When he finally got up from his meal, Macdonald said to himself: 'Thank you very much, Mr. Hoggett. I enjoyed that.'

II

When Macdonald got back to Cannon Row, he went to seek out a young colleague who was nicknamed 'Commander Gould,' because he had one of those encyclopædic memories which could produce the most diverse facts at short notice.

'Hullo, Jimmy,' said the Chief Inspector. 'I've had a letter from a bloke I don't know, but I seem to remember his name, although I can't place him. Perhaps I'm imagining it. His name's Giles Hoggett.'

'Good Lord, yes. He's the bookseller at Camford — at least he was. I believe he's retired. I've written to him sometimes when I couldn't get a book in London. Old Wetherby put me on to him. Good old Giles Hoggett. He found me a copy of *Bannister Fletcher* when I'd given up hope of getting it. He liked tracing out-of-the-way books; he'd got a sort of flair for it, like you have for copping an improbable poisoner. Hoggett's a north country bloke. I called in at his shop when I was driving that way. Big, long-limbed chap with one of those north country voices.'

'Yes. I see. Thanks very much,' said Macdonald.

His colleague put in: 'I say, you're not professionally interested in Hoggett, are you? He always seemed such a decent bloke.'

'No. I'm not professionally interested in him,' said Macdonald. 'Merely a human contact. I should like to meet him one day. Thanks a lot.'

He went back to his researches concerning the wool-trade reprobate, but one word in Mr. Hoggett's narrative stuck in his mind.

' 'Potters',' murmured Macdonald.

He turned back to one of those dreary police-reports, containing the evidence of a lorry driver who fared from Manchester and Liverpool to Leeds and the other Yorkshire cities.

'I have known Ginner for some time. I believe he was born in Lancashire, but he lived in Kendal at one time. He was generally in with a low lot — bookies and that. He had a row with some tinker folk at a coffee stall one day — something about recognising the old girl and something about a pottery. I think it was a pottery. It might have been a china-shop.' (Police query: Bucket shop?)

Macdonald pondered as he put the paper down.

'Pottery . . . Why not potters?' he asked himself, and then chuckled. This was wishful thinking with a vengeance, or wasn't it? He worked away at the ramifications of Mr. Gordon Ginner, and the more he thought about it, the more necessary it seemed to go to Manchester to consult with his colleagues there about the desirability of asking for a warrant to be made out. The evidence against Mr. Ginner was by no means conclusive; a skilful counsel would have made hay of it in no time, but it was obviously desirable to 'pull in' any one connected with the frauds in question.

Macdonald decided to write a brief report based on the essential facts he had culled from the papers which had been sent to him, and to hand in his own report without further comment to his Assistant Commissioner. This done, he decided to acknowledge Mr. Hoggett's effort, and wrote as follows:

'Dear Mr. Hoggett. I write to acknowledge the letter which you wrote at the suggestion of my friend Mr. Staple. I was much interested in the facts you described so clearly, and I will let you know at a later date if any official action be decided on. This acknowledgment is a personal one, so I can add that your description of your Lunesdale property made me envious. Yours truly, Robert Macdonald.'

III

When Colonel Wragley saw Macdonald that evening he said:

'You seem to be collecting some useful data about the coupon ramp, Macdonald. Do you think a consultation is advisable? The Manchester men would have no objection to a visit to London and something of the kind seems to be indicated.'

Macdonald allowed himself a chuckle.

'I'm sure the Manchester men wouldn't object to a London consultation, sir. For my own part, I should have no objection to a consultation in Manchester. To-morrow is Friday. The Sabbath cometh, when no man should work unless compelled by urgent duty.'

Wragley laughed good-humouredly.

'Have it your own way, then. You don't often suggest combining duty and pleasure, Macdonald. A week-end in Manchester isn't my own idea of enjoyment. However, good luck to you. I think you've made some very good points in that report, and the sooner we get this particular set of gentry in the dock, the better for everybody. This coupon business is an infernal nuisance, all the same. It's about doubled the work of the police.'

Macdonald agreed, but with inward reservations. He had no particular liking for Manchester, but Kendal had been mentioned in the evidence about Ginner and a week-end in Kendal was not to be despised. Moreover, the route for Manchester to Kendal undoubtedly ran through Lancaster. Whether Mr. Hoggett's discoveries had anything to do with any case on which Macdonald was employed was highly speculative, but since Mr. Hoggett had written a personal letter to that Robert Macdonald who was a friend of Mr. Staple's, the Chief Inspector saw no reason why he should not pay a friendly call at Netherbeck Farm.

Macdonald reached Manchester by midday on Friday. He had a satisfactory 'crack' with his colleagues, comparing notes on the London and Midland aspects of the case against Ginner, and determined to get a warrant out against that elusive gentleman. By four o'clock Macdonald had concluded his consultation, and shortly afterwards was in a train heading north for Lancaster, a knapsack on his back and a holiday feeling in his mind.

It was a fine clear evening when he reached Lancaster, and the grey mass of John of Gaunt's castle towered grandly above the Lune, a sombre silhouette which had majesty in its severe outlines. Macdonald found a car for hire in the station yard, and decided to trust to luck that the inn where he had stayed before would provide him with a bed. He could have telephoned, of course, but he knew quite well why he didn't stay to do so. The light would soon be fading, and he wanted to see Ingleborough again that evening.

He told his driver to take him as far as the hill above Garthmere — some mile or so from the main Lancaster-Carnton road — and soon he was driving eastwards from Lancaster, breasting the hills which climbed steadily up on the north bank of the Lune.

After twenty minutes' driving, he paid off his hired car and continued his way on foot.

Macdonald had a feeling for hill country and he liked walking. When he breasted the next rise he knew that his impulse to get out and walk was justified; this was the sort of country to be enjoyed leisurely, while a man was afoot. At the top of the rise he stopped and stared his full. There it was, just as he remembered it, grander than ever in the grey evening light. The great limestone mass of Ingleborough stood out blue against the pallid eastern sky, as fine a skyline as a man might hope to see; in sweeping lines the great hill reached from north to south across the horizon, a sleeping lion of a hill, sloping like a figure shrouded from head to foot, head to the north, feet to the south; in the far distance, over the lion's shoulders Penyghent and Whernside showed in mauve shadows the distant line of the Pennine Chain.

It was a silent prospect, meditated Macdonald. Speech seemed alien to that primeval mass. It stirred him in some way which he did not seek to put into words. He had wanted to see those hills again — and he was satisfied.

As the twilight deepened the wind freshened and Macdonald set out again at a good swinging pace. He knew his way; immediately to the south lay Garthmere, with the gaunt grey pile of the Hall merging into the surrounding shadows; ahead, to the east, Wenningby showed a few glimmering lights, and beyond, unseen, Chapelton-Lonsdale lay tucked away in the hills. Macdonald's inn, the Green Dragon, was a little to the north-east, in the direction of Borwick. Macdonald knew that if he carried on along the road parallel with the river he would pass Wenningby and he could take a turn to the left above Gressingham which would connect up with the Borwick road.

Half an hour's walking brought him to Wenningby — a group of stone farm-houses with mullioned windows.

He did not know which was Netherbeck Farm and he had no intention of visiting Mr. Hoggett that night, but quite apart from his detective calling, Macdonald felt a very human curiosity about the bookseller who had turned farmer. It was by chance that Macdonald became aware of Mr. Hoggett's proximity. He had just passed the last farm-house of the group and at the gate of a pasture a tall man was bending to fasten a gate more securely. His figure was only half-seen in the gloaming, but over the gate was a cow with a white patch on her forehead, and she was bawling lustily while making every effort to impede the shutting of the gate. Behind her, two younger beasts bellowed encouragement.

'No, Lady Clare,' roared a voice. 'I said '*No.*' You have plenty to eat in the pasture.'

'*That,*' said Macdonald to himself, 'must be Mr. Giles Hoggett . . . Lady Clare . . . well, she seems a recalcitrant lass.'

Abreast of the gate, Macdonald ventured: 'A fine clear evening,' spoken in the direction of the disciplinarian.

A pleasant voice answered him from the shadows:

'Aye; a good clear evening, but the wind's freshening. Have you lost your way by any chance?'

'No. I don't think so. This is Wenningby, isn't it? My name's Macdonald. Are you Mr. Giles Hoggett?'

There was a moment of silence. Then Mr. Hoggett said wonderingly:

'Did you say *Macdonald*?'

'Aye. You wrote to me, and as my business brought me up north, I thought I'd come and have a word with you. Will you be at home in the morning?'

'I certainly shall — but won't you come in now? My wife . . .'

'Thanks very much, but not now,' said Macdonald gravely. 'I'm sure your wife has enough to do to make her rations go round, and I'm not going to bother her at supper-time. To-morrow morning about ten o'clock? Good. Is that cow really in trouble?'

'Not at all,' said Mr. Hoggett firmly. 'That heifer is above herself. She thinks the world was made for her alone, including all the fruits of the earth in due season. She must learn a sense of proportion. I think the gate is safe now. I have mended it again.'

'I shall hope to make Lady Clare's closer acquaintance in the daylight,' said Macdonald. 'Are the lesser kine also of undisciplined habits?'

Mr. Hoggett laughed.

'My wife says so — but they're thriving. Well, I shall be glad to have a word with you to-morrow, Chief Inspector. Where are you staying?'

'At the Green Dragon. Good-night, Mr. Hoggett.'

'Good-night,' replied Mr. Hoggett, and turned vigorously towards the farm-house.

As Macdonald continued on his way he heard Mr. Hoggett calling 'Kate! Kate!' as he made for his own door. That would be Mrs. Hoggett, Macdonald hazarded.

As he hurried on in the dusk towards the hoped for hospitality of the Green Dragon, Macdonald wondered what Kate was like. His only data at present was her husband's statement that she considered his cows undisciplined. Macdonald was sufficiently urban to describe most bovines under the generic term 'cows.' The fact was that for all his detective ability he had never quite learnt the answer to the conundrum: 'When is a heifer not a heifer?' Apparently up here in the north they had their own usage for such terms.

4

I

'Ginner? No, I've never heard the name,' said Mr. Hoggett.

Macdonald was sitting by the fire in the living-room of Netherbeck Farm. It had taken no detective skill to observe that this room, probably the original kitchen of the old farm-house, was different from most farm-house kitchens. It was used as dining-room and living-room, and its furniture was good old wood — the dresser and 'spindle back' chairs and hard oak table of the Lancashire farm-house. They shone. So did everything else in the room. Macdonald felt relieved that he had wiped his shoes very thoroughly before entering. There was a fine log fire burning, for it was a chilly day, and the chair Macdonald sat in was a good old-fashioned rocker, but he noticed as he came in that a print of Holbein's 'Duchess of Milan' adorned one wall. It suited the room, and Macdonald liked it, but he regarded Mrs. Hoggett rather warily. He hadn't quite placed her yet; she didn't seem to fit into any ready-made category.

'There aren't any Ginners in this part of the world,' went on Mr. Hoggett, and Macdonald said:

'No matter. Now since you've told me all about your Wenningby Barns problem, and I have a free week-end, what about letting me see the place? I've already told you I am not here on duty, so my visit is not official. I have to make this plain, because we don't poach. I've no more status here than I should have fishing in your water without a permit.'

'Yes, I quite follow that,' said Mr. Hoggett, and his wife looked up from her knitting.

'You were asking about a man named Ginner,' she said. 'I've never heard the name, either, but when you mentioned poaching just now I thought of something. Giles, there was someone poaching on your water in August. I wonder if he broke into the cottage.'

Mr. Hoggett looked sceptical.

'I don't think it's very likely, Kate. The man you saw probably thought he was on the Carnton Anglers' water. They do make these mistakes. He wasn't a poor-looking fellow, was he? Wenningby Barns doesn't look the sort of place to attract a swell cracksman.'

Macdonald turned to Mrs. Hoggett.

'Can you remember anything special about your poacher?'

'He'd got a face I distrusted at once. I don't often take unreasonable dislikes to people, but the minute I saw him I knew he was a rotter. I just knew it. He wasn't a poor man, but he wasn't what I should call an educated one. He hadn't a north country voice. I should think he came from the Midlands, and he was probably something in the commercial traveller line. I only suggest that because of his assurance. He was the type you can't snub.'

Mr. Hoggett suddenly chuckled.

'Who's making things up now, Kate? You saw a fellow with a rod who said he wasn't fishing on my water.'

'. . . But he was fishing,' she protested. 'I saw him make a cast —'

'All right — and could you tell from the way he cast a fly that he was a commercial traveller from the Midlands who beats his wife and falsifies the petty cash? Could you swear by Almighty . . .'

'Shut up, Giles, and don't be an ass,' she retorted cheerfully. 'The Chief Inspector will think we're profane. Take him down to Wenningby Barns and bring him back in good time for dinner. I'm going to make an enormous ham omelette, so don't be late.'

Mr. Hoggett was still chuckling as he led Macdonald towards the brows.

'My wife took me to task — quite reasonably — for not being precise over the matter of evidence. She said I made things up to suit myself, and I ought to remember that in a court case I should have to swear to my facts — so I couldn't help getting at her when the boot was on the other leg.'

'Mrs. Hoggett struck me as a person who has respect for accuracy,' said Macdonald. 'She would be the first to admit that we all tend to read evidence so that it supports our own preconceived theories. For instance, you are sure that the potters broke into your cottage, and you find evidence to support it. Mrs. Hoggett believes her poaching gentleman was responsible. I have to remind myself at regular intervals that I am here on holiday and am not investigating anything but the countryside — and perhaps you, Mr. Hoggett.'

'Eh?' said Mr. Hoggett.

'Yes, you,' replied Macdonald. 'Weren't you once guilty of — playing Rugby football?'

'Rugger!' gasped Mr. Hoggett. 'I thought for a moment . . .'

'Yes. We can all feel like that sometimes. Did you

once play against a Police team in the Home Counties — many years ago. At Woodstock, wasn't it?'

'Guilty,' said Mr. Hoggett solemnly. 'It was in 1928 — one of the last games I played.'

'I sympathise. It was one of my last, too. I was 'borrowed' by the Home Counties Police team. I played Wing-Threequarter.'

'Well, well, well . . .' said Mr. Hoggett, and the two worthies stood still and regarded each other with increased respect.

'Having settled that, without either of us saying the world's a small place,' went on Macdonald placidly — 'say if you tell me some more about the other inhabitants of Wenningby. Are they all indigenous, so to speak?'

'No, not quite,' said Mr. Hoggett. 'This is the brow, by the way. I don't advise you to bring a police car down here. The leading inhabitant of Wenningby, by seniority in farming, is Richard Blackthorn of Great Gill. He farms nearly 200 acres. Then Edward Troutbeck of Wenning Hall, my nearest neighbour, would be next in rank. The Troutbecks have farmed here for four generations. Gilbert Clafton of Upperbeck is a young farmer — we have just passed his steading — but he is married to Richard Blackthorn's daughter. These constitute the wisdom of the inner Chapelry, so to speak.'

'The Witanegemot,' agreed Macdonald, and Mr. Hoggett went on:

'There are four other outlying farms, all held by natives, *but* in addition we have some members of the outside world. There is Mr. Vintner, who is tenant of a poorish-looking property on the Garthmere Road. He runs a chicken farm, not very successfully I imagine, but my wife tells me he is quite a competent painter.'

'A suspicious circumstance,' said Macdonald, and Mr. Hoggett agreed simply.

'I used to think so, but my wife thinks otherwise. Then there is Mr. Willoughby, the tenant of Mr. Shand's water. Mr. Shand owns land further down the river and has land adjoining mine. Mr. Willoughby leases a cottage of mine . . . But there he is.'

They had descended the brow and were walking along the level towards the cottage in the dales. A short, stoutish man, carrying fishing tackle, was approaching them. Mr. Hoggett greeted him in friendly tones.

'Good-morning, Mr. Willoughby. Have you been fishing so early?'

'Good-morning, Mr. Hoggett. I thought of trying for a fish, though the water's not too good — the river's fallen quickly, but I'm feeling annoyed. Someone has broken into my fishing hut up in Chough Close. I'm going to notify the police.'

'I'm sorry to hear that,' said Mr. Hoggett. 'Has anything been stolen?'

'My waders. It's most annoying. Quite unobtainable to-day. This is the first time such a thing's happened. The padlock was wrenched off. Have you noticed any suspicious characters about, Mr. Hoggett?'

Mr. Hoggett stood and scratched his head. He didn't look at Macdonald, nor did Macdonald look at him. At length Mr. Hoggett replied:

'I haven't seen anybody down here, Mr. Willoughby.' He spoke slowly, and the stout man replied hastily and testily:

'No? Then I'm going straight to the police. I consider it to be my duty to do so, and I'm very much put out about my waders. Perhaps you can tell me the appropriate officer to consult, Mr. Hoggett.'

Again Mr. Hoggett scratched his head. Macdonald with an expressionless face and a straw in his mouth, was staring towards the river. Mr. Hoggett said:

'I think Sergeant Cobley's your man, Mr. Willoughby. His headquarters are at Carnside, but he lives at Nether Pollock. If you care to use our telephone, my wife is at home.'

'Thank you, Mr. Hoggett, very kind of you to suggest it. I'll go straight up.'

The stout man bustled off and Mr. Hoggett turned to Macdonald.

'I don't know if I acted incorrectly,' he began, and Macdonald laughed.

'Well, if you did, I'm in it too,' he replied. 'In my opinion you were most discreet. This is *not* my pigeon, it's the Sergeant's. What a pity!'

'Why?' asked Mr. Hoggett.

'I was enjoying myself,' said Macdonald. 'I hoped your cottage affair would turn out to be a good leg-pull and that I should be asked to fish in your water. Now it's all up. The local men will have to investigate and I shall have to behave like a responsible official who knows his place—which isn't here. In other words, I shall have to report—and Sergeant Cobley will resent my intrusion from the start.'

'But look here,' said Mr. Hoggett earnestly, 'now you're here, you might as well come in and see the cottage.'

'...and the bogie; and Jacob's Buttery,' added Macdonald. 'All right—but the Sergeant *will* be annoyed.'

Mr. Hoggett looked very thoughtful.

'You're free for the week-end,' he said cajolingly,

'and you're a friend of John Staple's, and you came here before for haymaking, and it's quite natural you should come and see me if you like fishing. I'll lend you my gear —'

'Thank you very much, Mr. Hoggett. One day I'll remind you of your offer, but it won't be to-day. Life's not like that. I say, I like your cottage. You don't want to sell or lease it, do you?'

'I might consider it,' said Mr. Hoggett mendaciously. 'Now this is the point at which I observed the wheel tracks and footprints. The bogie's in the hay barn. Come right in.'

II

Mr. Hoggett brought Macdonald back to the farm just after midday. Mrs. Hoggett, with commendable reticence, did not worry Macdonald with questions about the 'Loss of the Iron Dogs.' She fed him extremely well, with the most magnificent soufflé omelette Macdonald had seen for years, followed by an enormous apple pie with thick cream. She explained that Rosie had recently calved, and that her milk would not be put 'on the road' for a day or two, and if Macdonald did not care for Cholostrom he could say so. They talked about cows and calves and heifers and stirks, about ewes and tegs and tupps, about the problems of dairy farming and the mentality of cows, and Macdonald enjoyed himself very much. It was after they had finished the meal, and had drawn their chairs round the fire that Macdonald said:

'I have enjoyed my morning very much, Mrs. Hoggett, and I have enjoyed the sort of dinner you can only get in a farm-house. I'm only sorry that I've got to get back to my job, and that your husband has got to report to Sergeant Cobley that his cottage has been entered by some unauthorised person. Before I go, will you look at these photographs and tell me if you can recognise any of them?'

Mrs. Hoggett took the photographs and sedately put on her glasses. Macdonald watched her, as she studied each in turn, laying them carefully on the table after each had been scrutinised: she was leisurely, but not slow. With just such an air of cautious enquiry a scientist might have examined an unidentified specimen. At length she picked one out and handed it to Macdonald.

'That is a photograph of the man I saw fishing on Giles' water some weeks ago. I do not know any of the others.'

It was Mr. Hoggett who broke into startled speech.

'Are you sure, Kate? Let me see. What an extraordinary thing . . .'

He seized the photograph and Mrs. Hoggett said calmly:

'Put on your specs, Giles, and don't look at it upside down . . .'

By the time Mr. Hoggett had examined the photograph, he also was of the belief that the face Mrs. Hoggett had claimed as her poacher's was familiar to him also. His wife took a poor view of his statement.

'Could you *swear* you've seen him, Giles? If so, where?'

'I'm not certain. Can *you* swear to him, Kate?'

'Yes. I can. Anywhere. This is a photograph of the man I saw just below Jacob's Buttery on August 31st. I've remembered the date. It was the day the stirks broke out when you were carting with Richard Blackthorn in Parson's Intak. I found Nanette in the dales and Patchey and Kitty in the river.'

Mrs. Hoggett would make a good witness, thought Macdonald. She only said she *was* certain of a thing when she really was certain, and she added chapter and verse with exemplary clarity. A judge would appreciate Mrs. Hoggett, meditated the C.I.D. man — but the jury would like her husband. It was Mr. Hoggett who asked the inevitable question (for all his north-country forebears, he was a very human individual and not ashamed to voice his curiosity).

'Who is this?' he inquired flourishing the photograph.

'He is named Gordon Ginner,' said Macdonald. 'I have been told he once lived in Kendal. I can't tell you anything more about him now, because I have got to regularise my position.'

Mrs. Hoggett studied him.

'Isn't it detective etiquette to pick up evidence in your spare time?' she enquired. 'I should have thought it was praiseworthy.'

Macdonald could not for the life of him tell if her question were serious or not.

'I think you probably know the substance of the answer to that question, Mrs. Hoggett,' he replied. 'I had a consultation with my colleagues in Manchester. When that was over, I was free to go my own way for the week-end, but if I intend to carry on as a police official in this district, it is up to me to get into touch with my country colleagues. I don't wish to be regarded as a snooper from London.'

'Aye,' said Mr. Hoggett. 'That's sense. I see just what you mean — but I'm sorry your week-end has been marred.'

'There's one thing about it,' chuckled Macdonald. 'My week-end may be prolonged — and if so, I'll wet a line in your water before I'm through.'

He turned again to Mrs. Hoggett.

'Thank you very much for your hospitality,' he said. 'I only hope you won't regret that your husband ever wrote and told me about the theft of the iron dogs.'

Mrs. Hoggett considered a moment.

'It won't be any use regretting it,' she said. 'If owt's amiss, as we say up here, it's got to be looked into.'

'Quite right,' agreed Macdonald. 'That's the way to look at it.' He paused and then added: 'Do you mind telling me — were you born in London?'

'Yes. I was. Why?'

Macdonald chuckled.

'I thought you were,' he said, and Mr. Hoggett scratched his head.

'I wonder what he means by that?' he enquired — but Macdonald did not answer him.

III

The Chief Inspector set out, regretfully, 'to regularise' his own position. Having borrowed Mr. Hoggett's bike he went to the nearest call-box (he was far too canny to phone from Netherbeck Farm). He first got in touch with the Acting Chief Constable — the same impetuous gentleman who had been instrumental in first bringing him to Lunesdale on the occasion of old Robert Garth's death.

'Chief-Inspector Macdonald of the C.I.D., sir. You may remember me . . .'

'Macdonald? Indeed! I remember you very well,' barked the cheerful voice. 'I should be glad to see you again. What is it brings you up north, Chief Inspector? Are you co-operating again on the agricultural front? I'm told you showed promise at the hay time.'

'Evidently nothing escapes you, sir,' replied Macdonald. 'I came to Lunesdale for a week-end of walking — and fishing, if I could get it. As it happens I've had a different sort of bite — it concerns a case of mine and possibly one of yours. In the circumstances I thought it better to report direct to you.'

'Perfectly correct. Excellent. Now where are you at the moment, Chief Inspector?'

'I'm speaking from a call-box on the Chapelton-Lonsdale road. One of the farmers told me that Sergeant Cobley was in charge of this particular area — between Garthmere and Wenningby. I should like a word with him, with your permission.'

'By all means. You'd better come over to Carnton for a consultation. Inspector Bord will be on duty. The Superintendent is away to-day. He's at the Assizes. I'll see that messages reach them. Meantime, do you wish to see me personally — or would to-morrow do? I've the deuce of a lot in hand.'

'To-morrow would do, sir. I just wanted to notify you of my presence in your district, and to consult with your men over points which have come my way.'

'Precisely. Excellent. Quite in order,' barked the deputy official. 'Er . . . let me think. A call-box, you said. Could you ring back in fifteen minutes' time?'

'Very good, sir.'

While he waited, Macdonald strolled back along the road. In a dip, standing back from the road, was a sorry-looking little stone house, whose flagged roof sagged despondently, the shippon being semi-ruinous. There were a number of shoddy out-buildings, and some rusty wire and make-shift hen-houses proclaimed that the occupier had once kept a number of head of poultry. To-day, a few dispirited hens and some moulting ducks were half-heartedly seeking a living off old cabbage stalks. A tall lanky fellow was doing some repairs to a gate which was off its hinges. As Macdonald drew level a vicious, 'Damn the whole blasted outfit,' was uttered as the gate fell drunkenly askew once more.

Macdonald said: 'Can I lend you a hand? Gates are awkward things to lift.'

'Thanks. Don't bother. The whole contraption's rotted through. I think I shall cut it up for fire-wood. More use that way.'

'Certainly not a native,' pondered Macdonald.

The voice was an educated voice, but ill-tempered. The speaker was very lean, of almost boyish build, if he had straightened his round back, carroty-haired, blue-eyed; something about him was like a ferret, but he lacked alertness. He was slovenly, like his property, down at heel and none too clean, but not altogether unlikeable.

'If you move the gate away altogether, there'll be nothing to keep the cattle out,' said Macdonald.

'Then let 'em come in. They're welcome. You're a stranger to these parts, aren't you? I haven't seen your dial before.'

'I'm a Londoner, but I've friends hereabouts. Are you the painter someone mentioned to me?'

'Well — I paint. D'you want to buy a poultry farm — goodwill, enclosures, a few fowls and lease of ancient and picturesque dwelling?'

'If I did want to buy a poultry farm, I'd rather buy

one where the birds didn't show every sign of imminent decease. Those hens are in a bad way.'

The sandy fellow laughed, but his laugh was rueful.

'You're telling me . . . I ought to wring their necks, but I'm fed up with it. Hens ought to be easy — but they're not. D'you know how many diseases a hen can get?'

'I don't. On the whole I should think painting is less speculative.'

'It's as easy to starve on. I say, would you like to sit for me? You've no idea how difficult it is to get models round here. The farmers are all worth painting — but will they sit for me? No. Too busy.'

'I'll think about it,' said Macdonald, glancing again at the sagging roof beyond. 'Who's your landlord?' he enquired.

The sandy fellow did not take the enquiry amiss. Macdonald knew his type well enough; he'd have been more at home in the brasserie of the Café Monico than in this upland solitude.

'My landlord? Name of Shand. You're wondering why he doesn't mend that roof. He might if I paid my rent. It's a vicious circle.'

'I see. Well, I've got to move on. May I come and see your work one day?'

'For God's sake do. You're the only person I've talked to for days. They don't talk in these parts. At least, not to me.'

Macdonald strolled back to his telephone box. What on earth had brought a fellow like that to this place of solitude and toil? A man must work to get a living from the sour soil of that poor holding.

. . . Hens ought to be easy . . . 'Poor devil,' thought Macdonald, as he lifted the receiver again.

5

I

Sergeant Cobley did not go out of his way to make difficulties. He accepted Macdonald's tactful explanation of his presence in Lunesdale without question, and was anxious to hear what the Yard man had discovered for himself. Macdonald had found time to pay a call on John Staple in the interval between telephoning to the Chief Constable and meeting the Sergeant, and was able to quote that worthy's opinion that 'summat was amiss' in the dales. Cobley had already received reports from Mr. Willoughby about the 'entering and breaking' of the fishing hut and Mr. Hoggett had dutifully rung up and reported that certain items were missing from Wenningby Barns.

Cobley said: 'Mr. Hoggett is probably right in his surmise about the potters doing both jobs. I've notified all stations to look out for them. Oh — here's the Inspector.'

Bord, who entered the room at that moment, turned out to be a tall, fair fellow, lean and sinewy, with powerful sloping shoulders and very big hands. 'A reliable lad in a scrap, that one,' thought Macdonald, as they shook hands. Bord was a north country man all right, and Macdonald took to him at once. Cobley was encouraged to repeat his report about the burglarious doings in the valley, and then Macdonald weighed in.

'I came up to Manchester to consult about a case

which has been passed on to our department,' he said. 'You've probably noted the routine enquiry: a man named Gordon Ginner disappeared from his lodgings in Marrington in August. We found he had rooms in London — in Pimlico — but he hadn't been seen there for weeks. It's probable that he is concerned in the coupon racket which has been carried on in the wool market. That was where I came in.'

Bord nodded. 'Aye. We noted it — but we've nothing to report up here.'

'By chance, I've happened on a curious piece of evidence,' went on Macdonald. 'You know John Staple, the Garthmere bailiff?'

'Aye. A friend of yours, I'm told,' said Bord with a grin which showed his strong white teeth. Macdonald nodded.

'Staple's a man I've a great liking for,' he said. 'Now you know his friend, Mr. Hoggett?'

'I've heard of him. He's well known in the valley. His folk have held land there for generations, tho' he was a bookseller by trade until he took to farming.'

'So I gathered,' said Macdonald. 'I saw him to-day because I was interested in what I heard of the burglary at his cottage. Admittedly it wasn't my business, because I wasn't there on duty —'

'We won't quarrel about that,' said Bord cheerfully. 'What was it you discovered about the cottage?'

'Mrs. Hoggett said she'd seen a man poaching on her husband's water at the end of August, and suggested he might be the housebreaker. She gave a good description of him. So good that I showed her a packet of photographs I'd got in my pocket. She identified one of them as the poacher — this one. You've seen it in our notification. It's Gordon Ginner. I should say

Mrs. Hoggett is a reliable witness, and she's prepared to swear to her identification.'

'By gum,' murmured Bord, and Cobley said:

'That's a rum go, that is.'

'Now about the thefts at Wenningby Barns,' went on Macdonald, and proceeded to detail them.

'I'll get you to come down there with me,' he added. 'I'm in agreement with John Staple and Mr. Giles Hoggett that the thefts are suggestive, especially coupled to the fact that the cottage is close to one of the deepest pools in the river. In other words, we'd better investigate Jacob's Buttery and the adjoining reaches. I say 'we,' but at the moment I've no official standing in the matter. It remains with you and your Chief Constable to decide if you want me here.'

Bord laughed — a cheerful chuckling sound.

'Between ourselves, Chief, no need to be so damned official,' he said. 'You've come to us and laid your cards face upwards on the table and I'm all for co-operation in the Force. If so be as you'd come it over us — well, I'm a Lancashire man myself and I don't truckle to Londoners ower-easily — but treat us fair, as you've done, and we've nought against you. Aye, I'll be glad to work with you. As for our old man — well, he'll be happy enough to have you; we're still short-handed, and this looks like being a job of work.'

'It does that,' agreed Macdonald, 'and what's more it looks like being a job we could do best together. If this man Ginner has been up here, your local knowledge will help to trace him.'

Bord meditated a moment.

'Aren't you pretty sure where you'll find him?' he asked.

'No. I'm not,' replied Macdonald. 'I think it's long

odds that something has been hidden in the river: the weights indicate that — but why the chain and hook? My notion would be that the hook's been used as an anchor, to prevent anything getting adrift. With the sort of stream you get at that bend of the river twenty pounds of weight might not be adequate to ensure that a thing stay put. Also, by means of the chain and hook you could recover the sunken object if you wanted to. From what I know of Ginner, he might well have a lot of papers he'd rather not carry about with him. That's all surmise of course. Does anything else suggest itself to you on the evidence we've got at the moment?'

The Sergeant put a word in:

'We don't know that it was the same party broke into the fishing hut and the cottage,' he said, 'but I reckon it was. Mr. Willoughby hadn't been down fishing of late. August was too fine and the river too low. Seems to me the thief might've looked in the hut first, to see if he could find what suited his purpose and then tried the cottage next.'

'That's quite reasonable,' assented Macdonald, and Bord put a word in:

'There's waders gone from the hut, an old coat, cap, and creel from the cottage. Seems to me the thief might well have walked off looking the dead spit of an old-fashioned angler. Not a bad idea at all. No one looks twice at a fisherman in Lunesdale.'

'I quite agree,' said Macdonald. 'Also the waders and brogues would successfully conceal any footprints. I wish we could fix the time at which the thefts took place. All we know at present is that they occurred between the time the Hoggetts were last in the cottage — on August 28th they say — and September

15th, when Mr. Hoggett went down there. Mrs. Hoggett saw Ginner on August 31st, but she did not go into the cottage that day.'

'We shall have to find out if any of the Wenningby farmers was down in the dales between those dates,' said Bord.

Macdonald nodded agreement. He didn't add that he'd already made a few extra enquiries himself on that score. Mr. Hoggett had told him that everybody in Wenningby had been busy in the harvest fields during the first fortnight of September. The only one of the farmers who had gone down to the dales was Richard Blackthorn, who had some young beasts pasturing at the foot of the scarp, some half mile below Wenningby Barns. Macdonald had had a few words with Mr. Blackthorn, asking him if he had seen any one in the dales on his visits of inspection. The old farmer eyed Macdonald shrewdly: the leisurely, independent judicial stare of appraisement which the C.I.D. man connected with the dalesmen.

'You're asking me if I saw 'anyone,' ' he commented. 'Happen you mean anyone from away.'

'I said anyone,' persisted Macdonald, 'from away and from here as well.'

'I shall have to think a bit,' said the farmer. 'Won't do for me to go telling you things too hasty like, and having you running in my neighbours just in case.'

There was a twinkle in the shrewd long-sighted eyes, and Macdonald put in:

'I'm from o'wer the Border, Mr. Blackthorn. Hasty like's not our motto in the Highlands.'

'Eh . . . but you're from London, too,' chuckled the other. 'Happen I saw Bob Fletcher time and again when I was in the dales. Aye, it's a funny thing, because he lives across the river.'

'Then what was he doing the Wenningby side?' asked Macdonald and the other roared his delight.

'He weren't this side. 'Twas his own side he was on, and we had a crack ower the stream, same as we've done this dun'-a-many years. That just shows you mustn't be ower hasty. Now I might ha' seen my son-in-law down by the river, and happen I saw Mr. Shand one day afishing in his own waters, all in order, and John Staple, he came along the river after one of his heifers. The beasts'll ford the river when it's low, and Mr. Fletcher, he's got a bull over yonder. Eh! but I'll have to think this out, Mr. Macdonald. I can't go making rash statements.'

'That's right. You thinks it over, Mr. Blackthorn, and I'll come and ask you again another day.'

'Aye. You give me time. Now I mind I did see two strangers one day. I can tell you that.'

Macdonald bided his time. This was going to be another leg-pull, and he knew it.

'T'was two A.T.S. lassies. They'd walked all the way from Caton bridge, and that's a powerful long way. They wanted to know where they could get a bus to take 'em back. 'You can get a bus at Aughton church at three o'clock,' I told 'em. 'Three o'clock on Friday that is, to-day being Wednesday.' Now you just give me time, Mr. Macdonald, and I'll give you a plain answer when I've given my mind to it.'

So when the Inspector said: 'We must ask the farmers,' Macdonald felt he was on safe ground when he said:

'Aye, and give them time to think about it. I feel I could do with a bit of time to think things out myself. In any case, I've got to ring up my own boss and tell him I've found a job to do up here, if you decide you want co-operation. Now what about this business of investigating Jacob's Buttery? We shall need a drag.'

'Aye, and a boat, too, and that's not so easy as it sounds, Chief. You can't scull a craft down the Lune like you can on the Thames; there's too many rapids. We shall have to cart a boat by road on the south side of the river and get it down to the water over the holm land. Quite a job that'll be.'

The Inspector scratched his chin.

'Whatever it be that's chained in Jacob's Buttery, Chief, it's been there for some days, hasn't it? D'you reckon it can bide till Monday?'

'I reckon it can,' agreed Macdonald.

The plan suited the Chief Inspector well. There were quite a number of things he would like to do on his own account on Sunday. True, he had said that the Sabbath was a day when no man should work, but following his own devices in Lunesdale did not seem oppressively like work to Macdonald. He concluded his talk with Bord by saying:

'All this is on the assumption that your Chief Constable sees fit to apply to C.O. for co-operation.'

'He'll see fit all right,' said Bord. 'Anyway, you're here.'

Macdonald laughed.

'Aye. Location will be ninety per cent of the reasoning, to parody the old adage. In any case, we want to clear up this clothing-coupon racket, and since Ginner has appeared in Lunesdale, my job lies here, so I think we can regard it as settled and leave the authorities to deal out the official agreements.'

'Suits me,' said Bord simply. 'I'll be happy to work with you, Chief.' And Cobley, from the background, muttered:

'Aye. That's champion,' and rubbed his large hands together in satisfaction.

II

As soon as Macdonald had left his colleague he found a convenient call-box and telephoned through to Mr. Hoggett.

'Macdonald speaking. Do you think I could stay at the cottage in the dales for the week-end?'

'Aye. Come when you like. I'll go down and light a fire and see there's some food. When will you come?'

'You've got a car, haven't you? I'll see you get some extra petrol if you use any for me. Could you come and pick me up at the Carnton-Borwick cross-road in an hour's time.'

'Aye. I'll be there.'

'Thanks very much — and I'd be obliged if you wouldn't go to the cottage again before I join you.'

'Right. I'll be at the cross-road in an hour's time.'

Mr. Hoggett was waiting in his car when Macdonald arrived, and when he had got in the C.I.D. man said:

'It's like this, Hoggett. It's a safe bet that there have been some illicit doings in your valley. What's the nature of them I don't know, but I want to avoid any show of police activity at present if I can. If anyone in these parts is watching out, the sight of your car isn't going to interest them nearly as much as the sight of a police outfit. Then I suppose you do lend the cottage to your friends occasionally?'

'Aye. That's very sound,' said Mr. Hoggett. 'I think

it'd be a good idea if I stayed at the cottage with you. It's quite a usual happening for me to have a friend or two down there for fishing.'

'Thanks very much,' said Macdonald, though he chuckled a bit to himself. Mr. Hoggett wanted to be on the spot while his own private mystery was being investigated. In most cases, the Scotland Yard man would have refused the offer of company, both tactfully and firmly, but he had a feeling that Giles Hoggett might be very useful. He had that same quality which (unbeknown to himself) had endeared Macdonald to the haymakers. He'd got the sense to do as he was told. Perhaps Macdonald felt confidence in his companion because he remembered him on the Rugby field. Hoggett had been a very good forward, not only because he was fast, but because he was cunning. He had shown himself a past master of the wiles which induced his opponent to think he was going to do just what he wasn't going to do. Looking at the long-headed fellow beside him, Macdonald summed the matter up with a Scot's reticence which Mr. Hoggett would have approved.

'I might do worse than have him there.'

'I've got some food in my haversack at the back,' said Mr. Hoggett. 'It'd be best if we put the car away at the farm as I always do and then we can walk from here. By the way, my Wenningby neighbours know who you are, but they won't mention you to anybody else. One thing about a small community like ours is that you do know your neighbours.'

'Yes. That must be very pleasant — but don't you ever miss Camford, and the book shop?'

'No. I'm doing what I always wanted to do and I want to go on doing it more than ever,' replied Giles

Hoggett. 'Here we are. Now if you can take the milk and that basket of plums . . . good. I like cooking. I've got the cottage keys . . . I'll just go and get my rods to add a little verisimilitude . . .'

By the time he was walking down the brow with Mr. Hoggett, Macdonald not only looked the part of an angler on holiday — he felt like it, too. It was quite a long time since he had carried such an assortment of goods, and it was evident that Mr. Hoggett made no conservative estimates concerning the amount of food two men could put away in a week-end.

Arrived at the cottage, Mr. Hoggett took off his coat and looked business-like. He nodded towards the hearth, which Macdonald had already examined that morning.

'Are you through with that? We shall want a fire.'

'Of course. You carry on with the fire. I've got a sample of the ashes and I'll just go round with an insufflator. I'm hoping for some nice portable finger-prints — on cups and plates and so forth. I've got a copy of Ginner's prints with me, so we can soon check up.'

'Good. I've brought some extra crocks and tools and a couple of saucepans so that I needn't touch those in here,' said Mr. Hoggett. 'My wife and I were very careful not to touch anything here, just in case . . . Do you care for mushroom soup? — and I've got sausages and tomatoes and plenty of eggs and a plum pie my wife sent . . . and there's the cream and a jar of honey . . .'

'Look here, Hoggett,' said Macdonald. 'I'm a Londoner and I haven't had food in such quantities for months. Do, for the good Lord's sake, leave off talking about food at least for half an hour while I do a spot of work. How can a London policeman do his stuff while you ask if he likes cream in the mushroom soup? The answer's in the affirmative, anyway.'

'Aye. I get you,' rejoined Giles Hoggett, and relapsed into silence, so far as his tongue went, though he seemed very efficient with the fire and his crocks and pots.

Macdonald went through the cottage in a very business-like way. He had soon got evidence that Gordon Ginner had been in the cottage; his fingerprints showed up plainly in two places: on an old cigarette tin which had been left on a shelf in the recess by the chimney piece (a beautiful clear print this one) and on the upright of the door. Macdonald was interested to find that there were very few fingerprints traceable; most of the surfaces had been wiped, so that his powder only showed up a series of smudges, and the old cups and plates and mugs on the dresser had also been wiped. The C.I.D. man made a thorough job of it, using his camera and flashlight outfit. He concluded that the housebreaker (or housebreakers) had not been upstairs in the cottage, for none of the furniture or other surfaces had been wiped in either bedrooms or on the landing. A thin film of dust lay undisturbed on chests and tables, and these, together with washing-bowls and ewers, showed a complication of fingerprints, many of them children's prints.

It was growing dusk by the time Macdonald had finished his examination, and Giles Hoggett called to him asking if he should close shutters and curtains before lighting the lamps. Macdonald agreed, and having put away his gear, he came back into the living-room of the cottage conscious that he was pleasantly hungry. A magnificent wood fire blazed up the open chimney, and Mr. Hoggett was ready with bowls of mushroom soup, while a vast mixed grill waited sizzling on the hearth as second course, with plum pie with thick cream to follow.

Macdonald sat down with his feet stretched out to the blaze and took his bowl of soup.

'Thank you, Hoggett,' he said, and gazed round the comfortable ancient room and back to the roaring fire. 'A man might do worse than live here,' he said meditatively. 'Why the devil do we equate civilisation with cities?'

'I've often wondered,' said Giles Hoggett placidly. 'I suppose my wife and I have turned our backs on most urban amenities and we're certainly in process of shedding the bookishness we were reared in, but it's a good life, and a fire like this one seems worth more than the proximity of cinemas and shops.'

'Aye,' agreed Macdonald comfortably.

They consumed their supper in companionable silence, and at length, having piled up the plates and pans in the adjoining small kitchen, they lighted their pipes and returned to the fire.

'Man, you're a grand cook,' said Macdonald gratefully. 'Now say if we get a few points cleared up before we both sleep the sleep of repletion. How many routes are there by which a man could arrive at this place?'

Giles Hoggett took his time over answering and then he said:

'It's like this, Macdonald. It depends on the weather conditions. You want to know about routes to the cottage at the end of August, the time when my wife saw the poacher?'

'Aye. That's about it.'

'Route one you know. Down the brow, the way we

came. Route two, by the river bank upstream from Garthmere bridge. It's a rough path, and not many would come that way because the path's overgrown and difficult to follow. It runs through the woods and it hasn't been kept clear of recent years. Route three, by the river bank walking downstream from the Knabb — that's a farm by the river a couple of miles to the east. Route four, by the right of way across Tom Profert's land — the Middle Upfield. Route five, by fording the river from the southern bank. You can do that when the river's low.'

'If a man wanted to reach the cottage unobserved, which route would be best?'

Mr. Hoggett scratched his head thoughtfully.

'Not by the brow, because he'd have to walk through Wenningby, and though you might not think it, hardly any stranger passes unobserved by somebody. Not by Knabb — that's a tidy-sized farm, and it's close to the river. Not by Garthmere — there's too many folk working in the fields. If I wanted to reach the dales unobserved, I'd leave the main road by the Upfields' turning. There are three Upfields — Near, Middle and Far Upfield, and two farm-houses to each. You see, those steadings are remote, and the houses were built in pairs for safety's sake in days when marauders had to be reckoned with. It's lonely land and they're small farms. You can follow the track through Middle Upfield down to the woods above the river and turn upstream by a path through the woods. Forty minutes' walking from the main road would bring you to these dales, and the track's marked on the Ordnance Survey. I'll show it to you to-morrow if you like.'

'Good.' Macdonald yawned comfortably and stretched his long limbs. 'D'you care for swimming?'

he asked.

'Aye. I like swimming well enough — but the river will be cold with all the water that's coming down from the hills.'

'Need you remind me of that?' said Macdonald, leaning closer to the fire. 'When you bathe from here, where do you take the first plunge?'

'Our bathing pool's a couple of hundred yards downstream by the big willow tree. You can get a good swim from there to Jacob's Buttery, over the rapids.'

'Losh keeps! Rapids, are there? Well, I'm going in for a dip as soon as the sun's up the morn's morn.'

'I'd better come in with you to see that you don't drown,' said Giles Hoggett. 'It'll be a thought chilly . . . but maybe you'll enjoy it.'

'Maybe I shan't,' groaned Macdonald.

6

I

Macdonald, warm, well-fed, and just comfortably tired, bent to knock his pipe out on the hearth, and as he looked up he became aware that Giles Hoggett was listening intently, staring at the door as though he could see through it.

'There's someone moving out yonder,' he said, and listened again. Macdonald listened, too, but he could hear nothing: the silence seemed unbroken — and the silence at Wenningby Barns was profound. Nevertheless Giles Hoggett was listening so that his long ears seemed to be more pointed in the effort of hearing.

'He stood still for a bit; now he's moving towards us,' he said. 'It's odd . . . no one ever comes down here after dark.'

Macdonald could hear the footsteps now; they were coming steadily nearer, until they stopped close at hand.

'He's opened the gate. He's coming in,' said Mr. Hoggett, and turned to the door of the cottage.

'Wait and see if he knocks,' said Macdonald quickly. 'If he does, keep behind the door as you open it.'

'Aye,' said Mr. Hoggett sagaciously.

A second later there was a drumming on the door. Obedient to Macdonald's instruction, Giles Hoggett kept well behind the door as he opened it.

'Who's there?' he asked.

'Is that you Mr. Hoggett? It's Barton Shand. Can I come in?'

'Of course. Come in, Mr. Shand. We don't often have visitors after dark at Wenningby Barns — but it's a fine evening. I see the moon's quite bright.'

Giles Hoggett's pleasant voice was as serene as if he were greeting an expected guest, but the visitor looked far from serene.

'Shand . . . the adjoining land-owner,' registered Macdonald's mind as the two men turned towards the fire.

Mr. Shand was a tall fellow, a thought taller than Giles Hoggett (who just missed six feet). He had a fine head of white hair and a rather heavy, fleshy face with deep-set dark eyes; he was the sort of man who could have been described as 'of commanding presence,' for he was well-poised and held his head with a touch of arrogance that was not unbecoming. Macdonald, of all men the last to be impressed by 'a commanding presence,' noted that Mr. Shand's figure had a tendency to obesity in the under waist, and that his cheeks sagged a little under his fine dark eyes. Hoggett was less impressive at first glance, but Macdonald approved of his lank northern spareness, his big shoulders and the way he stood on his feet, as though there was always a spring behind that easy stance. For no known reason, and rather unkindly, Macdonald thought that Hoggett could tackle the bigger man with every prospect of success — but Hoggett was firmly linked with the Rugger field in Macdonald's mind. The conversation which ensued, however, held no hint of bellicosity.

'I'm sorry to butt in on you like this, Hoggett,' said Barton Shand, speaking more easily now, though he was obviously out of breath. 'The fact is I saw the light through the cracks in your shutters and I wondered if there was a housebreaker on the premises. I just thought I'd make sure nothing was amiss.'

'Very good of you, Mr. Shand. I'm grateful for your thoughtfulness. We're just down here for the weekend, but the cottage is often empty. Won't you sit down awhile?'

'Thanks. I should be glad of a sit. Running's not so much in my line these days. I've been having the deuce of a time, Mr. Hoggett.'

Mr. Shand sat down heavily in the big wooden armchair pushed forward for him, and ran a hand through his ruffled white locks. Macdonald subsided silently into his own chair and Giles Hoggett sat on the edge of an ancient Victorian couch.

Macdonald noticed that Mr. Shand had recently had a tumble; his good raincoat was still thick with wet mud and slime.

'I've been very much put out by this business of thieving down here,' went on Shand. 'I went in to see Willoughby this evening, and he told me about his hut being broken open. He also said the police had told him you'd had burglars down here.'

'Well, that's putting it a bit strongly,' said Giles Hoggett mildly. 'I did report to the police that some unauthorised person had been in here and lighted a fire and taken some food — but burglary seems rather a strong word to use.'

'Can you define the term burglary for me?' demanded the other in rather testy accents.

'Certainly,' said Mr. Hoggett, promptly and urbanely. 'A burglar is one who breaks into a house by night, that is, between the hours of nine and six, with a felonious intent. I have no idea what time the unknown visitor entered this cottage. He did not break in — so far as I can ascertain. I do not know if his intent were felonious.'

'Come, come, that's mere quibbling, Hoggett. However, I should be interested to learn if you have any ideas as to the identity of your . . . er . . . unauthorised entrant.'

'Why, yes, I've got an idea of my own, but as my wife very properly reminds me, I have no evidence,' replied Giles Hoggett. 'I believe it's the potters.'

'I don't agree with you. I don't agree with you at all,' said Shand peremptorily. 'I have some evidence I can put forward myself; but it's nothing to do with the potters. Far from it. I had a word with the police about these accusations against the potters. Far from having been proven, these accusations were all very wide of the mark. I know nothing at all about the potters, but the police have satisfied themselves that the Golds were improperly accused. Now I have a very different suggestion to make — especially after my experiences this evening. I have a tenant who, speaking in confidence, is a very untrustworthy fellow. It won't tax your intelligence very far to know who I mean, Hoggett. That fellow at Thorpe Intak — Vintner by name.'

'Aye. The artist,' replied Hoggett. 'My wife tells me he's a very competent painter.'

'A fig for that!' retorted Mr. Shand. 'I can tell you he's very far from being a responsible tenant. Now when I left Willoughby's cottage this evening I ran my car along to the top of the brow in order to turn, and I saw a man disappearing down the brow. I turned my headlights on, and there was no mistaking who it was.

It was Anthony Vintner. I can swear to that all right. Now can you suggest any good reason why Anthony Vintner should be skulking down the brow after dark, Hoggett?'

'Yes, Mr. Shand,' replied the imperturbable Giles. 'I can suggest a number of reasons. The man's an artist. He may well have been studying the effect of moonlight on the flood water. It's really very beautiful, Mr. Shand. He may even have been composing poetry — about the moonlight.'

Giles turned to Macdonald with a gentle naïveté which nearly reduced the C.I.D. man to an outbreak of the mirth which had been welling up in him.

'There are some lines of Sir Walter Scott's about moonlight, Jock, perhaps you can recall them,' said Giles.

Macdonald played up.

'If thou wouldst view fair Melrose aright,
Go visit it by the pale moonlight,
For the gay beams of gladsome day
Gild but to flout the ruins grey.'

The C.I.D. man rolled out the lines as a Highland minstrel might have pronounced them and had the pleasure of seeing the muscles twitching round Hoggett's close shut lips. Mr. Shand was obviously annoyed by this levity and he cut in:

'Vintner *may* write poetry and he *may* paint pictures, but neither supposition explains why he first ran away from me and later tripped me up. I called to him when I first saw him, and instead of replying, he hurried on down the brow. I followed him. I was convinced he was up to no good. It's infernally dark on the brow, and just at the steepest corner I was tripped up by a stick thrust between my ankles. I took a proper toss — it winded me for the moment.'

'Hard lines!' said Giles Hoggett. 'I'm very sorry you had a tumble, Mr. Shand, but can you be certain you were tripped up? The ground is very treacherous on the brow and there are some fallen branches which came down in the gale. It's very easy to trip on the brow after dark.'

'I am *quite* certain I was tripped up,' retorted Mr. Shand, 'and I'm also certain that Vintner went on ahead of me along the dales. That's why I came to investigate when I saw your light. Now I think you should consider this matter seriously, Hoggett. Here is this fellow Vintner. He hasn't the money to pay his rent; his chicken farm is derelict and he's to all intents and purposes bankrupt. I wouldn't put it beyond him to do a little safe thieving. Now this cottage of yours — it's deserted for weeks at a time. He may well have thought it worth while to break in and see if there were anything of value here.'

'But there isn't,' said Giles Hoggett. 'At least, nothing of value in terms of money.'

'Are you quite sure?' said Shand.

He got up and stretched a hand towards the shelves in the recess beside the chimney.

'Those old books, for instance, Hoggett. I remember looking at them one day when you asked me to come in and shelter awhile — last Spring it would have been. I was surprised at the time that you risked leaving them down here . . . This one, for instance. Fine old binding, tut . . . tut . . . mildewed. Really, Hoggett, not fair to a good book to leave it against these damp walls. Damp plays the devil with books, y'know.'

Macdonald was more diverted than ever. It seemed that Mr. Shand did not know Giles Hoggett's avocation before he turned farmer. Giles remained deceptively mild; he even looked politely grateful for the information.

'Damp?' he said gently, taking the ancient little volume in his hand. 'I'm afraid it's been damp for a long time, Mr. Shand . . . 1837 . . . That's quite a time ago. H'm . . . that'd be my grandfather Ramsden. Yes, he was born in 1825. He went to Wenningby Grammar School. We had a Grammar School here as late as 1870, Mr. Shand. Perhaps the book is damp, but it's been here a long time, and I doubt if anybody wants a text book of English grammar written in the Latin tongue.'

Macdonald took the book from Giles Hoggett and read the doggerel written on the title page:

'John Ramsden is my name,
England is my nation
Wenningby's my dwelling place,
And Heaven my destination.'

MAY 6, 1837.

It was a nice little book, and Macdonald was surprised when he realised that an impulse flashed through his mind to put the mouldy little volume into his own pocket. He hastily returned it to Giles Hoggett and looked across at Mr. Shand, who was fussing over the other books on the shelves.

'H'm . . . classics . . . Well, Hoggett, I should have these valued. You never know . . . Have you got them catalogued? No? So you may have lost something valuable. Vintner's just the sort of chap who'd spot a valuable old book.'

Giles Hoggett sat by his own fireside, his stockinged feet stretched comfortably to the blaze — he had forgotten to put his slippers on again when he went to the door. His hands were thrust well into the baggy pockets of his ancient tweed breeches, his hair was a bit tousled and his face not quite clean — he'd cooked the supper over an open fire — but Macdonald always recognised innate dignity when he saw it, and without moving a muscle Giles Hoggett achieved real dignity at that moment.

'I have no catalogue of the books save that in my own memory, Mr. Shand. I grew up with those books, just where they are now. I know every one of them. I know also that not one of them would be priced at higher than sixpence by any bookseller of repute. They have, as I told you, no monetary value, but they have value to me. I know them — and they are all there. Nevertheless I thank you for your concern regarding them.'

Mr. Shand looked slightly non-plussed. Macdonald, who was a good judge of men, summed up the situation pretty accurately. Barton Shand was a land-owner — quite a sizeable land-owner. He could probably have bought up Giles Hoggett's acres — if he had the chance — without missing the money thus spent. He had probably seen Giles Hoggett mucking out his own shippon and milking his modest dairy herd. Barton Shand wanted to put Hoggett in his place; he wanted to do it very much, to condescend to a simple country neighbour and show him his ignorance, but his intention was not working out according to plan. Mr. Shand gave a good resounding snort.

'Very well, have it your own way, Hoggett, but I have my own opinion on the matter and I'm not likely to change it.'

He got up, and then added: 'If there is nothing of value in this cottage, how do you account for the fact that it was . . . er . . . entered?'

'I said nothing of monetary value, Mr. Shand. There was food and fuel and shelter — all valuable commodities on occasion. There were some old coats. These things may have been valuable to itinerant hucksterers. I don't think they would have even tempted a man like Vintner. He may be broke, but I don't think he's hungry, and his clothes are rather better than my own.'

'I deprecate this readiness to make a scapegoat of the potters. It seems to me an unjustified and unworthy attitude.'

'I respect you for what you say, Mr. Shand. I feel rather the same about Vintner. He's a fool with poultry and he hasn't the sense of a louse over housekeeping, but he's not a bad chap taking him all round.'

'Perhaps you might think otherwise if he were a tenant of yours, Hoggett.'

'Oh, I shouldn't have been so unwise as to let him the tenancy of a rural property,' said Giles genially. 'Now can I see you up the brow, Mr. Shand? It is, as you say, rough going, and it's dark under the trees.'

'No thank you, no thank you. I can find my own way. I wish you good-night.'

Mr. Shand went to the door and made the best exit he could, observing that the moon was still bright.

Giles Hoggett closed the door and returned to the fireside. 'The man's an ass in some ways, but he's not a bad landlord,' he said. 'I've known worse.'

'What did you think of his explanation of his arrival here?'

'Oh, I think he was telling the truth — he's a truthful man under the pompous stuff. He probably did see Vintner. The latter has been painting the valley in moonlight. Kate saw his picture. She said it was 'arbitrary' and advised me not to buy it. Do you know what an 'arbitrary' painting is?'

'I think so, Hoggett. And do you imagine that Vintner tripped up his landlord?'

'No — though I wouldn't put it beyond him. He's got his own sense of humour. I've no doubt Shand tripped over a broken branch and thought he was being attacked.'

Macdonald stretched himself thoughtfully.

'Would you care for a walk, Hoggett? I heard you mention the moonlight over the flood water.'

'Aye; it's a fine sight.'

Without further comment Giles reached for his shoes and started pulling them on.

'If you take the small lamp upstairs and set it on the landing, we can put this one out before we open the door,' he observed.

'You're a thoughtful chap,' said Macdonald. 'If I open the bedroom doors there'll be enough light shining through to give the right impression.'

'Aye,' said Mr. Hoggett.

II

The harvest moon was just past the full, and it seemed to sail overhead in a sea of luminous iridescence, due to the vaporous clouds in the high steely vault of the sky.

Giles Hoggett closed the cottage door quietly behind them, and the two men stood still by common consent until their eyes were accustomed to the delicate black and white of the world outside. The air was cold and very still, and at first the silence seemed unbroken. It took Macdonald some seconds to attune his ears to the distant sounds of the night: the gurgle of the becks, the call of a beast in the holm-land far across the river, the faint jarring cry of a night bird, and another queer sound closer at hand, which he realised was the munching of a beast (Cow? Stirk? Heifer? Bullock?) in Richard Blackthorn's pasture.

Giles Hoggett, as certain as a cat on his feet in the shadows of the cottage, preceded Macdonald to the gate and took a few steps forward before he touched the other's arm.

'Shand's car. He's got his headlights on.'

Hoggett's low deep voice seemed to be but an echo of the murmuring becks in Macdonald's ear. Glancing upwards towards the top of the scarp he could see the glow of the headlights for a second or two and then the faint sound of jarring gears put in by an impatient hand.

'He's taken the turning by the church,' murmured Hoggett.

Macdonald, keen of ear and keen of vision, admitted the other chap had got him beaten in both respects. Here, in his own valley, under the night sky, the dalesman heard and saw more quickly than the London detective.

'There's someone moving yonder — in the dales downstream . . .' said Hoggett.

He turned to the right, westwards, walking parallel

with the river, and Macdonald followed. On his right was the wooded scarp, sloping steeply up from the valley meadows; to his left some ancient low thorns were between him and the main stream. Macdonald fell behind a little, deliberately. Hoggett ahead of him knew the ground and could risk moving forward, loping, as it were, at a surprising speed, considering he made no sound. Macdonald felt the water over his shoes as he stepped through a small beck and perceived that he had passed the shadowing thorns and was now on the open dales. The moonlight shone white over the wet fog grass and made paths of radiance in the flood water, and the willows which fringed the river bank stood out black, their trunks rising from the water now; to his right the woods reached in impenetrable blackness to the level of the shining dales. Macdonald had time for a fleeting acknowledgment of the beauty of the moonlit valley; surely any painter might wish to study the black and white of trees and shining water — and then he forgot the loveliness about him as he realised that Hoggett had halted and stood immobile for a second before he squatted low on the sodden ground. Macdonald followed suit, and a second later he saw a sight suited to the fairy black and white of flooded, moonlit Lunesdale. A figure was running over the grass, and for a second Macdonald thought he was bewitched. The slight figure was clad only in singlet and running shorts, it seemed, white in the moonlight, and the slender limbs shone white too, while the head shone pale gold — a pixie eldritch figure in the cold moonlight. Hoggett seemed to have no feelings about fairies. Suddenly he was off, running at an astonishing speed, flat out, a long angular blackness, splashing through the flood water like a steeplechaser.

Macdonald was not slow off the mark himself. With an absurd feeling of exhilaration he raced after the other, and he admitted afterwards that he wasn't really chasing the eldritch figure of the fugitive — he was racing Hoggett. 'Damn the fellow . . . he's older than I am,' was the reaction of a distinguished member of the C.I.D. as he sent the flood water flying under the moon.

Macdonald always believed that he gained several yards on the straight, but it was Hoggett who brought the chase to an end. He tackled in the proper spirit and the proper place, and next second the air was lively with vituperation by no means fairy-like.

'Well, I'm very sorry, but you shouldn't have run away,' panted Mr. Hoggett. 'If you behave like a lunatic you must expect to be treated as one.'

He had staggered to his feet, gripping his sodden captive. This was no sprite; Macdonald could see him now. It was the poultry-farming painter. Clad in a manner more suitable for the tropics than for Lunesdale on a perishing cold evening in the back-end, Anthony Vintner's teeth were chattering as he swore and went on swearing.

'Now stop it,' said Mr. Hoggett, shaking him vigorously.

('Just the voice he uses to Lady Clare,' thought Macdonald.) 'Your coat's on the old thorns yonder,' continued Giles severely. 'We'd better get it, or you'll be getting pneumonia — and dying like those hens of yours.'

Suddenly Vintner laughed, and his laughter echoed across the valley in peal after peal of mirth.

'Damn and blast you, it's funny all the same,' he

gasped. 'I thought you were my landlord. I meant to ditch him by the fence. All right, where's my coat? Don't pinch, confound you. I'm not running away from you, Mr. Giles Hoggett. Have you got a hot toddy in that cottage of yours?'

'No, I haven't — and I'd say you don't need one,' retorted Hoggett. 'You're a rotten runner anyway. You can have a cup of tea and get dry while you're explaining why I shouldn't get you certified.'

III

They found Anthony Vintner's coat just where Mr. Hoggett had said they would find it — hanging on the old thorns. Macdonald admitted (very handsomely) that he hadn't noticed it as he passed, and Giles Hoggett said modestly, 'Well, you see I know the shape of those trees pretty well.'

'Yes,' agreed Macdonald. 'You're several tricks up this evening — but I'll diddle you yet.'

'Are you playing boy scouts?' demanded Vintner cheerfully; in spite of his chattering teeth he seemed very gay.

It was Giles Hoggett who replied:

'You're on my land,' he said solemnly, 'and I don't hold with these goings-on. I'm behaving as a responsible landlord should behave. Go in — that's the gate.'

They trooped into the cottage, and Giles Hoggett got busy with the fire and kettle, while Vintner crouched over the blaze and Macdonald kicked off his sodden shoes, studying the painter the while. His slim build, white skin and carroty gold hair explained why he had looked so sprite-like in the moonlight — but his hair was wet, trickles of water still dripping from the wiry curls which defied the wet.

Giles Hoggett made the tea and gave each a large steaming cup.

'Can I have some sugar in mine, please?' asked Vintner with his irrepressible grin.

While he fetched the sugar-basin, Hoggett found an opportunity by dumb play to ask Macdonald which of them should open the inquisition, and Macdonald signalled 'You.'

Hoggett gave Vintner the sugar, and then suddenly barked out:

'What have you been doing down here?'

The voice was quite unexpected; in place of his usual gentle tones, Giles Hoggett barked out the question like a severe schoolmaster accusing a schoolboy in the tuck cupboard.

'What the deuce has it got to do with you?' demanded Vintner. 'You can't say I was trespassing — the river bank's got a path along it, hasn't it? — and if I was trespassing, I've done no damage.'

'Now you listen to me,' said Mr. Hoggett. 'There have been some very improper things happening here of late — at least two cases of theft and an alleged one of assault. If you can't give any explanation of your presence down here at night, I shall consider it my duty to detain you and hand you over to the police. Now I come to think of it, there have been a number of unexplained thefts since you arrived at Thorpe Intak.'

'Damn it all, Hoggett, you don't really think I've been thieving, do you?'

Vintner spoke in tones of injured innocence, but Macdonald realised the underlying tone of uneasiness.

'I've asked you what you were doing down here,' persisted Mr. Hoggett, 'and I'm waiting for an answer.'

'I came to study the valley in the moonlight. I'm painting an impression of it.'

'Very good. Why did you need to go in the river in order to study the moonlight? Why did you run away when you saw me? Why didn't you answer Mr. Shand when he called to you? Why did you trip him up at the bottom of the brow and then run away? Remembering that certain thefts have been reported to the police, I think they'll want to know the answer to the questions I have just put.'

'If I choose to paddle in order to study the moonlight it's nobody's business but my own,' retorted Vintner.

'You weren't paddling — you wouldn't have got your head wet paddling. Why did you run away when you saw me?'

'I told you. I thought you were Shand. He's a damned awful consequential bully and I hoped to see him take a purler in the flood water.'

Macdonald put a word in at last, meditatively.

'I'm not a painter myself, and I can't draw a thing, but how any man trained to use his eyes could mistake Mr. Hoggett's figure for Mr. Shand's I can't imagine. Not even in the moonlight. If Mr. Shand can run at all — which I doubt — he wouldn't look like Mr. Hoggett while he was doing it.'

Anthony Vintner turned and studied Macdonald with his impish light eyes.

'Hallo, Scotty. It's you is it — the chap with the chin. You're going to sit for me one day, remember.'

'Don't prevaricate,' said Mr. Hoggett. 'If Mr. Shand brings an action for assault you won't be improving your chances of acquittal by what you've just been saying.'

'Hi, steady on,' protested Vintner. 'You said I tripped him up on the brow. I didn't. He tripped himself up. He fell over a branch. I wasn't on the brow. When I realised he'd got out of his car I climbed over on to the bank and came down the fields. I don't like Mr. Shand — but I didn't trip him up. Can I have a cigarette?'

He reached out and took a tin which lay on the bookshelves beside the chimney, and Mr. Hoggett pulled a depressed looking packet of Stars out of his pocket and held it out:

'That tin hasn't had any cigarettes in it since 1939,' he said. 'You can have one of these. Well, I can tell the Sergeant that you came down to the river to study the moonlight over the flood water, that you took your coat off and hung it on a tree, that you got your head wet while you were paddling, and that you ran away from me because you hoped to trip up Mr. Shand. I think Sergeant Cobley will be interested.'

Vintner stirred restlessly in his chair.

'Look here, you're not really going to try to get me into trouble with the cops, are you? I think it's damned unfair. I haven't done you any harm and I don't believe you really think I've stolen anything. What's been stolen, anyway?'

'Various items from the dales,' responded Giles Hoggett. 'I'm very upset about it. The folk hereabouts are honest folk and I'm going to see that the thieving is put a stop to. I'm not satisfied with the story you've told, Vintner, and I advise you to think it over. I'll give you until midday to-morrow to make up your mind.'

'Make it up about what?'

‘About telling the truth. I know enough already to know that you haven’t told the truth so far.’

He turned to Macdonald.

‘Ought we to keep him here?’ he inquired.

Macdonald shook his head.

‘I think not. It’s probable that Mr. Vintner will decide for himself that he’d be wiser to be more accurate next time he’s questioned.’

‘Aye, let him think it over.’ Giles Hoggett sounded very solemn. ‘You can go now,’ he said, ‘but I shall be seeing you again shortly.’

Anthony Vintner looked both puzzled and uneasy; he looked from one to the other of the big solemn fellows and then shrugged his shoulders.

‘All right. Thanks for the cup of tea and the warm, Mr. Hoggett. You’re not being fair, which is a pity, because you’re the nicest chap in a day’s march hereabouts. I know you think I’m bats. I don’t mind that — but the other stuff’s a bit thick.’

‘You’ve only yourself to blame,’ said Giles Hoggett, and his voice was once again the low kindly voice which was his norm. Vintner glanced quickly at him and then made for the door.

‘Good-night,’ he said. ‘Sorry you think I’m a thief — because I’m not,’ and with that he walked out into the night.

7

I

After the door had shut behind the carroty-headed painter, Hoggett and Macdonald turned to one another with the same impulse — to grin. They both grinned. Then Hoggett said:

'What about another cup of tea? I'm thirsty after all that.'

'Aye,' said Macdonald. 'You did fine, Hoggett. That hoary chestnut about 'knowing more than you think,' — it impressed even me, and I've heard it pretty often. The point is — do you?'

'No,' said Giles Hoggett truthfully, stirring the teapot vigorously. 'What did you make of him, Macdonald?'

'Well, I'd say he's a bit of a twister. The point that interested me was that the chap was afraid. When you first copped him his shivers weren't all due to being chilly — and he was very relieved to find it was you who'd copped him. Now what was he afraid of? Certainly not of Shand. He didn't care a fig for Shand.'

'I'd say you're right there.' Giles Hoggett sat forward, warming his toes at the fire, deep in thought. 'He'd been in the river,' he said. 'He left his coat on the thorn trees and walked across the dales. He must have hung his shorts and vest on the willow tree, because they weren't soaked. I knew he'd been in the river, because his skin was so cold. What would he have been in the river for? I know he's a queer bird, but I don't think he took a dip just for pleasure. At the same time I shouldn't have said he was a scoundrel. He's mischievous, maybe, but not a real bad 'un.'

He looked up at Macdonald.

'I was surprised you didn't want to follow him — in case he bolts.'

'I don't think he will — especially after your broad hint about giving him twelve hours' grace to tell the truth. He didn't really believe you'd tell the police about him, I could see that. In any case, if he tries to do a bolt along your roads to-night, he'll be asking for trouble. There are extra men at certain points, and a laddie dressed only in a topcoat over pants and vest is going to be asked what he's up to.'

Giles Hoggett put his cup down.

'Did you notice he pocketed that empty cigarette tin?' he asked.

Macdonald nodded. 'Yes, I noticed. I hope to find out the reason for that some time. Meantime, before we both fall asleep, tell me a bit about those two other worthies I met to-day — Messrs. Shand and Willoughby. Shand's not a countryman, is he?'

'Not what I call a countryman. His people came from Barrow and his father had an iron foundry and made a lot of money. He spent some of it buying land in this district and his son Barton Shand bought more land. He only comes here occasionally. He has a big place in the Peak district. He's a business man really, but he fancies himself as a land-owner.'

'Iron foundry. H'm . . . Is he married?'

'Aye, and he's got a son. They say clogs to clogs in three generations. They think that'll be the way of it.'

'Do you? Where's the son?'

'In London, I believe. He escaped military service on account of poor physique. He's a poor sort of bloke; as near weak-witted as makes no difference. Shand's not a bad sort. He's honest, and I'd say he's truthful, and he's quite a considerate landlord if his tenants behave themselves. He's got a very nice wife — Kate's met her and says she's a great improvement on her husband. Incidentally he's a very good husband, deeply devoted to his wife.'

'Does Mrs. Shand come up here with her husband?'

'Not now. She used to, but I believe her health is pretty poor. Shand doesn't really care much about Lunesdale, but he's a conscientious landlord in his own way and he comes up here at intervals to keep an eye on his property; then he's a fisherman, of course. But what I think he really enjoys is the feeling that he's a 'Squire' — although we don't have Squires up here.'

'I was wondering if Mr. Shand could help us later on — if we need help — by giving evidence of any folk he has noted in the valley.'

'He'd be willing enough to help; but I don't think he'd be much use. He was away for ten days from the end of August onwards. In any case, Shand doesn't really notice much. He's too busy concentrating on his own impressiveness. He's no judge of character, otherwise he'd never have let Thorpe Intak to Anthony Vintner.'

'What about Mr. Willoughby?'

'Oh, he's a very decent chap. He's a wool merchant, from Leeds. He's a good fisherman, a good tenant and a pleasant neighbour. He rents a cottage of mine just above the beck, and he's Shand's fishing tenant.'

'One last question before I let you go to sleep: Is

your suspicion of the potters based on real evidence or on prejudice?'

Giles Hoggett took his time over answering, and the answer when it came was perfectly truthful.

'On prejudice; but it's worth bearing this in mind. We're slow in forming judgments hereabouts, and we don't often analyse the reason behind our judgments, but there generally is a reason somewhere. Leave me out of it and consider the opinion of men like Richard Blackthorn and John Staple. They have a very poor opinion of the Golds and both these men are sound judges of character. I admit that I have inherited a prejudice from my parents; they both distrusted nomads of any kind — here to-day and gone to-morrow, with no sense of responsibility, no settled work, skimmers of other folks' industry. But that's only my opinion, and as Kate will tell you, once I'm prejudiced, I'm unreasonable. Richard's a very fair man. You have a crack with him sometime.'

'Aye, that's sound advice,' said Macdonald, 'but can't you tell me a bit more about these potters yourself?'

A fresh gleam of interest lit up Mr. Hoggett's face, and Macdonald realised his companion was willing enough to talk now he made it clear that he didn't want his opinions to be regarded as objective fact.

'You know, Macdonald, the potters are an interesting phenomenon. It's a wonder some bright young student hasn't done a sociological survey of them. In an ordered society they are among the very few people who remain free. They *are* free, just like birds.' Mr. Hoggett scratched his head and went on with more certainty as his ideas developed.

'Robins have a fixed territory which they keep

to themselves and from which they exclude others: similarly these Golds have a territory of their own which they work, say from Carnton up the valley as far as Chapelton-Lonsdale. I'd describe them as the economic parasites for this district which they have somehow claimed as their own.'

Mr. Hoggett glanced at Macdonald as though wondering whether to proceed, but the latter reassured him:

'Go on. You're just beginning to be interesting. Develop your thesis and translate it into terms of everyday life.'

'Meaning ordinary plain Lunesdale,' agreed Hoggett. 'I admit the potters have their uses; they act as scavengers, so to speak, for the farmers. They take rabbit skins, mole skins, old iron, slag bags, and anything else that's accumulating at a farm, and they pay some sort of price for them. They'll buy rabbits which have been snared, and save the farmer the bother of taking them into market. They come along before Christmas and they'll pay an agreed price to be allowed to cut the berried holly. Oh, they have their uses — but farmers don't really trust them and they keep their eyes on them as far as they can. Even so, we have a feeling there must be a lot of things the potters pick up on the quiet. The upshot is there's a sort of irritated tolerance for them, and the irritation comes to its height when something of value is missing and the tendency is to blame the loss on to the potters.'

Hoggett paused again and then added:

'All the same, there have always been potters about the countryside; they're traditional and so they're tolerated. I expect even if I had the power to clear them out of the district I shouldn't exercise it. You see, they're part of the landscape.' He concluded apologetically: 'I don't suppose all this has helped you much — you try talking to Richard about them.'

'Thanks, I will. Next, can you tell me of anybody who knows the Golds as individuals and whose word could be relied on?'

'Aye. There's my cousin George. He's a doctor in Ingleforth. He's doctored the Gold family, and he's a very truthful man. George makes allowances — but he doesn't live right in the country.'

Here Giles Hoggett allowed himself the colossal yawn he had been suppressing heroically.

'All right. Go to bed,' chuckled Macdonald. 'That was a good run we had.'

'Aye. You'd better leave your socks to dry by the fire. Kate's very particular about damp socks. I'll wake you in good time for a swim. I've got to be up at the farm for milking by half-past seven. Good-night.'

'Good-night — and thank you for a good evening,' said Macdonald.

II

The morn broke with a promise of perfect weather. When Macdonald and Hoggett went outside, the sky was still warm hued with the gold of dawn, but swathes of white mist floated down the valley: on the dales the mist was thick to shoulder height, but Macdonald found his head occasionally emerged above the white wraiths, so that he could see the willow trees floating above the mist as though trunkless. It was very cold and Giles Hoggett looked chilly and glum. They raced together over the cold drenched grass, took off their coats by the big willow and plunged in. The chill of the water was breath-taking but Macdonald trudged downstream with a vigour which soon set his circulation going. In a minute or so he was in the rapids and found that all he had to do was to keep straight and get his head up at intervals to breathe. The river had fallen in the night, and when he got past the rapids Macdonald found the stream was not bank high as it had been the previous night. He called over his shoulder: 'You all right?' and heard Hoggett's answering voice. Then he turned towards the bank in the stretch known as Jacob's Buttery, and plunged to test the depth of the water. When he came up he had to fight the stream to get into the bank and found it a tough business — the water was still coming down at a terrific pace. Hoggett went past Macdonald on the current as the latter managed to grip an overhanging branch leaning out from the bank, and Macdonald had a breather and turned to see what Hoggett was doing. He (canny fellow), knowing the ways of this river, was getting in towards the bank by means of an eddy which saved him from battling with the stream as Macdonald had done.

'He doesn't want any saving,' thought the Scot, and dived down into the deep water by the steep bank.

He found that the roots of the willow had been scoured clean by the current, and he soon found something else. Giles Hoggett's sack was there, and the chain, and the iron dogs. The laden sack was chained to the willow roots and lodged tight in a recess where the river had undercut the bank.

Macdonald surfaced again and plunged into mid-stream — he wanted to swim for a bit in the fresh air and wash away the feeling of that clammy sack. He found Hoggett's eddy and swam inshore easily, where the other was searching the bank.

'You can get out. I've found your sack,' said the C.I.D. man.

Hoggett scrambled out with Macdonald close behind him.

'I want my coat. That river's damned cold,' said Macdonald.

They ran over the grass, providing astonishment and diversion for Richard Blackthorn's bullocks, who ran after them with the inquisitiveness of their kind. Hoggett asked no questions, but as he seized the rough towel he had brought out with him, Macdonald saw the unspoken question in the other's eyes.

'Aye. As you guessed for yourself. A grim business. I'm sorry.'

'Thanks,' was all that Giles Hoggett said, and then added:

'I've made some coffee. It's in the pot — and it'll be hot.'

They wasted no more words but raced back across the dales. The sun was just getting through the mist, and the pale gleams felt warm to the chilled limbs of the two swimmers.

III

A fine fire was roaring up the chimney and the two men got dressed before the comfort of the heat. Hoggett poured out the coffee and they were both glad of its scalding fragrance. It was not until then that Macdonald said:

'I think I'd better stay down here. Will you telephone

to Inspector Bord and ask him to join me here immediately. It's only seven o'clock now but the earlier the better. We oughtn't to attract much attention early on a Sunday morning. Tell him to send the Mortuary Van and stretcher on the south side of the river. You'll know the right place for them to pull up. We needn't carry a stretcher up the brow.'

'Right,' replied Hoggett.

Again he asked no question, and it was for that very reason Macdonald went on:

'It's a man's body, not a woman's. I knew from the size of his shoes. I can't tell you anything else.'

'Since there *is* a body there, I'd rather it were a man's,' said Hoggett simply. 'You'll want some breakfast. You know where things are. I'll be getting on up.'

He paused at the door, and added: 'Was that why Vintner was frightened? He must have got out of the river just about there.'

'Maybe.'

Hoggett nodded and turned away. Macdonald put down a solid breakfast in quick time; he knew that no man does a better day's work for an empty stomach. Then he went out again into the sunlit dales and walked along beside the river. He could see for a long way, up and down the peaceful valley: not a soul was in sight and he thought how often the dales must be solitary like this. The chances against meeting anyone here must be considerable.

Having assured himself that no one was in the vicinity, he began to go over the ground they had covered last evening. It was too wet to have held any traces, for the ground was still waterlogged, but he remembered where he had been when he first spotted Vintner running towards the woods, and he squelched methodically back and forth searching the ground. He hardly expected to find anything, but it was almost instinctive to search, and as he walked he put together the few facts which had emerged in this first unofficial period of detection. Gordon Ginner had been seen in the valley with a fishing rod on August 31st. (Macdonald accepted Mrs. Hoggett's statement as reliable. He knew a trustworthy witness when he met one.) Mr. Hoggett had found traces of wheels (probably the bogie) between the cottage and the river on September 15th: he had also found a torn fragment of curtain material caught on the thorns. Mr. Willoughby's hut had been broken into. The cottage had been entered by somebody who had used the key.

It was at this stage in his thoughts that Macdonald found a tin. It was lying in the grass some twenty yards from where Vintner had been running last night. It was a cylindrical tin, still bright, though patches of rust were beginning to show on it. Macdonald picked it up gingerly by its edges and observed that solder had been used to fasten the lid on. The tin weighed some ounces, but Macdonald thought from its size it would probably float in water. He had no idea if it was in any way connected with his case, but decided to carry it back to the cottage and examine it there. He remembered the odd fact that Vintner had appropriated the old cigarette tin which had yielded Ginner's prints.

When Macdonald had noticed that the cigarette tin had disappeared from the shelf, he had been quite willing to believe the simplest explanation of its disappearance — that Vintner had taken it because it was a useful tin to hold some of his painter's impedimenta, good tins being hard to come by at the present time.

Macdonald knew — none better — the enormous increase in petty pilfering even among respectable people in these days of universal shortage. An empty tin, lying on a shelf among a variety of junk — why not 'knock it off?' It was a misdemeanour so commonplace as to be almost universal.

At that moment, too, Macdonald had been willing to believe that Vintner's swim-suit might have been put down to eccentricity. He was a queer type, with all the artist's capacity for exaltation — and the moonlit valley had been enough to excite anyone of aesthetic sensibility and nervous temperament. Vintner seemed to Macdonald to have just the type of mind to do things which would be described as 'silly' by the unexcitable average person.

Macdonald carried his tin back to the cottage, and when he emerged again, he heard footsteps coming down the brow. It wasn't Hoggett. Macdonald had already registered the sound of his host's apparently leisurely paces and knew how deceptive was that seeming leisureliness. It wasn't one of the farmers — nor yet two of them. The newcomer's progress was more like marching than walking. Macdonald turned towards the brow and met Bord and a young constable, both of them looking quite out of place in the dappled light and shade of the rough path. Navy blue and white metal buttons looked odd there, pondered Macdonald — and then he remembered that he hadn't shaved and that his own shoes and flannel bags showed very recent contact with flood water and mud and slime. The C.I.D. man probably looked a bit odd to his spruce colleagues of the County force.

IV

It was full moon before Macdonald knew all that could be learnt from examination of the contents of the sack which had been moored to the recess in the river bank. It contained Gordon Ginner's body, and Ginner had been dead for a good many days. He had been killed by one heavy blow on the back of his head, a blow which had smashed through the skull as a coal-hammer smashes a lump of coal.

'Well, it's probable he didn't know anything about it, anyway,' said the Police Surgeon who first examined the body. 'It was as quick as shooting him . . .'

This disposal of the body had been very careful. It was fully clad, in a nondescript tweed suit and brown brogued shoes, and the limbs had been lashed together with salmon line. The sack containing the body was tied round again and again with cord (clothes-line), and the iron dogs had been skilfully attached to the cord with salmon line. The sack had been chained to the willow roots in one of the only stretches in the river where the scarp of the bank was never uncovered, even when the river was at its lowest.

Bord watched Macdonald during his examination: together the two men considered the knots which had secured the cord and the salmon line, and it was Bord who said:

'Those are sailors' knots. The chap who did this has probably been at sea at some time.'

'Not of necessity,' replied Macdonald. 'Sailors' knots are used almost universally. Firemen use them. The Civil Defence men — in London at any rate — were taught to make nearly all these knots during their training — the firemen taught them. Then scaffolders use knots to secure their scaffold poles. Packers in certain industries use them, such as cloth balers. The knots used here would be known to a great many types of artisans.'

They went carefully through the pockets of the clothes in the sack, but found nothing. The pockets had been emptied, tailors' marks cut from the clothes, laundry marks erased from the underclothes.

Macdonald considered all this and then said:

'In the ordinary course of events, the body would not have been found for months, perhaps not for years. The only way of finding it was by diving in towards the bank. Very few people bathe in the river. The Hoggetts and their friends swim in the summer, but they wouldn't have gone bathing again this year. By the time the body had been found, taking all probabilities into account, it should have been unidentifiable.'

Bord nodded.

'That's quite true. We've got you to thank for the promptness of the discovery.'

'Oh, no, you haven't. You've got to thank Giles Hoggett. If it hadn't been that he was an observant man — and a very shrewd one — I shouldn't have done anything about it.'

'I should never have put him down as a man who was particularly observant,' mused Bord. 'He looks rather a slow fellow. You were saying just now that the Hoggetts wouldn't have gone bathing again this year. It's equally probable that the cottage wouldn't have been used again this year, either — in which case Mr. Hoggett wouldn't have noticed the loss of his iron dogs and salmon lines until after the winter, by which time he might not have remembered anything about them. Don't you think it all points to the murderer being a local character?'

'Yes, at first glance it does — but we've got to remember that Ginner was seen in the valley. He isn't a local, not of recent years, anyway. What was he doing in Wenningby dales, why did he ever go inside the cottage? While the obvious reading is that a native of these parts committed this crime, it's worth remembering that someone 'from away,' as Hoggett says, may have got to know this lonely stretch of the river, and thought it was an ideal place to commit a crime without fear of observation. There's a lot of work to be done before we can risk any generalisation on the matter. Meantime we've got to consider the Inquest — and the less information that's published, the better. Identity not being in dispute, we'd better get it deferred for a bit.'

Bord nodded. He was thinking deeply.

'I'm thinking about that question of yours: why did Ginner ever come to Wenningby? He left his lodgings in the middle of August, of his own free will, apparently. Your evidence shows that he met some of his friends a day or two after he'd left home.'

Macdonald nodded, and Bord went on:

'Do you think he and his pals had tumbled to it that the police were on to their coupon racket?'

'Yes. They'd realised that all right.'

'Very well. Ginner cleared out, and he'd have looked around for some place where he could lie low. One of your witnesses testified that Ginner had lived in Kendal at some time. You put his age at forty-five. Assuming that he got to know Lunesdale as a young man, he might have known of that cottage in the dales then. It has been kept as a holiday cottage by the Hoggetts for years, and in winter it was seldom inhabited.

Is it possible that Ginner thought he might have lain low there for a bit without being noticed?'

'Yes, I should say it was, because Ginner was a townsman. Townsfolk never realise how observant countrymen are. No native of the valley would make the mistake of thinking he could live in that cottage for very long without being noticed. Although the farmers don't often come down to the dales, they do come regularly to inspect their beasts — and someone would have noticed something.'

'Yes, that's true. We want to find out when Ginner came to Lunesdale, and where he stayed before he came to the cottage. It's not going to be easy, because you see we have been watching out for him since we got your notification.'

'He was seen in the dales with a fishing rod on August 31st. It's probable he got some sort of permit for fishing, because a man who knows he's wanted by the police doesn't risk carrying fishing tackle without a permit of some kind. I must talk to Hoggett about that point. He knows all the ins and outs of the fishing rights.'

'Ginner could have bought a permit from the Carnton Anglers' Association. I'll see their secretary and ask him.'

'I believe the Anglers' Association has agents in the valley who can sell day permits to fishermen — one or two of the farmers act in this way,' said Macdonald and Bord chuckled.

'You've been acquiring a lot of local information. Mr. Hoggett again?'

'Aye — but I've hardly started yet. That chap knows Lunesdale as only a native can; it's from him and the other farmers I shall get the information I need most.'

'Well, good luck to you. You'll find you can't hurry them.'

'I know that, but at least they're sure of what they *do* know — and they know much more than most townsmen realise.'

8

I

It was late that same afternoon that Macdonald reached the steading known as 'Thorpe Intak.' It was a smallholding consisting of rough pasture reclaimed from the fells, and it was such poor land that even the optimists of the War Agricultural Committee had not suggested ploughing any of it. Ten of the fifteen acres was leased to Mr. Strongways of Farfell, who grazed sheep on the scrubby fell-side. Of the remaining five acres, two seemed to be in possession of a donkey and a goat, both the property of Anthony Vintner, whose hen-houses straggled forlornly over the fields immediately around his dwelling. Doubtless in times gone by stout-hearted smallholders had wrung a living from the unpromising land, for the stone house was ancient, but the property was well known as a heartbreaking one, and it was pretty obvious that Mr. Shand had been glad to let it to anyone hardy enough to take it, even to such an unpromising-looking tenant as Anthony Vintner.

Macdonald lifted back the gate, which still leaned drunkenly from broken sockets. As he walked over the sour grass towards the house, he found himself leading a procession; two hens, one of them almost bald, three ducks, and a goose in a bad way followed him hopefully; then the goat joined in. Macdonald had no enthusiasm for goats behind him and he turned on it threateningly until he saw the creature was in such a poor way that it swayed weakly on its spindly legs. The donkey was a melancholy but friendly creature. One thing seemed certain from the behaviour of the half-starved collection of creatures — they were not afraid of human beings. If Anthony Vintner didn't feed them, he evidently didn't ill-treat them otherwise, for they showed a pathetic confidence in the two-legged visitor.

Macdonald went and knocked on the door of the house, but got no answer. Trying the handle and finding the door open he went in and found himself in a kitchen which was like a domestic representation of chaos. Dirty plates, pans, cups and saucepans disputed possession of floor and table space with painting and modelling materials and empty cans. The fire in the range was out, but the range was still warm.

Macdonald went to the room door and called:

'Anyone at home?' He got no answer and found the door opened directly into what was probably 'the parlour' of the house. It was now a studio. Canvases stood stacked everywhere. On the easel was a study which Macdonald recognised easily enough. It was the picture of moonlight over the river valley which Mrs. Hoggett had described as 'arbitrary.' The adjective was a just one, inasmuch as the picture was composed in a deliberate series of conventional planes, but Macdonald found it beautiful. Somehow he forgave the painter for the squalor of his kitchen in looking at that cold vision of white light over the flood water.

Rather regretfully turning his back on the easel, Macdonald glanced at the canvases stacked round the walls. Anthony Vintner was a portrait painter of something more than competence. Here, unfinished, were portraits of half the inhabitants of Wenningby. Richard Blackthorn was there, with his jutting nose and far-sighted eyes. Gilbert Clafton's red head shone out from a background of sun-flecked willows. Giles Hoggett's long face and grey eyes stared studiously into Macdonald's own, and Mr. Shand's black eyes and white hair were treated with the wicked skill of the caricaturist. Couldn't the chap market his work, pondered Macdonald. He was skilful enough — and then, as he turned a canvas away from the wall he got a real surprise. This was a townsman's face, a pale, crafty, smiling, unpleasant fellow, with a leering mouth and a sly stare — and the face was the face of Gordon Ginner.

II

A noise in the kitchen made Macdonald jump for the door; it sounded as though all the piled crockery and cans had cascaded suddenly on to the stone floor, and then followed a silly surprised sound as the tremulous goat expressed the emotion which had overcome her as her hopeful nose had caused the landslide of kitchen utensils.

'Ba ba-ba-be-bee-e,' she bleated, and was answered by a human voice.

'Ba-ba to you with knobs on, confound you! It may be utility, but I will *not* have goats in the kitchen. Get out, Belinda. I know you're hungry, you poor old fool, but you can't eat tin cans.'

Macdonald, standing by the door, said sympathetically, 'Why not give her some mangolds or potatoes? You can get those easily enough.'

‘Good God!’ said the painter feebly. ‘You didn’t bring any in that car, did you? It’s Hoggett’s car; I felt hopeful when I saw it. He’s a very decent bloke is Hoggett. The trouble here is that there’s something wrong with the pasture; if it makes a goat sick it must be pretty bad. Mrs. Hoggett said it might be because she’d eaten the rhododendron bush — Belinda I mean — or else the yew berries. I’d no idea what a lot of poisonous stuff grew in a place like this. Have you come to sit? I haven’t got a canvas, but I could start a study on the wall.’

‘No, I haven’t come to sit. I’ve come to talk. Shall we go in the studio?’

‘Studio? Sounds good. I’ll draw the bolt to discourage Belinda, although it doesn’t really matter. She’s smashed everything that was left. God, what a muck!’

With a shrug of his shoulders, Anthony Vintner turned his back on the representation of chaos and accompanied Macdonald into the further room.

‘Not got a fag on you, have you? The fact is I’m broke. I haven’t a bean left.’ He pulled out the pockets of his trousers and shook them: ‘Not even a fag-end,’ he observed. ‘Oh, thanks a lot.’

Macdonald offered a packet of Players and lighted Vintner’s. Then he said:

‘My name’s Macdonald. I am an officer of the Criminal Investigation Department, and I am here on duty. I am going to ask you certain questions. You have not got to answer them, but if you refuse to I may have to take you into custody. That being so, it’s my duty to warn you that anything you say may be used as evidence.’

Anthony Vintner sat down suddenly on a backless chair as though his legs would no longer hold him.

'I thought something like this would happen,' he said. 'I've been dreaming of it . . . someone knocking at the door to ask questions. Do you know that picture of the 'Scapegoat'? Holman Hunt's, and damn' clever whatever they say about the pre-Raphaelites. I feel just like that, stupid, bewildered, hurt . . . you know the look on that beast's face. I know you think I'm as guilty as hell, although I don't even know what you're here for. I'm not. I've never done a thing to hurt anybody and I always make a mess of everything and get left to hold the baby. What's it all about?'

Macdonald pointed to the painting of Ginner and asked:

'Who is that?'

Vintner replied: 'About him, is it? I'm not surprised. He's a dirty dog.'

'Who is he?'

'Name of Baring. Thomas Harcourt Baring. I met him in a Morecambe pub. Very chatty. Said he was looking for a peaceful place to doss down in while he wrote a book. I told him he could come here if he liked to muck in with me. A pound a week, share and share alike. He stayed a week — and that was a week too long. When he left he took my notecase and the last packet of fags, damn him.'

'Why didn't you report it to the police?'

Anthony Vintner stared at Macdonald, stared with the same stupid pained glance which Holman Hunt had painted in the face of the Scapegoat.

'Haven't you any imagination?' he asked. 'What d'you think I'm here for? Or do you always hound us down again?'

'You've been in prison. Well, we don't hound you down. I didn't know anything about you. I'm here for two reasons. First, because you went swimming in Jacob's Buttery last night, second because the body of your Thomas Harcourt Baring was taken out of the river close to where you were swimming last night.'

'Oh God . . . It gets worse every time. It happened at school first. I was accused of pinching and expelled. Give a dog a bad name. It's gone on. I've always been landed with the blame. I'm a born fool, that's why. I thought I should be all right here, right away from anybody. Then I was so damned hard-up. Those ruddy hens began to die — and when Baring offered me rent I thought it was a god-send . . . And he's got done in. He would. That puts the lid on it. I'm done. You know that theory about certain sorts of events always coming to meet certain types of people? It's true. I'm one of those blokes who attract disaster — and sordid disaster at that.'

'I know that's a weak man's philosophy,' replied Macdonald. 'I've listened to you. Now you can listen to me. If you've done nothing to break the law you've nothing to fear from me. You've everything to gain by being frank, because it's as much my job to protect the honest citizen as to apprehend the rogue. Get that into your head and show a little spunk. I can't help you if you can't try to help yourself. You say you've done nothing against the law. Very well, answer my questions truthfully. What were you doing in the river last night?'

Vintner looked across at the canvas on the easel:

'You may not believe me, but it's true I went down there to see the moonlight. I walked from here, past Hoggett's place, and the world looked beautiful enough to make a man believe in the goodness of God. Somehow I began to hope again, to think it was worth trying. Then, just as I turned down the brow I heard a car, and then that beast Shand turned his headlights on and yelled out to know what I was doing. That spoiled it all. I hate Shand, he's a hectoring bully. I climbed over on to what they call the bank — the fields which slope down to the river, and I heard him go crashing down the brow like an elephant. He came a purler at the turn and I laughed like hell. I thought he'd go back, and I waited a little and saw him go into the cottage. Then it was all quiet again and I went on into the dales. You saw it — the moonlight over the flood.'

'Aye. I saw it.'

Macdonald's voice was quiet, but something in it seemed to encourage Vintner to go on.

'I felt a little mad. It was perfection. This place gets you somehow, even when you're hungry. I took my coat off, wondering if I dared risk a swim. I knew it'd be cold, but I like swimming. I walked on by the bank and thought of all sorts of things. I wondered if I could drown. It'd have been so easy last night — but I swim too well for that. Then I decided I would go in the river, however cold it was. I took my vest and pants off and went in by the big willow. Then I saw a tin. It was tucked between two branches and it shone. I remembered I'd seen Baring playing about with a tin when he thought I wasn't looking and I had a crazy idea he might have hidden my money. I got the tin, and then I wondered if he'd hidden anything else.'

He broke off, and Macdonald sat silent.

'I dived down by the bank,' said Vintner, and then seemed unable to go on. 'Well — you know. I climbed out, and then, just as I'd got my vest on, I realised there was someone else there and I thought of Shand.'

‘How did you know there was someone else there?’

‘Because of the bullocks. I couldn’t hear anything, but the beasts had turned facing the wind and were standing with their noses up. I knew they’d scented somebody — so I just ran. I can’t tell you why, but I ran for the woods . . . it was dark under the trees. Then Hoggett came after me. Of course I knew it wasn’t Shand running: I didn’t know who it was, but it seemed like an avenging fury — he can run like hell, can’t he? I was glad when he caught me. I’m not afraid of Hoggett, he’s a good chap.’

‘Then why didn’t you tell him there and then what you must have known to be true? You touched that sack —’

‘Yes I touched it . . . If it’d been you, you might have told, but not me. You’d have thought — what you’re thinking now.’

Vintner shivered and then burst out in a tumult of words:

‘How *could* I tell? I’m a gaol bird, a man who’s been quodded for fraud. How could I say, ‘There’s a corpse in a sack under the bank, chaps. I don’t know how it got there. I was just having a swim and I found it by chance.’ Just having a swim at midnight, with a frost over the grass and the water as cold as the Arctic . . . Oh yes, likely. I know by experience everybody always believes the best of me . . . If it’s been Hoggett by himself I might have told *him*, but not two of you. Not you. I thought you were a lawyer, you look like one, and I’ve always hated lawyers.’

‘You’d have had a better chance of being believed if you’d told us then and there,’ said Macdonald. ‘Here’s another question for you to answer: why did you take an empty cigarette tin from Hoggett’s cottage last night?'

'Cigarette tin?' Vintner stared. 'What does that matter? I believe I did pick up an old tin, I wanted one to keep my own cigarettes in — when I've got any. Everything gets damp here if you don't keep it in tins. Look in that cupboard. If I keep a pair of shoes in there for a week it goes mouldy. Everything goes mouldy in this place.'

'How did you happen on this place? Had you been here before?'

'Not here exactly. I stayed at Chapelton-Lonsdale years ago. An old uncle of mine came and looked me up after I came out of quod. He offered me £500 to try and settle down and make a living, a decent old boy. It was he who suggested poultry. I jumped at it. Seemed to me I could start again somewhere where nobody knew me. The old boy paid for me to spend a few months with a poultry farmer to learn the ropes, and told me to look out for some place which was fairly cheap. I came up to Lonsdale and fossicked round until I found this place. I liked it — the old house pleased me because I loathe those god-forsaken bungaloid places, and I liked the old thorn trees and stone walls. Of course I ought to have realised there was something wrong about it. It'd never have been empty if the land was any good — but I didn't think of that. It was cheap, so I took it and bought some old hen-houses and some stock and thought I was going to get on a treat — but you see.'

'Yes, I see.' Macdonald encouraged Vintner to go on talking, because he wanted to get to know him. 'Did it occur to you to disinfect the old hen-houses?' he asked.

Vintner shrugged his shoulders.

'Not until the hens started dying. Then I remembered . . . I suppose I bought the diseases with the hen-houses. Damn.'

'Can't you market those paintings? They're good.'

'You try it. It's not so easy. They fall between two stools. They're not bad enough to sell easily for pretty-pretties and not good enough to get on the line in the big shows.'

He got up and stood before the painting on the easel.

'If you like it, will you take it?' he asked. 'I'd be glad to think someone liked it. I suppose you're going to run me in?'

'No. I'm not going to run you in. I've no evidence that you've done anything against the law, though I tell you frankly you made a mistake in not telling what you must have realised last night when you touched that sack. Also I warn you not to try to bolt. You've got to stop here.'

'I shouldn't get very far, should I? You can't bolt without any money.'

Macdonald looked at the man's tallowy face — it was almost green as he faced the cold northern light.

'When did you have a meal last?'

Vintner stared back at the C.I.D. man.

'God knows when I had a real meal. I can't remember. I got some bread and cheese in Carnton just now, and some tea. I did a deal with a chap at some dirty pub. I sold him my petrol lighter and he let me have some food. The bother is that I haven't any matches now.'

Macdonald turned to the kitchen door.

'You'd better light that fire and make some tea. Perhaps it'll restore your wits. You need something.'

III

It was Macdonald who got the range lighted. There was plenty of wood and the kettle boiled quickly over the crackling sticks. Anthony Vintner just stared. Macdonald knew that stare: the man was half-starved: on top of that he had had a shock which had knocked him edgeways. Macdonald doubted very much if Vintner were quite as much the injured innocent as he made out, but he was obviously in need of a meal and of a chance to pull himself together. Macdonald looked around for a receptacle in which to put the tins and broken crocks: he saw an empty sack — and decided against it. He then found a large zinc basin and piled the debris into it, while Vintner still sat with a puzzled stare.

'Here you are — take these and dump them wherever you have a dump,' said the C.I.D. man, and Vintner obeyed like a child. When he came back the kitchen table at least was cleared.

'I wish to God I was neat and handy like you,' said Vintner, and Macdonald replied:

'I don't know what's the masculine of slut, unless it's Vintner. No man needs to make a pig stye of a decent kitchen. Have you got another teapot — or not?'

Bemusedly the painter opened a cupboard and found some more crocks — very much crocks, and washed them at the sink as he was bidden. Macdonald found the tea, made it in the cracked pot, and cut the loaf.

'Sit down and eat a meal and try to behave as though you'd got some wits,' he said, and Anthony Vintner sat down at the kitchen table and began to eat like a starving man. Macdonald poured himself out some tea, lighted his pipe and sat by the fire, pondering deeply. At last he turned to Vintner.

'Now you can answer some more questions — and the more truthfully you answer, the better for you,' he said.

They went on talking until dusk softened the mullioned windows: question and answer, question and answer. After a pause, Macdonald turned and looked hard at Anthony Vintner's pallid face. His eyes were shut, and he was fast asleep, slumped down on the kitchen chair. The man was so exhausted he had fallen asleep almost as he talked. What was the reason of that exhaustion? The effort of thinking ahead in that deliberate interrogation to which he had been subjected? The fact that he had not slept for nights because he dared not sleep? Macdonald did not know. There was an old sofa under the window: clearing it of its miscellaneous junk, Macdonald lifted the slight figure and laid it on the sofa. Anthony Vintner stirred a little, grumbled unintelligibly, and curled up like a dog, so fast asleep he was unaware of having been lifted.

Macdonald saw to it that the range was shut down, and then he went outside, closed the door firmly, and then drove Belinda and the donkey into the old pasture and tied up the ancient bed-end that did duty as a gate.

Macdonald was not quite sure what to make of Anthony Vintner, but he didn't like the idea of the goat and the donkey finishing the remains of the bread and cheese on the kitchen table. He paused as he left Thorpe Intak.

'A goat, or merely a donkey?' he wondered to himself.

IV

Just as he was trying to secure the drunken gate which gave on to the road, Macdonald saw a car approaching along the lonely road — a good, opulent-looking, well-cared-for car. It slowed down and pulled up just ahead of Giles Hoggett's less prosperous-looking vehicle, and Macdonald recognised the driver with a feeling of amusement. It was Mr. Barton Shand, who had wanted to instruct Mr. Hoggett about the value of old books in Wenningby Barns. Macdonald quickly schooled his expression to one of official gravity. He and Giles Hoggett had been free to indulge in flippancy last night — but it seemed rather a long time ago.

Mr. Shand got out of his car and walked back towards the Chief Inspector with a frowning, troubled face.

'Good-day. Am I right in believing that I speak to an official of the Criminal Investigation Department?'

'Yes, sir. My name is Macdonald, and I am here on duty. Last evening, when I saw you in Mr. Hoggett's cottage I was off duty, so far as official proceedings were concerned.'

'We need not discuss that, Chief Inspector,' rejoined the other tartly, 'though I should like to make it clear that what I said then was not spoken in jest. I gather that the police now have reasons for a serious investigation in this valley.'

'That is quite true, sir,' rejoined Macdonald, 'though I should be interested to know how you came by that information.'

'It seems not improbable to me that the whole of Lunesdale is aware of it,' retorted Mr. Shand. 'The police van on the Caton road and the presence of police officers and the nature of their burden across the Garthmere holm-land this morning was plain enough for all to see.'

'Forgive me if I challenge that statement, sir. Some care was taken to avoid undue obviousness, if I may put it that way. I know that you, for instance, were not on the Caton road this morning, and I ask you again how you came by your information.'

'If you used your eyes, Inspector, you would have noticed that that stretch of road, river, and holm-land can be observed from the fells on the south side of the river. I own some land on that side, and during my brief holidays here I take a gun with me for some rough shooting — rabbits, hares, wild duck — anything is welcome as an addition to rations in a town these days.'

'Yes. I see,' replied Macdonald readily. 'As you say, a Londoner is slow to observe what is plain to the countryman. I am always ready to acknowledge my indebtedness to those who help my shortcomings in that respect. Mr. Hoggett, for instance, has been most helpful.'

'An excellent fellow,' rejoined Mr. Shand, 'and well versed in local lore — but obtuse, Chief Inspector. Obtuse. However, you do not wish for my views on that matter. I should, however, like to ask you for certain information if you are able to disclose it. You have, I assume, just come from seeing my tenant here at Thorpe Intak. I am much troubled in my mind about him. You can see the state into which this holding has fallen.'

'It doesn't need much detective skill to observe that,' rejoined Macdonald. 'Vintner has neither the industry, character nor physique to enable him to make a success of any rural undertaking.'

'He is a crooked, slovenly rogue in my opinion, and nothing will make me alter it,' retorted Mr. Shand. 'I want to get rid of him and put in another tenant. My reason for coming here to-day was to see him and to tell him so. I intend to let him off his arrears of rent, provided he moves out immediately — and I consider that that is a very generous offer.'

'I don't know much about rural tenures myself, sir,' rejoined Macdonald, 'so I can't offer an opinion on that matter but I would ask you to defer your interview for the time being.'

'For what reason, Inspector?'

'First, because I want Vintner just where he is until I know a little more about him. Next, I think if you evicted him now — or attempted to do so, he would probably cut his throat. He is just at the stage when any additional difficulties would bowl him over. Whether Vintner was connected with the crimes I am investigating I am unable to say, but I think he may be able to produce some useful information if he's carefully handled.'

'Humph. How do you know he won't bolt?'

'I don't think he would get very far. I am having the roads watched — and Vintner is no fellsman.'

Mr. Shand frowned;

'It's very annoying,' he said. 'I wanted to get this matter settled before I returned home. My home is in Derbyshire, and I only come here for visits to keep an eye on my property.'

'If you could make it convenient to stay here a few days longer, sir, it might be a considerable help to me — and you would probably be able to regain possession here with a minimum of trouble.'

'I must ask you to enlarge on those points, Inspector?'

'Certainly. In the first case, I want all the information I can get as to who has been seen in the dales — and you are a fisherman. Next, when Anthony Vintner has answered all my questions and recovered his equilibrium to some extent, I think you will find no difficulty in getting him to accept your offer — but I must ask you to leave him alone for the time being.'

'I see. Well, Inspector, every responsible citizen is taught that it is his duty to assist the police. If I can help you, I will certainly stay.'

'Thank you, sir,' rejoined Macdonald politely.

Mr. Shand cast another glance at his derelict property.

'That man Vintner will one day get his deserts,' he said profoundly.

9

I

When Macdonald got back to Wenningby Barns that evening, he found Giles Hoggett cooking supper for him. The first course was trout fresh from the river; Hoggett cooked it exceedingly well and Macdonald enjoyed it very much. He also appreciated Hoggett's unusual ability to refrain from asking questions — it was a very rare virtue. After they had eaten and cleared away the dishes, they sat by the fire and Macdonald said:

'Will you tell me about fishing rights here? I want all the information you can give. You have fishing rights on this side of the river only, I take it?'

'On both sides,' replied Hoggett. 'The fishing rights here depend on the ownership of the dales, and that fact takes us back a very long time in history. The dales, as you probably know, are narrow strips of land at right angles to the river. In ancient times every man in Wenningby had one or more dales, as this valley land was the most fertile land in the settlement. It was shared by everybody, quite equitably, and the curious thing is that ownership of the dales took on account of the river as a boundary, some of the dale strips continuing in a straight line across the river — you can see the dale stones on the other side; they mark the strips. Consequently because my family own some of the dales to-day we really have fishing rights on both sides of the river.'

'Then you, like Mr. Shand, own land on both banks?'

'Yes. My dale strips go right across the river. They're let to Richard Blackthorn: he cuts the hay and stores it in the barn. In the winter he keeps some cattle in the shippon here and they consume the hay cut from the dales. We have a clause in our agreements to the effect that the hay must be consumed on the premises — that is to ensure the fertility of the land. The dung from the shippon is spread on the land again. However — you want to know about fishing rights. The answer is that I own fishing rights on both banks where I own the dales, and so, of course, does Shand — and the contiguous land-owners.'

'Doesn't this arrangement involve complications sometimes?' queried Macdonald, and Hoggett nodded.

'Yes, it has caused quite a number. As you can see for yourself, the dales are so narrow that while fishing you are off your own dale, and on to someone else's in no time, almost without knowing it. The arrangement my father made with the Garths was this. (Downstream their dales and ours are alternate in some places.) Mr. Garth and my father agreed to fish right across each others' dales, both sides of the river. That was all right until Mr. Garth let his fishing to the Carnton Anglers' Association. Quite profitable to him, but very annoying for us. It meant that while the old arrangement held, we shared the fishing with about two hundred Carnton Anglers — not our idea of a fair division. There was a good deal of unpleasantness for some time, and at last we compromised by the Anglers fishing from the dales on the south side of the river, while the Garths and ourselves continued to fish right along on the north bank, so far as the dales are concerned, though farther upstream the rights are ours alone.'

'I see — but isn't it a bit difficult to know when to warn anyone off? For instance, when your wife saw Ginner fishing, in your water, how did she know he hadn't a permit from the Garths?'

'She could be certain of that when she first asked — and she did ask — why a man was fishing on that stretch, had it been with permission of the Garths it would have been stated immediately. Actually if I give anyone a permit to fish I make a habit of letting the Garths know, and Miss Garth does the same for me. There is very little fishing on our side except for our own families, who are all well known. The 'Anglers' fish on the other side.'

'But legally you both have the right — by ancient usage — to fish either side up and down each other's dales, save for the gentlemen's agreement.'

'Yes. That's true — but our stretch is a long way from anywhere and we don't have much trouble these days.'

Macdonald fell into a reverie for a while, and then he started talking. Warm, rested, and well-fed, he felt disposed to talk again. He told Hoggett about the portrait of Gordon Ginner and Vintner's account of his acquaintanceship with Ginner and his history of himself.

'I think all that is probably true, as far as it goes, but I doubt if it goes all the way,' said Macdonald. 'My own belief is that Vintner knew Ginner before he saw him in the pub in Morecambe, and that he was unwilling to have him as a lodger but was afraid to refuse.

Vintner said that Ginner went off early one morning, a week after he had first arrived. He gave September 1st as the day of Ginner's departure. Incidentally Vintner knows a good deal more about various items in this case. How did you first get to know him?'

'He has been sketching between here and Garthmere all the summer, particularly along the valley. He was always very pleasant and asked if we minded his going on our land. I was glad for him to do so and my wife was interested in his painting. He's done some good studies of Ingleborough and the view over the Wenning to Hornby.'

'So you got used to seeing him about down here?'

'Aye. He was down here most days in the summer.'

'Will you describe the coat you missed from this place?'

'It was a very old raincoat, lined with a sort of green tartan and supposed to be reversible. It was so old it was almost a pantomime garment, and it was very long and full. We all used it down here for years, and then I took it into use on the farm when things got short, but Kate objected and I brought it down here again in case she destroyed it. She said it was a moth-eaten menace.'

'Vintner said he saw an old tramp in the valley, early in September. The tramp must have been wearing your old raincoat turned inside out, plus George's fishing cap and your father's steel-rimmed glasses.'

'Good gracious!' exclaimed Hoggett, and Macdonald went on:

'The point which interests me is this. Vintner obviously knew about the coat and the cap and the glasses — but I've no proof that he ever saw anybody in them, or, if anybody wore them, that it wasn't

Vintner himself. The trouble is that I can't take everything he says at its face value without further proof because I think he's made up so many yarns in his time he's got into the habit of it and doesn't tell the truth except by accident.'

'Let's get some dates down and see how it all fits in,' said Giles Hoggett, and Macdonald agreed.

'That's the idea. Got a sheet of paper? Good. We'll both do a calendar of our own and see what we can fit in. My first date is August 15th, when Ginner was last seen at his lodgings.'

'August 15th,' murmured Mr. Hoggett. 'We cut Richard Blackthorn's oats on August 15th. It was wonderful weather. I'd say no one in the place was down in the dales that week — we worked on by moonlight.'

'Vintner met Ginner in 'The Bunch of Grapes' on August 24th,' went on Macdonald, and Giles Hoggett intervened:

'The Georges stayed here — at Wenningby Barns — from August 21st to August 28th. I'll just put that down on mine.'

'I will too,' said Macdonald. 'It may be relevant. Who are the 'Georges,' by the way?'

'George is my cousin, a doctor. His name is George Castleby. He has a wife, Margaret, and the two children, Giles and Eleanor, called Nell. They stay here once or twice every year and there's nothing they wouldn't notice between them. You'll see George this evening some time. I rang him up and he's coming to talk to you about the potters.'

'Good,' said Macdonald. 'Now I think our next date is August 31st, when Mrs. Hoggett saw Ginner fishing. Now the 'Georges,' if I may use the family term, left here on August 28th. That interests me because, according to Vintner, Ginner had no rod with him. Where did he get one?'

'Here,' said Giles resignedly. 'I suppose he took Uncle Henry's.'

'It seems probable to me,' agreed Macdonald. 'He must have mooched around and observed when the Georges left. Did you come down here on the day they left?'

'I came down to help them carry their gear up the brow, though I didn't actually come into the cottage,' replied Hoggett. 'I've been thinking of what you said about Ginner 'mooching round.' He could have heard quite a lot that would have been useful to him. There was a lot of gear to carry up, and it necessitated double journeys. I remember George was the last to come up and he was going to go back for the key which he had left behind, and I called to him not to bother. If he'd left it in the usual place that would do, and I'd go and fetch it later.'

'Yes,' mused Macdonald. 'That might explain a lot. I had a look at the land bordering the brow — you call those fields the 'bank,' don't you? Anyone could hide behind those holly trees on the bank and hear everything that was said by anyone on the brow without being seen by them.'

Giles Hoggett nodded.

'Yes, I've realised that. We all talked pretty freely. The children said what a pity it was that no one was going to be at the cottage again for so long, and Margaret said she'd left everything arranged for the winter. That means that nothing was left on the floor downstairs which could be damaged by flood water if the river rose high enough to flood the cottage. We are always careful to move mats and rugs and hassocks upstairs and not leave any boots or shoes to float about if the water does reach the cottage.'

'I see. The general trend of the conversation indicated that no one would be staying in the cottage, and I expect it would be safe to assume that no one would ever go down there after dark when the place wasn't being lived in?'

'Aye, that's true enough.'

Both men fell silent for a moment, and then Giles Hoggett spoke again, studying his calendar.

'Ginner didn't come to Thorpe Intak until August 25th and the Georges were staying at Wenningby Barns until August 28th. If Ginner's body had been in the river for a fortnight when it was found, he wouldn't have had many days to study conditions at Wenningby Barns while it was unoccupied.'

'Aye,' agreed Macdonald. 'That's sound reasoning, Hoggett. You're thinking that a rogue like Ginner would have wanted to know a bit more about Wenningby Barns than he could have learnt from what he overheard when the Georges were leaving.'

'I don't want to accuse Vintner of aught,' went on Hoggett. 'I told you that I didn't size him up as a bad lot, but I reckon he's a weakling — got no moral stamina. Vintner had plenty of opportunities of studying conditions at Wenningby Barns when it was empty. It's more than probable he knew where we kept the key, and he'd have certainly known that no one ever goes down there after dark in the usual way.'

'Are there ever occasions when anybody goes down to the dales after dark?' enquired Macdonald.

'Aye, if the river rises unexpectedly,' was the reply. 'I remember one night when we all went to bed at the usual time and Richard Blackthorn came and woke us about midnight. He *knew* the river was rising, though we'd all judged it'd be safe till morning. We were down there all night; one of Richard's men had failed in his duty to drive the beasts up over the river and they were cut off.'

For once Macdonald forgot the thread of his detection as he pondered over Hoggett's words. 'The beasts were cut off?' he asked.

'Aye. They stood huddled on a little island of higher ground. We knew where they were, though we couldn't reach them.'

'But what could you *do*?' asked Macdonald.

'Nought. We just waited. The river began to fall before dawn and we knew they were safe. Richard drove a wedge of wood into the ground hard by the gate there. He said: 'If t'water don't reach yon peg, they're safe.' It came within inches of it — and then began to fall. It rained that night . . . But this isn't detection, Macdonald.'

'Quite true — but thanks for the story. Now where are we? It seems probable that Ginner learnt all the details he needed about the cottage from Vintner, who'd had opportunities to observe it.'

'Aye, that was probably the way of it. Do you think Ginner imagined he could live in the cottage until the hue and cry after him died down?'

'No, I don't, because in my judgment all men of Ginner's type make certain demands on life. How far is this place from a pub?'

Hoggett scratched his head.

'You should know. You've been staying at the nearest one.'

'The Green Dragon. Call it four miles there and four back. Eight miles of hilly walking. I can't see a man like Ginner settling in a primitive cottage with eight miles of walking between him and a drink — and you can't buy spirits in bottles where you're not known these days.'

'Then what did he come here for?' demanded Giles Hoggett.

'I'd risk a guess he came here in order to meet somebody,' replied Macdonald. 'It'd have been a good spot for that. It's safe after dark: it's an easy spot to describe because it's the only cottage right by the river for miles, and the approaches to it are marked on the Ordnance Survey Map. Here are the probabilities as I see them. Ginner was concerned in a large theft of clothing coupons. His part in the ramp was the dispersal of the coupons — passing them on in comparatively small numbers to others who were concerned in cashing them, as it were. If Ginner wanted a safe rendezvous for meeting his clients, this cottage had a lot of advantages. It is within motoring reach of the industrial towns of the north; it is approachable from the Yorkshire wool trade towns, via the Leeds to Lancashire railway line, and yet it's a place where the police don't come. 'Wenningby Barns,' — oh, that's Mr. Hoggett's cottage. Nought to do there.'

'Aye, that's all true enough,' agreed Giles.

'There's another piece of evidence which fits in,' went on Macdonald. 'While I was in the dales this morning I found a tin with the lid carefully soldered on. Anthony Vintner said he saw the tin last night when he was swimming. It was wedged in the willow roots by the bank. That tin contains a large number of the stolen clothing coupons. It occurs to me that Mr. Ginner had hit upon a good safe hiding hole for his most valuable, but very incriminating, property.'

Again Giles Hoggett scratched his head.

'Then, if I follow you, Ginner wasn't killed in order to get possession of his loot? It'd be a fool's trick to kill him before you knew where he'd hidden the stuff you were killing him to obtain.'

'Aye, so it seems to me,' rejoined Macdonald. 'Isn't that footsteps outside, or am I imagining things?'

'That's George,' replied Mr. Hoggett.

II

George came in with a quiet 'Good-evening' and settled down by the fire looking exactly as though he belonged there and had never been farther afield than Wenningby village. There was a strong family likeness between the two cousins, though the doctor lacked the farmer's healthy tan. George was not so lank and lean as Giles, and his glasses gave him a more studious air, but his low deep voice was so similar to Giles Hoggett's that Macdonald had an occasional uneasy feeling that someone was playing at ventriloquism.

George (Macdonald had quite a difficulty in remembering to address him as Dr. Castleby) lighted a cigarette, stretched his feet to the fire and enquired about the river and the trout his cousin had caught before any other topic was mentioned. Macdonald was aware of a serene sense of continuity which he could not quite put into words. These two men were like links in an unbroken chain: here they were in Lunesdale, as their forefathers had been before them, sitting by the same hearth, warming their feet at the blazing logs which had been cut from their own woodlands, talking about the river, the floods, the fishing, the cattle and the harvest.

Macdonald, whose Scots shrewdness was far from lacking in imagination, suddenly realised how transitory he and his organisation were in contrast to something that was changeless in these two natives of Lunesdale. It had seemed so incongruous that a cheap cheating rogue of a townsman should have got himself done to death in sordid manner in the dignity and silence of the fell-guarded valley — but listening to the murmur of the low-toned voices, the C.I.D. man realised that this incursion of alien crime did not so much as scratch the deep serenity of this place. It had happened here, but it did not belong here. The voices of Giles Hoggett and George Castleby brushed it all aside as irrelevant, and the essential peace of the valley re-establshed itself as though Gordon Ginner had never existed. ' . . . all the beasts of the forest are thine . . . and so are the cattle upon a thousand hills . . .' The immemorial words were running in Macdonald's mind when Giles Hoggett said:

'About the potters . . .' and George murmured:

'Aye, the potters,' and brought the C.I.D. man back to reality.

'It's the Golds you want to know about,' said Dr. Castleby. 'They have a headquarters by the Clunter — a stream which runs into the Lune some ten miles from here. There's some level waste ground there which has always been common land and they have their vans and encampments there very much like gypsies — although the potters aren't gypsies. There's no real Romany blood in any of them, they're nomads, but native nomads. They travel about with their carts, huckstering and bartering, but they always come back to the old pitch in winter. It's not a bad life — and the potters aren't bad folk. I think they get the blame for a lot of mischief they're innocent of, because the settled folk of farmsteads and cottages are always suspicious of the nomad.'

'I don't like the Golds,' put in Giles Hoggett, his voice mild but obstinate. 'The old man's got roguery ingrained in every line of his villainous old face.'

Dr. Castleby chuckled:

'So much for your judgment, Giley, my lad. You say 'old face.' Reuben Gold isn't much older than yourself. I doubt if he's over fifty-five and his wife is under fifty. I know they look old, but they live hard — and drink hard when they've got the wherewithal.'

'Hang it all, George,' protested Giles Hoggett. 'You must have underestimated. I can remember Reuben Gold for years. He's never looked any younger.'

'That's your opinion, but it's wrong,' said Castleby. 'I'm fifty this year. I started practising in Carnton as old Gregory's junior partner when I was twenty-five. That's when I first doctored the Golds. Mrs. Gold came to me one night with a child on the back of her cart — a boy of eight or nine. He'd got pneumonia. I had the dickens of a job to persuade her to let him go into hospital — but we pulled him round. She's never forgotten. These potters are like gypsies inasmuch as they never forget a grudge and never forget a kindness. Many's the time I've been embarrassed by a basket of eggs left on my doorstep. They still bring me mushrooms and blackberries and even posies of flowers.'

'Well, well, I'd never have thought it,' murmured Giles. 'Did they bring you any fat ducks last Christmas? Never mind, George, but you told me something else I don't know. I'd no idea they'd got a child.'

George paused and turned to Macdonald.

'I take it that I can regard this as a professional consultation — that is, the facts I state are for your information professionally, Chief Inspector, and won't go any further if they're irrelevant to your case?'

'Yes. You can rest assured of that, Dr. Castleby.'

'Very good. We don't repeat gossip, and we don't usually repeat facts we've come by in the course of our practice, but you are investigating a murder case and circumstances alter cases. Now, Chief Inspector, leaving Giles and his hunches out of this, have you any real reason for connecting the Golds with your problem?'

'I've no direct evidence,' said Macdonald, 'but there is one rather curious circumstance. Hoggett says that when he first discovered the theft of the iron dogs, he found in the dales a piece of old curtain material which had been used for wiping off some mud and which I think will prove to have blood stains on it. Mrs. Hoggett gave the curtains of this same material to the potters. Another piece of it was in Anthony Vintner's house. He had used it as a paint rag and it was stained all over with oil paint. I asked him if he knew the potters and he denied having spoken to them at any time. When I asked him where he came by this piece of paint rag he said that he hadn't the least idea.'

'Ah, George. This is where you can produce a little evidence,' put in Giles Hoggett. 'Did you ask the children if Aunt Kate ever gave them some striped orange curtain material when they played Red Indians?'

'Yes. I asked them, and they were quite positive they had never had any such material, and had never seen any near the cottage. Eleanor remembered the curtains up at the farm, because Kate used them when we played charades last Christmas, but they were then intact — not torn up into pieces.'

'Well, that does lead to the conclusion that the potters have had some connection with the case,' said Macdonald. 'Either the Golds brought a piece of material down here, or else Vintner did. Do you know Vintner, doctor?'

'I've seen him down here with his easel. He shows every sign of undernourishment and anæmia.'

'He also shows when he's telling lies,' rejoined Macdonald. 'As a rogue, he's very unsuccessful. Every time he wittingly tells a lie he peers round at one to see if one's swallowed it. When he tells the truth he doesn't bother to scrutinise his auditor. I only mention this because I believe he was telling the truth when he said he'd no idea where his paint rag came from. My question about it didn't disturb him.'

'In that case one can make an assumption that Vintner found a bit of the curtain stuff lying about somewhere down in the valley — where the Golds had left it, and that Vintner picked it up to use as a paint rag,' suggested Giles Hoggett.

Macdonald nodded.

'That'll do for the moment. Is that enough evidence to convince Dr. Castleby that I'm justified in asking questions about the private lives of the Golds?'

'Yes, I think so,' replied George. 'I was talking about the boy who had pneumonia. It was in the winter of 1922 — my first winter in Carnton. Mrs. Gold was then about twenty-six and the boy about eight. She begged me never to say anything about the child to her husband. The child was hers, but not his. It wasn't my business and I didn't ask her any questions, but when the little lad recovered I told her he'd better go to a convalescent home. He was still weak and not fit to live in their camp. She told me some rather involved story about the child being tended by a foster mother and said he'd been born in wedlock but the father had died. I remember she was very insistent about the child not being a bastard. Once again, it wasn't my business. We don't stop to ask if a child's legitimate or not before we tend it. I had my own ideas about what had happened in the matter of Mrs. Gold's child — but I asked no questions.'

'That was why she trusted you,' observed Macdonald. 'There is nothing the nomad fears so much as the relentless questioning and form filling of Means Test Officials and Charitable Societies. Most of the tramp and gypsy type, in my experience, would rather die of cold and starvation than submit to the interrogations of well-meaning officials.'

'That,' said George, in his deepest murmur, 'is profoundly true.'

'But since you have admitted to having your own ideas about the Gold progeny, doctor, won't you give us the benefit of them?' asked Macdonald.

'Aye, but they're simple enough. The boy's father deserted the mother after the birth of the child and the mother joined forces with Reuben Gold. She is married to Gold — I happen to know they married in the Preston Registry Office. I've no real knowledge of Mrs. Gold's earlier history, but I believe she wasn't one of the potters' community originally. I think she was the daughter of a smallholder in the fell country around Kirkby Stephen, and I'd hazard a guess she ran away and got married and was later deserted. The reason I believe she was married in the first place was that she was evidently afraid she'd told me too much.

You see she'd been through a legal marriage ceremony with Gold, and if the first husband deserted her without a divorce she'd committed bigamy — and knew it. But most of this is surmise on my part. I admit I was interested at the time. Mrs. Gold was a fine-looking young woman, and at eighteen, when the boy was born, she was probably a very lovely girl.'

'This,' said Giles Hoggett, 'is where I do a little arithmetic. The Gold child was eight in 1922 . . . born, 1914, present age, thirtyish. How old was Ginner?'

'Over 45. Probably between 45 and 50.'

' . . . once lived in Kendal . . . call him 50 . . . in short Mrs. Gold's first husband was Ginner, the son being Anthony Vintner,' murmured Giles Hoggett.

'Elementary, my dear Watson. Too elementary,' replied Macdonald. 'Life's not as easy as that — but I do feel the story Dr. Castleby has told us causes me to ponder.' He turned to George. 'What was the child like — if you can remember anything about him?'

'He was a fine little lad, with carroty hair.'

'What did I say?' demanded Giles triumphantly. 'Of course he's Vintner . . .'

'I don't think so, Giley . . . I remember the boy had odd eyes, one blue and one grey, like his mother — and Vintner is over thirty, quite a lot over thirty.'

'Well . . . I'll go into that later,' said Giles imperturbably. 'But what about Ginner being the first husband? It answers everything, motive, means, opportunity —'

'But without evidence,' said Macdonald. 'However, it leaves me with plenty to do. I shall have to trace the past history of the Golds and of Anthony Vintner. We are already trying to work back along Gordon Ginner's history.' He paused, and then said to Giles Hoggett: 'It evidently entertains you to make up a story which fits the facts. I wonder if your ingenuity will work to the extent of producing a story which accounts for the various factors we have been considering? It isn't altogether an idle question. You know this place, and you are observant of your fellows. It may be that you will tell me something useful when you are least aware of it.'

George Castleby chuckled.

'As a compliment, that's a back-handed one, Giles, but I hope you accept the challenge. I'm prepared to sit back and enjoy the reconstruction.'

10

I

Giles Hoggett sat forward, his feet on the hearth, his elbows on his knees, and he began his recital very solemnly:

'We are considering the death of a man who was murdered in this valley. So far as the evidence goes, he was a stranger here, a man concerned with certain illegal dealings in the industrial Midlands, yet the evidence goes to show that he met his death at the hands of someone who knew the conditions of this valley and could utilise that knowledge. At the same time the murderer was lacking in a sense of detail and of real understanding of the inhabitants, for it did not seem to have occurred to him that any intelligent construction would be put on the theft of various trivial objects from this cottage.'

George settled more comfortably in his chair.

'That,' he said, 'is a very promising beginning,' and Macdonald murmured, 'Aye, a very sound beginning,' and Giles Hoggett went on:

'The only evidence which directly connects any specific persons with the crime is the curtain material which my wife gave to the potters. A fragment of this was found caught on the thorns some hundred yards from this cottage, another fragment among Anthony Vintner's painting materials. We have George's evidence that Mrs. Gold had a son, born in

1914, previous to her marriage with Reuben Gold. It also seems possible that Mrs. Gold's first husband deserted her. Assuming George's theory about Mrs. Gold's origin in a smallholding, near Kirkby Stephen, one can reasonably imagine that as a young girl of seventeen she ran away with a plausible rogue: perhaps the girl got hold of some money which had been concealed by her father — the thrifty suspicious fellsman of that remote hill country would like enough hide his savings in the house rather than trust a bank. With the money as a lever, the girl achieved her marriage lines — and then, when the money was spent, the rogue deserted her. She would have been used to hard work and a hard life: perhaps she earned her keep among other casual labourers in the seasonal jobs of potato lifting, fruit picking, and hoeing. Her child was born, and put to a foster mother, and the girl met Reuben Gold, also earning money by potato lifting or such like, and he fell in love with her. Experience had taught her to bargain. She gave nothing away, and she induced Gold to marry her, keeping her own secret about her child, and with their joint savings they bought a horse and cart and joined the ranks of the potters from whom Reuben was derived.'

'Well, well! All considered that's a good effort,' said George. 'From what I know of the facts, you've made a good job of that reconstruction, Giley. Mrs. Gold *did* once work in the Preston country, fruit picking. I know that.'

'Go on,' said Macdonald. 'I thought this might be useful, and it's even better than I hoped. You know this country and I don't. Go on.'

Giles Hoggett lighted another cigarette and stared at the fire. He was quite obviously taking this very seriously, and trying hard to work out his thesis. He spoke slowly, but his voice had a natural tendency to dramatise his thoughts, and he was curiously convincing, as though he spoke of something he really knew, rather than of theories he was developing. Without elaboration, in simple clear-cut phrases, he made his story come alive.

'Sarah Gold had the cunning which often goes with the primitive peasant intelligence so often underrated by townsfolk,' he went on. 'She kept in touch with her child, but concealed his existence from her husband. The boy had a mixed inheritance, on the one side the shrewd tenacity of his fell forebears, plus the less stable but more imaginative cunning of his father. The boy ran away when his schooling was over at fourteen, and he developed his gift for drawing and became a painter.'

Giles Hoggett scratched his head and added:

'I can't tell you much about the boy. I can't see him very well . . . mischievous, lively, but with the unstable element which always attracted him to bad companions and the seemingly easy path of petty pilfering. Perhaps he did have an uncle, somewhere up in the hill country: perhaps the uncle did think he would give the boy a chance to settle in the country and raise chickens . . . I don't know, but I don't think a north country uncle gave him £500 to waste on hens which would certainly die . . .'

'Leave the boy for the moment, he's not in your line of country,' said Macdonald. 'Go back to the Golds.'

'Aye, the Golds,' said Giles Hoggett. 'They rubbed along all right. It was a hard life, but they were both shrewd at a bargain and they valued their liberty. Their horse and cart gave them mobility and they call no man master. Sarah Gold was able to save a bit — thrift was in her blood, but she and her husband were opportunists: they bought what they could, they saved what they could, and they stole what they could. They were too clever to be bowled out and they flourished according to their own standards. This brings us to the present day and to the appearance of Sarah Gold's first husband in these parts. Ginner had been involved in many transactions of questionable legality and he had a large acquaintance among lewd fellows of his own type. He had also run a profitable side-line of paying attentions, with matrimonial suggestions, to elderly ladies with some amount of capital. It seems not unreasonable to imagine that his first essay at obtaining money in this way had encouraged him to run the risk of marrying divers widows in suitably distant localities.'

George laughed aloud here.

'Steady, Giley, steady! You're giving too much rein to your imagination.'

'Oh no, he isn't,' said Macdonald equably. 'Dr. Castleby may not know that Ginner's disappearance was first reported by a middle-aged lady of comfortable income and no pretensions to beauty. The very first idea I had about Ginner was that a likely looking fellow of under fifty, of his known proclivities, could have had only one motive in proposing marriage to a slightly bearded, teetotal, Nonconformist widow of sixty — and if once, why not frequently? Hoggett is on sound ground there.'

Giles Hoggett did not laugh at all. He was entirely serious and working very hard.

'This brings us to Ginner's appearance in the Lunesdale country,' he said.

II

'Ginner heard from some of his friends that the police were on his track,' went on Giles. 'He didn't wait to be arrested. 'No, not me, old chap. Nothing of that kind of mutt about me,' he would have said. 'I'm going to beat it. He who steals and runs away, lives to steal another day.' Beat it, that's the idea . . . but where? Then he thought of the north — the fells around Kirkby Stephen . . . cold, dour, remote . . . and the country folk have long memories. No, not there. Somewhere nearer to civilisation, somewhere within reach of a pub and a cinema and a railway line. Morecambe Bay. Why not? It'd do as a starting point.'

Giles Hoggett broke off and turned to Macdonald.

'That bit about Ginner being in a pub in Morecambe, it struck me as probable — completely in character. If he played with the idea of concealing himself up here, Morecambe was such a likely point of departure. Morecambe in August, crowded with trippers, the very thing! Then he met Vintner. He'd seen Vintner before, used him maybe, on some swindling venture, and had some hold on him. When Ginner learnt that Vintner had a lonely house on the fells above the Lune he said to himself, 'That's the ticket. That'll do while I have a look-see' — and he went to Thorpe Intak and looked around. He saw Vintner's painting of this cottage and asked about it. An empty cottage, furnished, a long way from anywhere. No one likely to be there all the winter. Just what he wanted. He could even risk making a date with some of his pals to raise a bit of money. After all, he'd got those coupons, and they were worth the devil of a lot if he could market them. He'd have had to think it out very carefully. He wouldn't have risked writing letters, in case they fell into the wrong hands. No use finding a nice safe hidey hole like the cottage and then giving away the secret. No. I reckon he did some telephoning. There are plenty of public call-boxes to be found on the main roads if you look for them. He probably had an A.A. key, too, and he could have used those boxes.'

'Quite true. He had. And he probably did,' said Macdonald. 'I'm looking into that, Hoggett. Some of these rural exchange operators have long memories.'

'Did you find the A.A. key on him?' demanded George Castleby.

'No, but we found an A.A. receipt among his papers. We found nothing on him. I've no doubt he had a key ring in his pockets when he left home. It's one of the things I want to find. Go on, Hoggett.'

'He did some telephoning,' said Giles, earnestly taking up his story exactly where he had left off, 'and it was while he was waiting about outside a call-box one day that the Golds passed him in their cart. Ginner hadn't changed all that in the course of twenty-five years. Sarah recognised him — but, of course, Reuben had never seen him. Sarah hadn't forgotten how her first husband had treated her, and she made up her mind, then and there, to get even with him if she could. Of course, Ginner didn't recognise Sarah — a thin, weather-beaten white-haired gypsy of a woman. If she was beautiful as a girl, she's not beautiful now . . . I think the Golds saw Ginner enter Thorpe Intak. Sarah said nothing — but when she got the opportunity, she had a talk with a young fellow in the encampment, and offered to make it worth his while to follow Ginner and find out where he went and what he was doing. And this,' announced Giles Hoggett, with earnest directness, 'is where the bits of curtain come in. Sarah tore up some strips of the stuff, and told her sleuth to lay a trail — a bit of the stuff on a thorn bush, with other signs which all the tramps and potters can recognise, to lead her to her quarry.'

'Bravo, Giles! That's a good effort,' chuckled George. 'I wondered how the dickens you were going to bring in the curtains.'

Giles turned to Macdonald with earnest dignity.

'It isn't so silly as it sounds,' he said. 'The potters do leave signs, just as the tramps do, and that stuff is very distinctive.'

'It isn't silly at all. It's a very interesting point,' said Macdonald. 'Let's have the rest of your story.'

George suddenly snorted.

'If you're going to tell me that Sarah Gold killed Ginner and tied him up with salmon line and wheeled his body across the dales on your bogie, I tell you straight out I don't believe you,' he said trenchantly. 'The Golds may pilfer. I've no evidence to that effect, but it's not improbable, but Sarah Gold did *not* bash her first husband over the head with a coal hammer —'

'I never said she did,' said Giles indignantly. 'I've been thinking over my suspicions of the Golds. I still believe they stole my ducks, and they once milked my cows when I was in Lancaster, but I don't make any other accusations at all. If you'd only be as patient as Macdonald is, I'll tell you just what did happen. Sarah Gold followed the trail laid from the high road to this cottage, and when she got here she had the fright of her not very virtuous life, for one of Ginner's disreputable urban accomplices had followed Ginner here, knowing that he possessed the haul of coupons. It was this scoundrel from the slums of an industrial city who killed Ginner in order to steal the coupons. Once he'd killed him, he had to hide the body, and being here he *saw* the iron dogs and the chain and the salmon line, and he used them. Being a townsman he hadn't the sense to realise they'd be missed and he thought it would be all right, so he waited till nightfall and then hid the body in the river, and Sarah Gold saw him at it. She was frightened and said to herself 'Better say nowt. Better see nowt. Better know nowt' — and she cleared out as fast as she could and told her husband she was going to see her old sister up at Kirkby Stephen, her being in a bad way — and that's why Sarah Gold hasn't been seen on the road recently.'

Macdonald laughed: not in the least scornfully, but in appreciation of an effort at reconstruction which he was the first to admit contained some very ingenious ideas, plus a real knowledge of possibilities.

'Congratulations, Hogget. That was a very fine effort. You have included most of the facts and not strained probabilities too far. The beginning was very good indeed, but the conclusion was a masterpiece of wishful thinking. You have persuaded yourself that the culprit was a scoundrel from the slums of an industrial city, and that even the potters of Lunesdale leave court without a stain on their characters.'

'Dog does not eat dog,' said Giles with dignity. 'George is probably right about Sarah Gold. Perhaps she didn't even steal my ducks — altho' they *were* stolen. I'm going to make some tea. I'm thirsty after all that talking.'

He seized the kettle and turned towards the door

(the water at Wenningby Barns had to be fetched from the beck). Suddenly Giles turned back towards Macdonald.

'We ought to have had Kate here. She always spots the weak points in my reconstructions.'

'Yes. She was born in London. Londoners are a great race,' chuckled Macdonald.

Giles Hoggett looked pained at this conclusion but forbore to argue and went out with his kettle. George Castleby turned to Macdonald.

'From your own point of view as a C.I.D. man, did you get anything valuable from Giles's imaginative effort?' he enquired.

'Certainly I did. He gave me some very useful ideas, and I'm far from disdaining ideas when I'm off my own beat. I encouraged him to do it that way because he was so interested in his own reconstruction that he produced his ideas without sterilising them by analysis if you follow me. It often happens that if you can get a chap talking about his own environment without the feeling that he's on oath, as it were, he produces something useful in the way of local colour which a newcomer to the district wouldn't have thought about.'

'Yes. I follow that, and I admit I was jolly interested in Giles's story — but a story it remains. Incidentally, do you really think you have enough evidence to connect the potters with this crime?'

'I have enough evidence to make it desirable — and justifiable to investigate them. Those pieces of curtain material need to be explained. Moreover, they constitute a link between Vintner and the potters, which also needs investigating. There is another point, which I observed immediately I had read the letter your cousin wrote to me. A lorry man who knew Ginner slightly put in his evidence that Ginner had a number of 'low friends' and that he once had a row with one of them 'about a pottery' or something like that. Now I gather that this row occurred at one of those road-side coffee stalls where lorry drivers pull in for a hot drink. It was on the road between Liverpool and Crewe. Now it seems quite possible to me that the 'low friends' who started the dispute with Ginner may have been tinkers or members of the gypsy tribe — that is, brethren of the road who may well have been acquainted with the potters of North Lancashire and Westmoreland. I tell you this because I'm hoping you'll be willing to help me a little further, Dr. Castleby.'

George's expression lacked enthusiasm: in fact he looked far from happy.

'Well, Chief Inspector, I am willing to admit my civic responsibility and my duty to help the police, but in my profession we are very averse from exploiting the confidence of our patients. I have told you what facts I knew, because you were justified in asking for them, but I can't combine detection with doctoring. That idea goes all against the grain.'

'I see that,' replied Macdonald, 'and I'm not asking you to do any detecting. The thing I want is confirmation of a fact which you mentioned, but without any degree of certainty — that Mrs. Gold came originally from a farm or smallholding in the hills near Kirkby Stephen. If you can ascertain that, it may save me a great deal of time. As you know, all marriage certificates in England and Wales are filed in Somerset House. Searching with hardly any data is a wearisome and time-wasting performance, though it is astonishing what can be done by a skilful and determined searcher. If I had the name of the district plus the maiden name — if possible — of the bride, I could save one of my men a lot of trouble.'

'I'll try and get you the name of Mrs. Gold's birthplace, but I doubt if I shall arrive at her maiden name,' said George. 'If it's any help to you, I can tell you that her son was named Stephen, that he was born in July, 1914, and his birthplace was Preston. I think his mother would have registered the boy's birth, because she evidently laid considerable store on his legal status — maybe with the hope of his inheriting something from his father.'

Macdonald studied the other's thoughtful but noncommittal countenance. With his large glasses and composed expression George Castleby looked both bland and reticent.

'The child's name was Stephen,' said Macdonald. 'A not very common name these days. Have you any other reason for assuming his mother's native place was near Kirkby Stephen?'

'I think it's probable — very probable,' said George blandly. 'Here's Giles with the kettle. Any fresh ideas, laddie?'

'I'm bursting with information,' said Giles. 'Anthony Vintner told me that he originally studied painting in Preston. He went later to a London Art School.'

George looked interested.

'Preston . . . Well, if it's a coincidence, it's rather an odd one.'

Macdonald looked sceptical. 'It doesn't impress me,' he said. He turned to Giles Hoggett. 'Did he tell you that when he was trying to sell you a picture?'

'Yes. Why?'

'Shrewdness on his part. Vintner's sharp enough to

know that you'd feel more sympathy for a man trained in the north. Think of his voice, Hoggett. Could you imagine for a moment that Vintner was reared in the north of England? He learnt to speak in the south of England. It's unmistakable. You spent over twenty years in Camford, Hoggett, but it didn't alter your voice. I've been living in London since I was ten years old but nobody thinks I was born there when they hear my voice. A northern accent is ineradicable. Anthony Vintner's voice is not the voice of north Lancashire.'

'Yes. That is perfectly true,' said Giles Hoggett. 'I ought to have thought of that. All the same Vintner must have had some knowledge of this part of the world: I don't think he hit on Lunesdale by sheer chance.'

'Perhaps his friend Ginner suggested it to him,' said George. 'Incidentally, I'm far more disposed to think of Vintner as the culprit than either of the Golds. I admit Reuben Gold is a rough customer, and might well have a savage temper when he has been drinking, but this job doesn't seem in keeping with what I know of him.' He turned to Macdonald. 'Would it have been necessary to bc able to swim to have concealed the sack where you found it?'

'I think so. You would have had to be quite a good diver for one thing; the chain was neatly and strongly hooked on to the willow roots several feet below the surface. Also, when I was in the river, the stream was very strong and it was difficult to get out and scramble up the bank without being washed downstream. I think swimming must be considered a necessary part of the murderer's equipment.'

'Reuben Gold can't swim, and both he and his wife are afraid of water — Mrs. Gold has almost a phobia about it,' said George, getting to his feet. 'Well, Giles, I must be off. I'm sorry to say that if I had been asked to provide a reconstruction by the Chief Inspector, I should almost have been hypnotised by the fact that you and I have all the necessary knowledge and qualifications which would have enabled us to commit the murder successfully and then to hoodwink the Chief Inspector by subtle detection of our own nefarious doings. Isn't that so?' he concluded, turning to Macdonald.

'Undoubtedly. The more I see of both of you, the more I realise the truth of Dr. Castleby's observations,' rejoined Macdonald serenely. 'At the same time, if it turns out that you did do it, I shall retire from detection and buy Thorpe Intak, to share the thistles with the other inhabitants.'

'Very handsomely said,' rejoined Giles Hoggett. 'George, I'll see you up the brow.'

'Good-night, Chief Inspector. I shall hope to see you again some time — unprofessionally.'

'Good-night, doctor — and thanks very much,' replied Macdonald.

11

I

Macdonald sat over the fire and pondered. He had been very much interested in Giles Hoggett's imaginary narrative. Admittedly it was not detection, but various points were suggestive to Macdonald's mind, and indicated different lines of research to be followed. He sat in the silent cottage, meditating that it was probable that Gordon Ginner had sat just where he was sitting now, listening, perhaps, for the footsteps of an unexpected visitor. Even as he pondered over this, Macdonald also was aware of footsteps outside: two men were approaching the cottage. One was Hoggett, the second a shorter man who took more footsteps to cover the same ground. Macdonald sat and waited until Hoggett opened the door.

'There's a visitor for you,' he announced. 'Kate sent him along and I met him just as I left George.'

'Reeves!' exclaimed Macdonald. 'It's good to see you. Have you brought me some news?'

'That's it, Chief. The A.C. sent me along with his compliments, hoping I'd be useful.'

'Good for him,' said Macdonald. 'First I'll introduce you to my friend Mr. Giles Hoggett, who is our host here. Hoggett, this is Detective-Inspector Peter Reeves, a hundred per cent Londoner, and one of the best arguments in favour of London ever produced there.'

'Good-evening, Mr. Reeves. I'm very glad to see you here, and I'm much impressed by the Chief Inspector's testimonial. Have you just come from London?'

'Yes, sir. I reached Lancaster at nine o'clock and got a lift from a farmer named Troutbeck. There are some good-hearted folk hereabouts. I expected to have to foot it.'

'You must be hungry,' said Giles Hoggett promptly. 'I'm afraid we've eaten all the trout, but I've got a lot of eggs if they'll help.'

'Eggs — in the plural? Glory! I haven't met eggs in the plural for years. Doesn't sound real these days.'

Reeves stood by the fire, a trim well-balanced figure, always on his toes; he was six inches shorter than Hoggett, and looked like a schoolboy with his neat dark head, slim figure, and cheerful grin.

'Do you like your eggs boiled, fried, or scrambled?' enquired Mr. Hoggett. 'There are plenty of tomatoes and some soup.'

'Sounds good to me,' said Reeves. 'If you'll trust me with the frying pan I shall enjoy doing the cooking.'

'Right. I'll get the eggs and tomatoes and leave you to it, while I see about some coffee.'

Once again Macdonald thought how adaptable Mr. Hoggett was. Reeves was a Cockney; his quick speech and mobile lively face made him as unlike Hoggett as a monkey is unlike a mastiff, but the two men cooked over the same fire in perfect amity, not getting in each other's way, and obviously enjoying one another's odd ways and speech.

When Reeves sat back with a cup of coffee, after putting away his own notion of scrambled eggs plus tomatoes and fried onions, Macdonald said:

'What's the news from the Metropolis, Reeves?'

'I've got a line on Ginner, Chief. I've been running round in circles after him, like a kitten chasing its own tail. I knew he hadn't been called up for the Forces — groggy heart or something — but I reckoned he'd have had to do Civil Defence of some kind. He was in Pimlico the first year of the war, and when the first bombs came down he beat it to the Midlands. I got that from the Civil Defence bloke who organised the street Ginner lived in. I followed up on information received and traced him to Warwick. He was in the N.F.S. there for a while and later got transferred to Midchester, still in the N.F.S. I got chatting with some of his mates in the Fire Service there. It's a safe bet that if a chap ever talks at all, he'll talk while fire-watching. Lord, the stories I've heard from the dumbest blokes God ever made while we were on that job. You've got to talk. You can't help it.'

Macdonald chuckled. 'I know. Very sound, Reeves.'

'Applied psychology,' murmured Mr. Hoggett.

'Fruits of bitter experience, sir,' replied Reeves with his quick grin. 'Ginner was an alias, Chief. I reckoned it would be. It's funny to think the chap got himself bumped off here, all in the midst of peace, perfect peace. He'd take such a lot of trouble to arrange bolt-holes. He was Gordon Ginner in London and Midchester. He was Thomas Harcourt Baring in Liverpool — he's got a room there, and an identity card, too. His real name was George Garstang. I got that from a bookie in Midchester who served in the N.F.S. with Ginner and managed to make him tight one night. Ginner must have been pretty well sozzled, because he got to the weepy and confidential stage. Ginner — I'll go on calling him that to save confusion — was born in Preston, in 1900 — I've looked up the records in Somerset House. His father was a commercial traveller who died in 1902. His mother once lived in Southport but had had a married sister in Chapelton-Lonsdale. The Preston people found that out for us. Ginner's mother (Mrs. Garstang) came to London when her husband died. In 1910 a Mrs. George Garstang died in Battersea. She'd worked as a barmaid. I reckon that's Ginner's mother, because I've checked the records in Somerset House. Jenkins spent all yesterday trying to find someone who remembered Mrs. Garstang and found a body in the Balham High Road who'd known her. This old girl name of Peabody — remembers the boy as a precocious young varmint, but she says he used to go and stay with an aunt in the holidays somewhere up in the north. That'd be the Chapelton-Lonsdale aunt. His father had no sisters. Somerset House again. Marvellous what you can find out there once you've got a real name to start on.'

'There you are, Hoggett. That's what real detection is, ploughing through old death, birth and marriage certificates at Somerset House,' said Macdonald.

'Plus applied psychology or the fruits of bitter experience, whichever you prefer to call it,' replied Hoggett. 'The story's come full circle again — with Chapelton-Lonsdale at the centre.'

'That's near here, isn't it?' asked Reeves. 'I thought it would be. There's nearly always some sense in real life stories. If there weren't we'd all go bats in our department. If a chap like Ginner with a Cockney accent like mine and lodgings in Pimlico gets his ticket in a place like this, miles from anywhere, it's not just chance. There's always a connection somewhere.'

Reeves looked around the ancient room in which

they sat. 'Old, isn't it?' he asked meditatively. 'Centuries old. I bet this room's seen some doings . . . Funny to think of. There's a place called Garstang not so far away, isn't there? I've been looking at the Ordnance Survey. I suppose Ginner's people came from Garstang originally, it's a rum name. His ancestors might have lived in a cottage just like this one. He'd got rooms in Pimlico . . . nasty rooms. Flash. All cheap tawdry muck. Like Ginner. He came back here and got his ticket . . . as though this place was ashamed of him. Didn't like him. Wouldn't have him. Chucked him in the river and got rid of him. What was it you said, sir? Full circle . . . that's about it. It's often like that. Sorry I'm talking too much. It's this place. It's . . . got a feel to it.'

'Aye,' said Hoggett's deep voice. 'It's got a feel to it. I never imagined a London detective would say so, though.'

Reeves glanced at Macdonald, a swift glance, to find out if his superior officer did think he'd been talking too much. Reeves was as sensitive to atmosphere as a cat to the presence of a mouse. Macdonald was staring tranquilly into the fire, and Reeves went on talking to Mr. Hoggett.

'A London detective,' he echoed, in his clipped speech which sounded so thin after Mr. Hoggett's murmuring bass. 'You don't think much of Londoners up here, do you? You think of movies and jazz bands, fried fish and chips and chromium plating, when you say London. Crowded, isn't it? Stinks, too, foggy and dirty, with lots of swindlers, con-men and smash and grabbers. All that. Well, I'm a Cockney, born and bred. Proud of it, too. Went to school off Holborn, lived in Clerkenwell — and I can tell this place has got a feel to it. I know it's worth something. More than you can say about Clerkenwell, sir — but it is worth something, by heck, it is . . . What was the matter with Ginner was that he made no place his own. Just swindled his way from one place to another and cleared out when the balloon went up. Nasty customer, was Ginner — but his folks came from around here once. You get good 'uns and bad 'uns everywhere, not only in London.'

'Aye. You're quite right,' said Mr. Hoggett, and Macdonald seemed to wake up.

'We've quite a variety of jobs to do to-morrow, Reeves. I want to interview a gentleman named Gold myself: he's an itinerant hawker. What we call tinkers in the south; they call them potters up here. I suggest that you go to Chapelton-Lonsdale and see what you can learn there. I wonder if Mr. Hoggett would like to drive you there?'

'Aye,' said Mr. Hoggett with alacrity. 'I'll do that with pleasure. Is there any ban on my making a few discreet enquiries from people I know on the subject of a lady who had a married sister named Garstang?'

'None whatever,' rejoined Macdonald. 'I only make one stipulation. If you go with Reeves, you must undertake to do what he tells you — or not to do what he bans. He has got to control the expedition — but you'll find him a very reasonable skipper.'

'That'll be all right. I won't cause him a moment's anxiety,' rejoined Mr. Hoggett, 'and I shall enjoy enlarging my knowledge of him.'

'Thank you, sir. That's very kindly put,' said Reeves. 'I reckon we ought to make a good team. You know the people: I know the ropes. You can talk to the tradesmen and I'll do the pubs. Chatty places, pubs.

We'll work out a scheme so that we don't cramp one another's style. We don't both want to try the same people. If you tackle the parson about your old aunt's housemaid, I'll see the schoolmaster about my mother's cousin's wife — and I'll do the parish registers. I'm very hot on searching registers.'

Macdonald chuckled. 'This is in the nature of a sporting event,' he said. 'While I consider that Hoggett has the initial advantage, because he knows the country, I'm willing to bet that Reeves will bring back at least as much information.'

Mr. Hoggett made no reply, but he looked very determined, and skilfully sidetracked the conversation by making dispositions about sleeping accommodation.

'Reeves can have my bed,' he said. 'I will go up to the farm. My wife will be quite pleased to see me, she hasn't really much enthusiasm for detection in real life. Also, with Reeves here, I consider you are adequately protected,' he added to Macdonald.

After Mr. Hoggett had left them, Reeves said:

'Did he really mean that bit about you needing protection, Chief, or was he being funny?'

'I'm willing to do quite a lot for you, Reeves, but interpreting Mr. Hoggett is no part of my duty. I'll leave you to think it out. Do you get breakfast, or do I?'

'I will,' said Reeves. 'I know where the eggs are.'

'Right — but if you make scrambled eggs for me, I don't want onions in them.'

'No? They're tasty that way. You'd better have yours boiled. I'll see to it. I like this place, Chief — and I like *him*. I'm beginning to understand what he says right away now. He got me guessing a bit at first.'

'You got him guessing, too,' rejoined Macdonald.

II

Reeves woke up first the next morning. Macdonald heard him whistling in the kitchen while the fire crackled cheerfully up the chimney. Reeves came upstairs grinning all over his face.

'Shaving water, sir. Breakfast in half an hour. I like this outfit. Champion, as they say up here. It's very well organised, too. Everything to hand, nice and tidy and easy to find. That Mr. Hoggett must be a very useful husband.'

'The fact is that he's got a very useful wife,' said Macdonald. 'It's Mrs. Hoggett who's the tidy one. You must meet her, Reeves. She's an intellectual who uses her intelligence in country life.'

'Brains of the outfit?' asked Reeves. 'I shouldn't say her husband's any sort of fool though. Not half wily in his own way. Reckon I'd better leave the kitchen nice and tidy. I'm all for making a good impression. My kids wouldn't half like a holiday here next summer.' He chuckled, as cheerful as a schoolboy. 'Better keep it under our lids, sir, or half the Yard'll be rolling up here as a change from Brighton. There's some real butter in that larder. You know — yellow and creamy. Straight from the cow. Not Government stuff. I do like butter.'

'It's an ill wind that blows nobody any good,' said Macdonald.

Shortly after nine o'clock Mr. Hoggett and Reeves set off on bicycles. This was Mr. Hoggett's suggestion, so that Macdonald could have the use of the car. Reeves had Mrs Hoggett's bicycle, and he assured her that he was quite to be trusted with the ancient vehicle. Macdonald knew that Reeves was almost up to the standard of a circus trick-rider on a cycle, and he had no doubt that Mr. Hoggett would have an interesting ride.

Macdonald first made contact with Inspector Bord at Carnton, and gave him a resumé of 'information received.' Bord reported in his turn that Anthony Vintner had only left his house to walk to the pub and had not had any visitors; that Mr. Willoughby (whose waders had been stolen from the fishing hut) had rang up and made an appointment to see Bord that evening; that Mr. Shand had made a statement to the Superintendent protesting against Mr. Hoggett's belief that the potters were responsible for the thefts in the valley; and finally, that Reuben Gold had set out in his cart along the Carnton-Ingleton road, and that Macdonald would probably overtake him if he drove in that direction.

It was on a straight, bleak stretch of road that Macdonald eventually overtook the potter's cart. He drove past it, ran his car on to the rough moorland grass and alighted, standing well in the middle of the road with his hand raised as a signal to the potter to stop. The driver pulled up and sat regarding Macdonald with a stare which showed no sign of fear. He was a heavily-built fellow with a bearded face, an old cap pulled down low over his eyes. They were light coloured eyes, calculating and hard, very far from amiable.

'Reuben Gold? I am a police officer and I want a word with you. You can see my warrant. You had better tie your horse up to that thorn tree.'

Reuben Gold sat still, holding his reins.

'I'm well enough here. Police ha' nowt against me.'

'That's as maybe. You can get down and speak civilly, or you can drive on and refuse to speak at all. In which case you will be taken in charge and the contents of your cart examined.'

'For why?'

'Because of certain thefts which I am looking into. You'd better get down, Gold. If you've done naught against the law you've still got the same duty as every other man — to assist the police when you're called on to do so.'

The potter stared back, inscrutable and unafraid: at last he jumped down from the cart and led his horse on to the verge, still holding the reins. Standing thus he waited for Macdonald to speak.

'I am a police officer from London,' said Macdonald. 'I have come to this district to find a man who has been concerned in thefts in the Midlands. There have been some unlawful doings in this valley, and I want all the information I can get. First of all, what took you down to the dales just lately, Gold?'

'Nowt. I havena' been in the dales these past two years.'

'You'll have to repeat that on oath later, so better think again. I've no doubt you know all about laying a trail, and following one. I know how to follow one, too. Where did you get that bit of orange-coloured rag in your pocket?'

Gold stared hard at his interlocutor, but his face did not change.

'How should I know? I buy rags and such like bits and sell 'em to owd gaffer in Carnton. Mebbe the missis picked owd rag oot and stuffed it in ma pocket.'

'Maybe she did — and dropped some other bits along the trail. If it's poaching trout you were after, better say so. That's a small charge compared to the one I'm working on. What about the painter at

Thorpe Intak?'

'Yon's a gey gert fool, that's all I do know about him.'

Macdonald was feeling his way along. Standing on the fringes of this dour, fell country, he was aware of two arguments playing tug-of-war in his mind. The first told him that his evidence for connecting Reuben Gold with the crime in the river valley was so slight that any counsel would have laughed it out of court. The second, based on his own reactions to the tough fellow in front of him, was that Gold *did* know something, and that he had acquiesced in the order to get down out of his cart because he judged it as well to learn what lay behind that order.

Gold bore no resemblance to the tramps of the southern counties: neither was he of the gypsy type, alternatively cringing and threatening. This man was of the Norse type, independent, unafraid, rough and terse of speech, probably brutal when he was drunk, and dour at all times — but he *had* got down from his cart; he was watchful, and, for all his stillness, uneasy.

Macdonald tried another tack:

'Where is your wife, Gold?'

'What's that to you?'

'I want to see her. She hasn't been seen on the road with you these two weeks. Not since you were in the dales that night. She's got to be found.'

Macdonald, as often before when dealing with fellows of this type was following his instinct now. The conventional question and answer of police procedure were useless in dealing with this man who would produce nothing but negative answers. The only way of dealing with him was to find what he was afraid of. For all his set face and unchanging stare, Reuben

Gold was uneasy.

'How much do you know about police work?' asked Macdonald. 'If ever a charge has been made against you, you've been acquitted, haven't you? Gey gert fools, the police. Maybe — but this is different. If you've no other answer to give to my questions, the whole police force will be looking for your wife before the day's out, aye, and questioning everyone of your fellows, following up every deal you've worked, every journey you've taken. You know what I'm after, Gold.'

The big fellow came at him so suddenly that if Macdonald had not been tensed for the attack he would have gone down on the rocky ground — and stayed there. Macdonald had chosen his own field of action. For miles the bare fells were solitary beneath the grey skies: the road was as solitary as the fell-side. In stopping this man here, the C.I.D. man seemed to have offered him a plain way out — the way of violence known to every nomad in the world. There was no witness to this encounter on a lonely road. Macdonald side-stepped as Gold came at him and then hit out before the other had recovered his balance after missing his blow. Gold went down from the blow which had a trained boxer's power behind the punch, but he was too tough to be outed by one blow; he was up again in a second, crouching to spring for a wrestler's hold. Macdonald sprang back — he had no intention of playing that game, he knew well enough the other could likely break his back once he got a hold. It took two more punches to knock the stuffing out of the potter, but then he lay stunned on the grass long enough for Macdonald to get a pair of handcuffs on him and a handkerchief knotted round his ankles. All the time the old pony had stood quite still, indifferent to the performances of human kind.

Macdonald left Gold where he lay in the rough grass—grunting painfully as he recovered from a blow which would have laid most men out for hours—and the C.I.D. man, looking ruefully at his own split knuckles, went to investigate Gold's cart.

It was a quarter of an hour later that Inspector Bord arrived—the follow-up having been duly arranged by himself and Macdonald. Both of them, to quote the latter, were too canny to leave much to chance. Bord found the potter's pony grazing quietly on the poor grass at the road-side. Gold was sitting up, green-faced and grim, handcuffs on his wrists, an adequate handkerchief still professionally tied round his ankles. He was quite silent. Macdonald was sitting by the road-side, too, his knuckles plastered now. Beside him was a pair of waders and a bundle of rags, including some of Mrs. Hoggett's old orange curtains.

Macdonald got to his feet as Bord got out of the police car with his young chauffeur—the latter trying to look cool and professionally unconcerned. Macdonald addressed the potter:

'You got what you asked for, Gold. Next time you think of hitting a policeman, remember we're taught a thing or two before we get talking. You'll be charged with being in possession of a pair of waders stolen from a lock-up hut in the dales. I'll be seeing you later, when you've had time to think things out.'

He turned to Bord.

'I think we can get him into your car. Better leave his ankles as they are. I fancy he can kick. Can you send a man back for the cart? That's a very good pony. Never budged an inch. He's seen a thing or two in his time.'

12

I

Leaving Bord to deal with the silent Potter and the imperturbable pony, Macdonald turned the car westwards. His mind was busy with those bits of orange curtain material, and the more he thought about them, the more he was disposed to believe that Giles Hoggett had hit the nail on the head when he suggested that the rags had been used to mark a trail. What then could be the explanation of the rag hanging from Reuben Gold's pocket? A signal of sorts? Thinking it out, Macdonald came to the conclusion that here was a possible means of communication between illiterate folk. A fragment of the material could be handed on with the tacit message implied — follow this sign, or speak to the man who carries a similar one. With a chuckle, Macdonald thought how much Reeves would enjoy the chance of driving the potter's cart, perhaps with an orange rag tied jauntily to his whip.

Meanwhile, Macdonald determined to follow that route to Wenningby Barns from the main road which Giles Hoggett had described as the one most likely to be chosen by a person who wished to reach the river valley unobserved.

He found the Upfields turning without difficulty — a narrow farm road, marked by the platform for the 'kits' — the big milk cans which the lorry man collected every morning from all the farms round about. Macdonald ran the car on to some waste ground, locked it and pursued his way on foot. He could see the low stone buildings of the two farms which constituted the 'Middle Upfield,' and his way led between them, but he saw no signs of any inhabitants. The farm kitchens would open on to the yards, but their doors did not directly overlook the roadway, which ran between stone walls. Macdonald was intrigued by those stone walls. The one on his right was a massive piece of building, very deep and strong, with a coping of dressed stone and gaps at intervals in the lower stage of the wall. It was obviously of considerable antiquity and seemed to enclose a large property. The wall on his left was the usual 'dry walling,' crude but durable.

Immediately beyond the farmsteads, the ground began to slope towards the river valley. Choosing his way between various gates, Macdonald followed the slightly worn track down the sloping fields and was soon out of sight of the farm buildings. The only creatures to note his passing were a bunch of stirks and some dark-faced sheep, who looked at him with the enquiring and suspicious manner of their kind and bleated insults at him when he had passed. Huddled together in a group by the hedge they seemed to Macdonald to be doing their best to state that no one but a lunatic would choose that path, and in any case the lunatic had no right to be there.

Leaving the indignation party of bleaters to their legitimate pasture, Macdonald passed through a gate into the woods above the Lune. He had been conscious of the loneliness of the path while he was still in the pastures: once in the wood he seemed infinitely far away from human beings. The trees were close and the undergrowth thick: it was obvious that the path had not been cleared for years and it was difficult to follow, overgrown with bramble and rose suckers and treacherous with sodden leaves and fallen branches. At one stage he stopped because he realised he had missed the track and looking round to reconsider he saw something which might have been dead beech leaves: certainly there was a broken branch with yellowed leaves clinging to it, but there was something else — a scrap of orange rag, impaled on a thorny branch.

'Good for you, Giles Hoggett . . . but why? For what, and for whom?' he said to himself.

Back on the right track he walked parallel with the river and crossed a rocky gill where the beck splashed merrily down its course, and found for the first time he had a clear view down to the river and across the valley to the fells on the southern side. It was a beautiful prospect and a natural resting place, where the path was level and clearly defined and Macdonald looked around carefully to see if there were any signs of others having passed that way. He soon found something which did not in the least surprise him — an empty tube of paint. It was a Windsor & Newton tube and it had once contained Flake White. Although the leaf-covered ground showed no traces of footmarks, the traces of an easel and camp-stool were clearly discernible, where the pointed legs had made holes in the rich black soil. Here also were some frayed threads of orange cotton, where a fragment of the curtain material had once been planted. He followed the track until it brought him down through the woods to the edge of the dales and found that he had arrived at the wide level stretches where Giles

Hoggett had chased Vintner in the moonlight. It was evident that Vintner had made a beeline over the dales for the entrance to the woodland: there was a stile where the path through the woods reached the dales, and the woods were fenced off to prevent the cattle from straying.

Macdonald sat down on the stile, lighted his pipe and contemplated. It was clear that several people had used the woodland path of late; certainly Vintner had, as the empty paint tube and the marks of his easel testified. Almost equally certain one of the potters had, and left the trail marked by the scraps of curtain material. Macdonald could now see the usefulness of that particular stuff: its faded orange tone had camouflage value. It was possible to find the rags if you knew what to look for, but you could easily have passed them without noticing them, so well did the colour tone in with the fading autumn leaves. Pondering over the matter, Macdonald hazarded a guess that Gordon Ginner had had nothing to do with blazing the trail with those rags; it indicated a craftiness which was quite foreign to a towns-dweller whose lodgings had been described by Reeves as 'Flash. All cheap, tawdry muck.' If Ginner had marked the trail, he would have used something much less subtle than those tawny rags.

Sitting on the stile facing the dales Macdonald began to study the lie of the ground. Eastwards the track led to Wenningby Barns and the Brow — a quarter of a mile upstream. Westwards there was no path along the actual holm-land — it was necessary to go into the woods if you wished to walk in the direction of Caton and Lancaster, for the river had altered its course several times in the passing of centuries, and beds of shilla and some back-waters and tributary gills made the valley level too involved for a direct footpath. Nevertheless, it was obvious that fishermen would keep down by the stream and Macdonald decided to do some exploring off the track and see if he could find anything interesting in the pathless area between the woods and the river.

II

It was heavy going over the pastures where no path had been worn. The ground was still waterlogged from the recent floods, and the becks flowing down from the woods were still in spate, so that Macdonald wished he had gone back to the cottage for a pair of gum boots. However, he was soon so wet that nothing could have made him much wetter, so far as the legs were concerned anyway. An incautious step had resulted in being bogged almost to his knees, and he reflected that rock-climbing was preferable to mud-larking. For once the Lune was being captious with him.

It was shortly after he had negotiated a particularly sodden stretch that Macdonald was aware that he was not alone in the valley, and his spirits went up with a bound. (No man feels his best when he is being derided by river-mud which is camouflaged by a luscious growth of fog-grass.) Somewhere up against the woods, some fifty yards distant, somebody else was investigating this sodden stretch of valley, and Macdonald was pretty certain he knew who it was. The man was short and sturdy, a rather paunchy figure topped by an old hard felt hat. None of the farmers wore a hat like that; it had been bought for town wear, and worn so long that it had become a favourite possession to its owner. Macdonald had noted Mr. Willoughby's ancient hat when the latter had told Mr. Hoggett about the breaking open of his fishing hut. That hat sat on its owner's bullet head as though it were part of it — and now the hat and its wearer were keeping well out of sight against the hedge bordering the woods.

Macdonald forgot that the flood water was very cold and that the mud oozing in and out of his shoes was very uncomfortable: he ploughed on, as quietly as he could, paddled cheerfully through another beck, and came on his fellow mud-larker while the latter was still trying to lean well back into an intractable and inhospitable hedge of thorns.

'Good-morning, Mr. Willoughby,' said Macdonald. 'Are you in trouble? If so, can I help you at all?'

The stout little Yorkshireman glared back. 'May I ask who you are, and why you are trespassing on private land?' he asked belligerently.

'My name is Macdonald. I am an officer of the Criminal Investigation Department of the Metropolitan Police, and I am here on duty,' said Macdonald urbanely. 'In the course of my duty I must ask you to account for possession of the coat and the rod you have concealed in that hedge.'

'By goom, lad,' began Mr. Willoughby wrathfully, and then subsided a little. 'All right, all right. Not so much of the police officer to *me* if you please. It may look a bit queer, but it's all right really.' He hitched his own coat clear of the thorn hedge and went on, speaking excitedly: 'I've been very much put out by the goings-on down here, and I thought I'd look into it myself. I remembered I'd caught a glimpse of an old gaffer along here a few weeks ago — looked like a tramp, but he'd got a rod and creel. You may have noticed when you look along the valley it's sometimes difficult to see which bank an angler's working on — the river winds such a lot you can't follow its course.'

'Aye, I've noticed that,' replied Macdonald.

'I thought my old gaffer was on the other bank when I saw him,' went on Mr. Willoughby: 'then, thinking it over, I wondered if he hadn't been this side. This bit of land we're on now isn't Mr. Hoggett's land — it belongs to the Garths. You'll know the fishing rights? Mr. Hoggett and the Garths fish right along this bank, from Garthmere to the Knabb, where Mr. Shand's water starts. However — to cut a long story short — after my hut was broken open I remembered seeing this old man on the Garthmere dales, and I thought I'd take the liberty of walking along to see if I could notice aught. I reckoned it was some poaching game that was afoot. I found this coat and the rod caught in the stones in a beck just up there. I reckon the coat had been hidden in a hole and the flood water had washed it down. It's still soaked.' Mr. Willoughby poked at the coat with his rod and sniffed. 'Reeks of somewhat,' he said.

Macdonald watched him closely: the stout little man was very excited and his words came tumbling out. He stood in the wet ground oblivious of the water round his feet and the chilly wind, pouring out his story with vigour.

'Will you show me just where you found the coat?' enquired Macdonald.

'Aye. You follow me. It's not very far. That's Mr. Hoggett's coat. I must ask him when he missed it. I'm pretty sure it was the same coat that old gaffer was wearing when I saw him. It's time this sort of thing was put a stop to. I don't like it at all.'

Mr. Willoughby led Macdonald about fifty yards downstream, splashing vigorously over the swampy ground, and he then halted and pointed to a recess in the bank at the edge of the woods.

'It was there. You can see there's a hole in the bank just beside the beck. It looks as though the ground gave when the water was in spate and the coat was washed out and caught on the branches there. There's nought else there. I've looked already. The rod was thrust among the undergrowth.'

Macdonald had a good look. There was nothing to disprove Mr. Willoughby's story, and the explanation was quite a feasible one, but the fact remained there was something a bit odd about this verbose Yorkshire wool merchant. To Macdonald's mind he talked too much.

While the Chief Inspector was studying the bank, Mr. Willoughby went on:

'I tell you straight out, I'm a bit worried over all this. Seems there's something behind it. Y'know, when I first saw that coat it gave me a bit of a shock. Turned my stomach right over. Looked like a corpse, the way it was caught on those thorns, by heck it did.' He chuckled uneasily. 'Detection's not in my line, officer, but I thought I'd hit on something rum. Then, when I saw you coming along, I thought maybe I'd learn a little more if I just stayed quiet and bided my time. Of course I didn't know who you were. I reckon *you* thought you had spotted something rum when you saw me, eh?'

'I certainly wondered what you were doing,' rejoined

Macdonald. 'I'd be obliged if you'd come along with me to Wenningby Barns, Mr. Willoughby. There are a few points I want to get cleared up, and it's chilly standing here.'

'Very good, officer. There are a few questions I'd like to put myself, I admit. Very uneasy I've been. Now what shall we do about that coat? It's very wet, and not a savoury thing to carry. I tell you what. I've got a bit of line in my pocket. I'll just tie it round the coat and we can hitch the string on a stick and we'll carry it between us. Not that the coat'll be much more use to Hoggett, but he ought to have it back, eh?'

Macdonald agreed, and they went back and recovered the coat and tied it up with a length of line Mr. Willoughby obligingly produced from one of his pockets and hitched it on a stout stick as he suggested. The sodden bundle was surprisingly heavy, and Macdonald remembered Mrs. Hoggett's complaints about her husband's ancient coat; it had smelt, she said. Macdonald could assure Mrs. Hoggett that it was even smellier now, after the old tweed had been soaking in the flood water.

They reached the cottage without further incident, and Macdonald put on some dry sticks and blew the embers into a lively flame before he sat down notebook in hand to talk to Mr. Willoughby.

'As I've no doubt you've thought yourself, Scotland Yard doesn't send C.I.D. men to investigate cases of petty theft in the provinces,' began Macdonald and the other replied:

'Eh — but I've thought of that — and it wasn't petty thefts you were busy on over there by Jacob's Buttery, officer. What you were after 'twasn't for me to ask — but I reckoned it was something amiss, and maybe the thievings haven't been right out of the picture. Now what can I do for you in the way of information?'

'First, I want a list of the dates when you've been in the dales since the middle of August,' said Macdonald. 'I dare say that'll take a bit of thinking out, and I'll leave you to it after a bit. Next, I want to know the date you saw the old gaffer, as you described him, and I also want to know exactly who you've seen in the valley this past month.'

'Eh, but I think I can tell you all that plain enough,' replied Willoughby. 'Maybe you know I lease a cottage of Mr. Hoggett's up yonder. My wife thinks nought of fishing, and not much more of Wenningby. Southport's nearer her mark, so when I come here, I come by myself. Train to Hornby and then a taxi out here: very convenient having the line for Leeds. Now let me think. The first half of August I wasn't here at all. My manager was away on holiday and I was kept busy. 'Twas the third week in August I came here, on the Friday evening, the 20th that was. Eh, it was lovely weather, but not for fishing. The river was low, and so clear the fish could see you a mile away. I mind I stood by that pool they call Jacob's Buttery and you could see the river bed, 'twas that clear. I stood there and watched a salmon waving his tail in by the bank there where the willow roots show: eh, that was a fish — but catch him? No, not worth trying!'

'Do you fish in Mr. Hoggett's water?' enquired Macdonald. 'Jacob's Buttery comes in his reach, doesn't it?'

'Aye — that's Mr. Hoggett's water right enow. I didn't say I was *fishing* Jacob's Buttery, mind you, but I walked that way. Mr. Hoggett never takes amiss if I go over his land, altho' it's Mr. Shand's water I fish. I told you that bit about the water being so clear thinking it might help you. That pool was clear as glass until the weather broke on September 15th. Now I came again the last week-end in August — the 27th — but the weather was still the same and the river so low you could walk across it by the ford — aye and some of the cattle did cross, too, and a fair nuisance it was with the farmers all being busy harvesting. I remember that Dr. Castleby and his family were staying here, and the children were bathing that evening. I couldna' fish, but I spent most of the time down at the hut, doing a bit of creosoting and such like. 'Twas not that week-end I saw the old gaffer. No —' twas the next. I remember now.' He took out a pocket diary, saying: 'Saturday, Sept. 4th. Greenwell's Glory,' he read out. 'That's a very good fly. I went into Lancaster to get one, and to get a new gut line in the morning. I also bought some oil-bound distemper and some paint, meaning to do the cottage up a bit — but the weather was too good to stay indoors and I went down to the river again after tea. I walked down the brow — that's my favourite path — and I turned upstream towards Chough Close — where my hut is. As I told you the river was very low, and I walked out on to that shilla bank where the river takes a big turn. There's a pool there — not a very deep pool, but it's a favourite one for the trout. I'd got an idea I might try for a fish after dark. I'm telling you all this to explain how I saw the queer old chap in the long coat, because if you get on the top of that shilla bank you can see a long way down the valley.'

Macdonald nodded. Despite Mr. Willoughby's verbosity, his narrative was interesting to the detective.

'That was Saturday, September the 4th,' Macdonald reminded the other. 'You saw the old man that evening?'

'Nay, nay! Now don't you hustle me,' said Willoughby. 'I'm not much of a hand at telling a story, but I must tell it my own way. That was the Saturday: aye, I remember now. I lay on that shilla bank thinking how I'd arrange things: if you're hoping to catch a fish, 'tisn't much use to make a lot of noise first and startle every trout from here to Kirkby. What I didn't think of at the time was that if I'd had a mind to hide, the shilla was a good place to hide on. I reckon my old tweed suit's much the same colour as those stones. I mind I saw Mr. Shand walk past, and I chuckled a bit because he didn't notice me, and he and I always have a crack when we meet. The next two people I saw were a couple of young fellows, town lads I'd say from the look of them.'

'Can you describe them?' asked Macdonald, and Mr. Willoughby scratched his bullet head.

'I'm none so sure I'm much of a hand at that,' he said. 'One was brown headed and one was carrots, and I could see they'd got a towny colour if you get me — palish faces that didn't often get the sun. They came from downstream and they were walking towards the Knabb. I didn't see them come back. Mr. Shand, he came from upstream, and I saw him come back, in about half an hour, maybe. You asked me to tell you *everyone* I saw, mind you,' added Mr. Willoughby, and Macdonald nodded.

'Aye. Quite right. You're doing just what I want you to do.'

''Twas the next evening — the Sunday — first I saw the old gaffer,' went on Willoughby. 'I hadn't caught a fish on the Saturday evening, but I'd got a rise or two. There's a canny owd trout in that pool, and I reckoned I'd have a go for him after dark. I took a bite with me, and got my gear arranged just where it was to hand, and I went on the shilla bed about sunset. 'Twas then I noticed the old man downstream — a long way off, mark you, but he looked a scarecrow because of that long coat. I couldn't make out which bank he was on. I took it for granted 'twas the south bank, because the Anglers' Association fish the water that side — but thinking it over, I'm none so sure.'

He fell into a reverie, and Macdonald enquired sympathetically, 'Did you get your fish?'

'Eh, did I get him,' echoed Willoughby disgustedly. 'I heard him rise, aye, I heard him surface, and then he touched my line. I'd've got him if it hadn't been for some gert fool came blundering through the gate into Chough Close, making a row with that rusty chain on the gate. 'Twas all oop then,' he said sadly. 'That fish — well he didn't wait. I was real put out, mark you. I hollered right out, 'Damn you for a noisy lout!' — and I reckon someone was startled. I heard 'em run. 'Twas a funny go, all right,' he chuckled. 'I reckon they thought 'twas a banshee on the shilla bank, all in the dark. Like ma fish, they didn't wait. But I never saw them, so I can't tell you who 'twas. I gave it up then and went home. Eh, but 'twas a near thing!' he exclaimed. 'That fish . . .'

'Yes,' said Macdonald, determined at all costs to avoid a debate about the possible weight of 'that fish.'

'But didn't it strike you as odd — suspicious, even — that somebody should be down in the valley after dark?'

'Nay, why should it?' asked Mr. Willoughby. 'Up till then, we'd never had any trouble in the valley. The Wenningby folk—why I'd trust 'em with anything! Never was such honest folk, aye, and neighbourly. Why shouldn't somebody be in the valley after dark? 'Twas a real beautiful evening, warm and balmy. Maybe 'twas one of the farmer's sons come down to bathe after his long day in the harvest fields. As for them running, why 'twas natural enough when a voice had roared at them from the middle o' the river, seemingly. Of course they ran. I'd've run meself if it'd happened to me like that.'

'Was there a moon that night?' asked Macdonald.

'Aye, there was a new moon, but it had set before I began fishing.'

'When were you next at Wenningby?' asked Macdonald.

'The next week-end, September 12th, that was,' replied Mr. Willoughby. 'Again, 'twas no manner of good for fishing—but harvest weather, lad it was grand! I lent a hand with the carting—though I tell you I'm a bit old for that game. Sixty-two last birthday and not so spry as I once was—but I went for a swim, all the same, that evening. Nay, you needn't look so surprised, I've been a swimmer in my time, and it's not a thing you forget. About six o'clock it'd've been, and the air all still and warm, I took a dip from the old willow where Mr. Hoggett's put a diving board—not that you could dive that evening, the river was too low. 'Twas after my swim I saw the owd scarecrow again. I was having a rub down after my dip and I saw him by the bank with his rod and all, but 'twas on the further bank he was. That I do know.'

'Was the river shallow enough to ford?'

'Aye, if you knew the place to do it, opposite Wenningby Barns — you could wade across and easy just there — the ford's marked on the map, you'll find.'

'Was the old man fishing?'

'Aye, I'd say he was. I saw him make a cast. I didn't stay to mark much, mind you, because I'd no wish to get rheumatism and I reckoned I'd taken liberties enough for my age. I went back to my tea. And now you know why I've been poking around to see what I could see, Inspector. The rum thing is this: I've made a few enquiries, but no one's seen the owd gaffer but me — and if so be you ask me how I can prove I ever saw him at all, well, there's no answer. See him I did — but nobody saw him by Scawton Bridge, where t'anglers mostly make for the river, and no one saw him at Birka Farm, the other likely road. There you are, officer. Make what you can of it.'

Macdonald met Mr. Willoughby's steady, rather pugnacious stare, and at length replied:

'Since the coat was borrowed this side of the river and worn this side of the river, perhaps it's not surprising that no one saw it on the other bank, Mr. Willoughby. Here's another question for you to consider: have you ever noticed the potters on the road in these parts?'

'The potters? Aye I've seen Gold and his old woman with their cart. What have they got to do with it? I've never seen the potters in the valley.'

Macdonald listened for undertones, as much as for actual words. He knew that while Willoughby had been giving his description of things seen by the riverside, he had talked quite happily. Now, for the first time, his voice sounded quite different — not frightened, but guarded.

'What have the potters got to do with it, Mr. Willoughby? Can *you* tell me?'

'Nay. That I can't,' replied the other stubbornly.

Macdonald tried another cast: 'Have you ever taken the path up through the woods to the high road beyond the Middle Upfields?'

The other shook his head. 'Not me, I'm not much of a walker these days. I use the Brow to reach the river.'

It wasn't that, thought Macdonald. It was the mention of the potters which made the other on his guard. He tried again:

'I have reason to believe the potters have been down to the river, of late. I don't know why. Is it possible that the old man you saw wearing Mr. Hoggett's long coat was Reuben Gold?'

Again Willoughby scratched his head. He didn't answer for some time, and then he spoke uncertainly.

'I can't tell you either way. It might have been — or not. I can't swear it wasn't. The old chap had an old-fashioned cap crammed down on his head, and I wasn't near enough to see his face. I can't tell you if he had a beard.'

'If you couldn't see his face, you can't be sure he was an old man. Perhaps it was a young man who looked old in the distance in that old-fashioned coat and cap.'

'Maybe.' Mr. Willoughby looked at his watch. 'I've answered your questions as well as I could, officer, and I want to be away, up to the cottage. If there's aught else I can tell you — well, you know where to find me. I shall be there to-night. And if I think of aught else that can help, I'll let you know.'

'Very good,' agreed Macdonald. 'I know I've taken

a lot of your time. You think it over, and I'll see you again later.'

'Then good-day to you,' replied Willoughby.

Macdonald suddenly remembered something and called the other back. 'I forgot to tell you. I've found these waders of yours.'

'Eh . . . ?' Mr. Willoughby was evidently startled. 'And where did you find them?'

'In Reuben Gold's cart. He'll be charged with the theft before the magistrate — unless other offences are proved against him.'

'Well, I'm jiggered . . .' Mr. Willoughby pulled himself together and said: 'I'm grateful to you for your trouble. They were very good waders.'

'Aye, I noticed that,' replied Macdonald pleasantly.

III

A few minutes after Mr. Willoughby had gone, Macdonald heard footsteps outside and the door opened without preliminary knocking to disclose Mrs. Hoggett standing on the threshold with a basket in her hand.

'I've brought you some dinner,' she said. 'There's a pork chop, some sage and onions and apple sauce and a jam pie. It's Giles' dinner really, and you needn't be afraid to eat it because he'll be stuffing on meat pies in Chapelton-Lonsdale.'

'But that's *very* kind of you,' said Macdonald, realising with some embarrassment that Mrs. Hoggett was regarding his own damp and muddy flannel bags.

'If you look in the chest upstairs, there are some very old grey flannels of Giles', and some socks. Go and change at once. You're wet through,' she commanded.

Macdonald laughed, he couldn't help it. 'I haven't been spoken to like that since 1914,' he said. You sounded exactly like my mother when you spoke just then.'

'I'm sorry if I was too abrupt. I get used to speaking vigorously because Giles would never remember to change anything unless I tell him to, just like that. Perhaps you don't realise how you can get rheumatism from damp clothes on stone floors — and we don't want you to blame future decrepitude on to Wenningby Barns. The chest's in the bigger room,' she concluded.

Macdonald went upstairs, quite meekly, and changed into some dry clothes whose size made him realise that Hoggett wasn't as thin as he looked, and brought his own damp clothes down with him.

'Go and hang those on the line. They'll soon blow dry,' said Mrs. Hoggett. 'Your dinner's ready, all nice and hot. I'll leave you in peace now.'

'Oh, please don't do that,' said Macdonald. 'Won't you stay and talk to me? There are a lot of things I want to ask you.'

'If you want me to, I'll stay — but I didn't want you to think I came down here to cadge information.'

She sat down by the fire and looked round the room. 'You're a very tidy person,' she said. 'Giles would never keep this place as neat and clean as you're keeping it. It takes a bit of management, I know that.'

'The credit to-day is Reeves',' replied Macdonald honestly. 'He is very efficient domestically, and the first thing he said was how well this place is arranged.'

'I should think he's very efficient generally. I like

him,' she replied. 'If Reeves had killed that wretched man and put him in the river, he wouldn't have made the mistakes the other man did.'

'Would you like to enlarge on that?'

'Yes — if you like.' She lighted a cigarette, paused a few seconds, and then began: 'Giles told me his 'reconstruction story' when he got back last night. It was good in some places, poor in others. The beginning was good, when he said that the murderer *must* be a man who knew the valley to some extent and used his knowledge, but spoilt the plan because he had no sense of detail. Later on Giles spoilt his reconstruction because he both used his imagination too much and forced an argument that the murderer was a stranger.'

'I think your criticism is very sound,' said Macdonald. 'Would you like to try *your* hand at a reconstruction?'

'Not an imaginative one. I haven't that sort of mind. I don't have brilliant hunches, I can only reason. Have you realised what the murderer's initial mistake was — the thing that really gave him away? It was interfering with Giles' wood-pile and leaving the logs tumbled about. If it hadn't been for that, Giles wouldn't have come inside the cottage that day. He might not have come into this room for weeks, and if he had, he wouldn't have come in determined to look round to see whether anything was amiss. Ordinarily speaking, it's quite possible he wouldn't have noticed anything had gone. It was just because the wood-pile made him suspicious.'

'Yes. I see. It's a point which most people wouldn't appreciate.'

'Most people from *away*,' she corrected. 'The

wood-pile told me at once that it wasn't anybody from around here who'd done it, because the farmers and their men wouldn't have made that mistake. They'd know at once it'd be noticed, because they would have noticed it themselves. Yet the man who stole the iron dogs and chain wasn't a careless person. He had swept the floor and cleared the hearth — but he didn't know how to clear hearths properly. He tried to bury the empty cans — but he didn't bury them deep enough. Finally, he was the sort of person who wouldn't think that small valueless objects would be missed. I should argue from that that he wasn't a poor man, and he wasn't a very observant one, but he was quite good at looking for things when he'd made up his mind what he wanted.'

'In your opinion, Mrs. Hoggett, is Anthony Vintner capable of having done it? You see, he does fit the bill in many ways; he knows the valley and the river and the cottage — but he has no sense of country ways. It would never occur to him that a woodpile was an expert piece of work and that interference with it would give him away — but he did have Ginner staying with him, and nobody has seen Ginner alive since the day he left Thorpe Intak. I ask you because I'd value your judgment on the point. You talked to Vintner sometimes, didn't you?'

'Oh, yes. I went and saw his pictures and I like them. He's a clever painter and he's got an eye which really sees things, and he can be quite interesting to talk to on his own subject — but he's quite incapable of having committed this crime by himself, I'm certain of it.'

'Why?'

'Well, you've seen his kitchen, haven't you? If

Anthony Vintner had made a fire and opened tins of beans and sardines in this place, you'd have found sardine oil dripped all over the flags, bits of beans on the crocks and ashes trampled everywhere. He's like that, he can't help it. He just makes a mess with everything he touches in the house — and it would never, never have occurred to him to clear up the hearth. What's a hearth for, anyway? Ashes, isn't it? — well, leave them there.'

'Even if he'd noticed it was swept and clean before he came?'

'He wouldn't have noticed. There are some things he just can't see — and he can't reason, either. I've never met any man who was so incapable of thinking out cause and effect — and the murderer here *did* reason. Apart from that mistake about the wood-pile, most of his reasoning was sound.'

Macdonald nodded. 'Yes. I'm beginning to realise that. The place where the body was hidden was very ingenious. Did you know there was a considerable recess in the river bank below the willows in Jacob's Buttery?'

'No, but you'd be pretty safe to assume it. The stream is very strong round that bend, it washes part of the bank away every year. It's scoured part of the willow roots clear, so it would obviously undercut the bank beneath the willow.'

'I expect the fishermen get to know pools of that kind,' meditated Macdonald. 'The sack was chained in such a way that it would never have been visible from the bank above, no matter how clear the water was, and the undergrowth concealed it from view on the other bank. Also, owing to the way it was fastened in the recess, there was no likelihood of any fisherman fouling the sack with a cast. That part of the job was very well done.'

He paused and added: 'Did you notice that your husband's old coat has turned up? I've spread it to dry on the hedge at the back.'

'Where on earth did you find it?'

Macdonald told her and she frowned a little. 'That's the sort of story it's very difficult to prove or disprove. I'm awfully glad you're on this job, Chief Inspector.'

'Are you? I'm very glad to hear you say so. I was afraid you were wishing me at Jericho.'

'I'm not. I know that what's done can't be undone, and the police have got to investigate in Lunesdale. I'm glad you're here because you look obstinate. You're like me, you'll go on until you find out. It'd be awful if you didn't find out, because the whole story would be chewed over and over, and it'd be impossible to prove that Giles and George hadn't been mixed up in it.'

'That's quite true,' agreed Macdonald. 'Apart from the undesirability of leaving a murderer at large, it is essential to get at the real facts in order to scotch suspicion — whether it's your Giles and George, or Anthony Vintner, or the potters, who are suspected. Now can you tell me this: was Hoggett's old coat here while the Georges were staying here in August?'

'Yes.'

Macdonald valued that clear decisiveness of Mrs. Hoggett's. 'I asked the children about that — Giles and Nell,' she continued. 'Children notice things much more than grown-ups in some ways. If anything is moved from the cottage they always notice it. The old coat was hanging up by the door when they came, and the children used it when they put up a tent outside. Nell said it was hanging up by the door when they left, and that George's old cap was in one of the pockets. Their grandfather's spectacles were on the bookshelves. They're quite certain about those facts.'

'Thanks very much. I agree with you that children do notice if things are altered. I used to stay with my grandfather on his croft in Perthshire when I was a kid, and the first thing I did when I got there was to go round to make sure that nothing had changed. I liked the changelessness — it seemed valuable, somehow.'

Macdonald looked round the ancient room: 'The steading up there wasn't very different from this — quite as primitive and probably older.'

Kate Hoggett's face lighted up. 'Oh, now I understand. It seemed so odd for a London C.I.D. man to be so at home in a place like this. I can see you're good at it — you don't make a mess like most people who're only accustomed to modern equipment.'

Macdonald laughed. 'I'm glad my native housewifeliness passes muster — but you talk to Reeves some time. He's a hundred per cent Cockney, but he's as adaptable as a chameleon. However, we mustn't dispute about that. I want to know if you'll come up through the Middle Upfields with me — I've left the car up there — but I really want to know if you notice anything different from usual — anything at all.'

'Yes, of course I'll come. I know the path very well, but I don't suppose I shall be any good at detecting things. The children would probably be better.'

'Children aren't on in this act,' said Macdonald. 'It's not really a game. No. I think you're the person I want, and while you are walking up you can tell me every single thing you can remember about the time you saw Ginner in the dales.'

They had an interesting walk together, but Mrs. Hoggett did not have the chance of spotting the pieces of her old curtains on the brambles and thorns, because, greatly to Macdonald's interest, these had been carefully removed from the places where he had seen them only that morning.

13

I

When Macdonald reached the cottage again after his walk with Mrs. Hoggett, he found a totally unexpected sight. There were two men in the garden, and they were apparently clinched in a life and death struggle, swaying crazily with locked arms and bent backs, heaving slowly back and forth. When Macdonald first caught a glimpse of the locked struggling figures, he was just about to race for dear life to investigate them, when he realised from their clothes (their heads being unobservable) that the two combatants were Giles Hoggett and Reeves, and their activity was a Westmoreland wrestling bout. As Macdonald opened the gate, they broke apart and Mr. Hoggett said breathlessly:

'Aye, that's better. You had me that time.'

Reeves brushed back his dishevelled hair and faced Macdonald with his cheerful grin.

'We're exchanging lessons, Chief. Mr. Hoggett's teaching me a bit about the wrestling technique up here, and I've been showing him some Ju-jitsu tricks.'

'Very valuable for both parties, provided you don't break each other's backs in the process,' replied Macdonald. 'Can you throw him, Reeves?'

'In wrestling, you mean? Not me — but I'm getting on. I could put him where I want him the other way. Come on, chum!'

The next second Mr. Hoggett was attempting a newly learnt hold on Macdonald, but the latter was just quick enough to avoid it and eluded his host while Reeves chuckled.

'The position was right, but you've got to be quicker than that.'

'And *that,*' said Macdonald, 'is enough for the moment. Have you brought me any news?'

'Aye!' they declared in unison, and Macdonald laughed aloud.

'If you go home and say 'Aye' to your wife, Reeves, she'll think you've got a screw loose. Come on in, and what about it? Who got first news?'

They went into the cottage together, and Mr. Hoggett said: 'Reeves won easily — but I picked up a few items later. He'd better tell you his part of the story first.'

'Well, I was lucky,' said Reeves modestly. 'I told you I should try the pubs, I always get some news in the local. There are five pubs in Chapelton-Lonsdale, varying from a two-star R.A.C. hotel to some small beerhouses in back streets. Ever been there, sir? You ought to, it's a queer old town; all stone houses, even the poor ones. I put my old raincoat on and my working cap and I strolled into one of the lesser dives. Beer pretty short, but more conversation than I'd hoped. I told the tale about a friend of my dad's, a traveller named Garstang whose sister-in-law once lived up here. Funnily enough there was an old chap in the bar who used to travel in dry goods and he told me to go to the Spotted Bear and ask for old Tom Brough. Tom was there all right — he'd been a carrier on the Chapelton-Kendal roads for fifty years and he said he knew the party I meant — Mrs. Soper. She once lived on Albert Terrace, and she had a nephew in London used to come and stay with her, name of Garstang. Tom Brough said he'd taken the boy on his rounds with him once or twice, only he was such a young limb he'd had to leather him. Mrs. Soper left Chapelton in 1918, and Tom Brough says the last time the boy stayed with her was in 1914. That's my little lot. Now Mr. Hoggett had better carry on — he did all the rest.'

Giles Hoggett took up the story. 'Reeves and I met for lunch by arrangement at the old bridge,' he said. 'I had had a disappointing morning. I called on the Vicar, but he was a newcomer — he'd only been inducted in 1924 — and he couldn't help. Then I tried the schoolmaster, but he was worse, and I was very glad to knock off for lunch. My routine work is not good,' he added sadly. 'I tend to get disheartened by rebuffs.'

'You're learning, chum,' put in Reeves with his irrepressible grin. 'You go on with the story.'

'Once Reeves had found out the lady's name, it put fresh life into me,' said Giles Hoggett. 'I felt I could go asking questions with much more authority, if you take me. I went back to old Bob Pritchard — he's the harness maker — and asked him to tell me who were some of the older and more respected tenants in Albert Terrace, so that I was armed with an introduction as it were. I called on a Mr. and Mrs. Braithwaite and told them I'd come from Mr. Pritchard — and we had a real talk. Amos Braithwaite, (he's eighty-two this year) had been coachman to old Dr. Johnson, and he remembered my Uncle Henry. Well, he remembered Mrs. Soper, too, *and* her sister, who became Mrs. Garstang. The maiden name was Baring and their parents lived in Appleby.'

Here Giles Hoggett paused, as an orator might wait for applause, and Macdonald was quick in acclaiming the point.

'Bravo, Hoggett! Triumph of routine work!' he said, and Reeves added:

'What did I tell you? These stories do make sense if you stick to them. Ginner called himself Baring on some occasions — it was a name that was familiar to him, and that place Appleby's somewhere north of Kirkby Stephen where the doctor said Mrs. Gold came from. It all fits. I bet young George Garstang-Ginner went up to stay at the old home in Appleby sometime.'

'Now it's you who's going ahead of your data, Reeves. You're catching it from Hoggett,' said Macdonald.

Reeves chuckled. 'All right, Chief — but it *does* make sense, all the same. We're getting somewhere.'

Mr. Hoggett continued: 'Amos Braithwaite had not a very high opinion of either Mrs. Soper or Mrs. Garstang. In fact he was distinctly uncomplimentary about the latter lady and seemed to think she'd got just what she deserved both as regards husband and offspring — however, you'll like to know some more of the family history. It's very enlightening. Thomas Baring, father of Anne and Grace, who became Mrs. Soper and Mrs. Garstang, was an inn-keeper. His daughter Anne married a railwayman, a navvy employed on the permanent way. Before they came to Chapelton-Lonsdale, the Sopers lived in Tebay. Do you know anything about Tebay, Macdonald?'

It was Macdonald's turn to chuckle — he had not expected to be examined in topography, but he felt fairly confident on this occasion.

'My home is in Scotland, Hoggett, and my way home has frequently taken me through Carlisle. Tebay is a station on the main L.M.S. line between Penrith and Oxenholme junction. A very good centre for a linesman to live. It's after you leave Tebay that the line begins to climb Shap Fell. Every railway man in the world knows of the Shap gradient.'

'Aye. You can pass on that,' said Hoggett, 'but it's more local knowledge we need. Tebay is on the head waters of the Lune, and the main road from Kendal to Kirkby Stephen passes through Tebay. You said that Ginner had lived in Kendal at one time, and since he stayed with his railway-linesman relatives in Chapel-ton-Lonsdale he'd have been familiar with all the places in the Kendal-Tebay-Kirkby Stephen country. So it's not surprising that he knew a bit about Lunesdale.'

'He ought to have known better, oughtn't he?' put in Reeves sotto voce. 'He hasn't even the excuse of being a Londoner.'

'That worm is too antiquated to get a rise out of this fish,' replied Mr. Hoggett with dignity, and he turned to Macdonald again. 'Mrs. Soper left Chapel-ton-Lonsdale in 1918 after her husband died, and she went back to live at Tebay again. She was then in her early forties in Mr. Braithwaite's opinion. That would make her around seventy now.'

'If she's alive,' put in Reeves.

'I see no reason why she shouldn't be,' retorted Mr. Hoggett. 'One can count on greater longevity in the north than in the south of England. It would be a very interesting drive from here to Tebay,' he added thoughtfully, 'and one could reach Kirkby Stephen on the same day.'

'I reckon that's a very sound idea,' said Reeves appreciatively.

II

There was a silence for awhile after that. Macdonald was evidently cogitating hard and he said at length:

'We are collecting a lot of odds and ends of information which look as though they will fit into the picture some time, but they're unco-ordinated at present.'

'Like Mr. Vintner's kitchen,' murmured Giles Hoggett.

'Oh, I wouldn't say it's as bad as that,' rejoined Macdonald, 'but the bits and pieces need some reconsideration. I'm going up to see Vintner again shortly, and I hope to get him placed in the picture: after that I'm going to see if Gold will be more forthcoming — and I want more help from you, Hoggett. Gold is concerned in this somewhere, but it's important to remember that the crime was carried out in the dales, by the river. The potters don't frequent the dales, do they? The potters keep to the roads.'

'Aye,' rejoined Hoggett. 'I've never seen the potters down by the river.'

'Isn't there anything that could have taken them down to the river?' persisted Macdonald. 'For instance, you can get good prices for rabbits in the Black Market, and a fortune for hares. Do you think the Golds could have gone down to the dales on a rabbit snaring expedition? Poaching, in short.'

Mr. Hoggett shook his head slowly. 'I don't think so. No, I don't think so. If they had set snares or traps they'd have been noticed by some of us. Richard Blackthorn would have noticed. He knows all the rabbit runs and burrows. If he'd seen anything of the kind he'd have said so, and we should all have heard about it.'

'Well, if not rabbits, what about fish? Mr. Willoughby told me he sometimes went fishing after dark.'

'Aye. I've done it myself sometimes. When the river's low and the water's very clear you can't get a fish in daylight, but they'll sometimes rise to a fly on one of the pools after dark — but the potters don't go fly-fishing. No. Of course there's a possibility of another sort of poaching. I've heard of it being done, but I've no evidence it's ever been tried in our valley. If a charge of explosive is detonated in a pool the fish are killed or stunned and they can be picked up with very little trouble. Now I don't think the potters could get fish that way themselves — but if other folks did, the potters might be employed to take the fish away. Aye, that's a possibility. The potters might provide safe transport for the loot.'

'That's an idea,' agreed Macdonald, 'but wouldn't you have heard the explosion?'

'Perhaps — but that's not to say we'd have noticed. They detonate in the quarry on the fells across the river, and we're used to the sound.'

Reeves put a word in here: 'That's just the sort of game a chap like Ginner would have liked — not too much work and plenty of profit. There are salmon in this river, aren't there, as well as trout. Salmon's worth big money these days.'

'I'm still thinking about those bits of curtain stuff, Hoggett,' went on Macdonald. He related his experiences of the morning, ending up with the fact that when he retraced his steps through the woods the orange rags had disappeared. Reeves immediately put in:

'Willoughby? It looks mighty like it.'

Mr. Hoggett looked perturbed. 'No. Not Mr. Willoughby. That goes all against the grain. I can't imagine Mr. Willoughby tying bits of rag on to bushes. It's all out of the picture. Why should he? — and he wouldn't poach anyway.'

'Those rags are connected with the potters,' said Macdonald. 'They lead to and from the potters. Now Hoggett agrees that the potters keep to the roads with their cart, they don't come down into the river meadows or the woods, so they wouldn't know their way cross-country as it were. Isn't it possible some one laid a trail with those rags so that Reuben Gold could follow it without getting lost? Even after dark, provided he'd got a torch, he could have followed that trail.'

'That's all right,' agreed Reeves, and Macdonald went on:

'Hoggett, you suggested, quite reasonably, that the potters were most likely to be concerned in transport if there were any illicit dealings. It's not beyond the bounds of possibility that Ginner used them as intermediaries to transport his own letters and packages, and maybe that orange rag in Gold's pocket *was* used as a signal.'

'Yes,' said Giles Hoggett, 'I think that's quite likely — but I don't see Mr. Willoughby taking any part in that sort of thing.'

Macdonald went on: 'I think it's reasonable to assume that those rags were removed this morning by someone who knew I had taken an interest in them. Now the news that Gold had been detained by the police and his cart impounded may have got round surprisingly quickly. So far as I could see, the spot where Gold and I met was quite solitary, but I'm beginning to realise the fell-side can have eyes — as Mr. Shand reminded me concerning the events of Sunday morning. Some friends of Gold's may have seen or learnt what happened and decided to come and remove the rags from the trail.'

'Aye, that'd be it,' said Giles Hoggett more cheerfully. 'Now that other point you mentioned — about the old man who wore my coat. You have now two witnesses who have seen him, one of them a reliable witness.'

'Aye,' said Macdonald thoughtfully. 'Anthony Vintner said he saw him and so did Mr. Willoughby — but how do I know that it wasn't Anthony Vintner who was inside the coat Mr. Willoughby saw?'

'He said an *old* man,' pointed out Mr. Hoggett.

'Aye, so he did, but any man might have looked an old man in that coat and cap.'

'It was a good coat,' protested Mr. Hoggett sadly, and Macdonald replied:

'It still exists — as a coat: Mrs. Hoggett wouldn't call it a good coat, but such as it is it's hanging on the line to dry.'

'Eh?' cried Mr. Hoggett joyfully, using every vowel as one vowel in that indescribable Lancastrian query. 'Where is it?'

'Out yonder. It's wet — *and* it smells.'

'All good tweed smells,' rejoined the owner.

He hastened outside and returned with the weighty and noxious garment. 'Let's put it on Reeves and see what he looks like in it,' suggested Hoggett blithely. 'George's old cap's here, too. Good. Come on, Reeves.'

'You try it on yourself, chum,' protested Reeves, but Hoggett said firmly:

'No. That's no good. The coat fits *me*, it's my coat, and I admit I look an old man in it, but you're still a young chap, Reeves. We can get an idea of what a young man would look like in my coat — a reconstruction, you see. That's the idea, now the cap. Well, well, *what* a difference. Hi, stop . . .'

Macdonald collapsed into helpless mirth. First, the sight of Reeves in the antique garment which reached right to the ground topped by George's ancient soft tweed hat was enough to make any man laugh, but Reeves had his own ideas of a 'reconstruction.' Swift as thought, he had lifted the long skirts of the preposterous old coat and flung its capacious folds over Giles Hoggett's head, and the two were wrestling together under the voluminous tweed.

'Stop it!' roared Macdonald. 'This enquiry is getting completely out of hand. Hoggett, you've got just what you deserved, and as for Reeves, the north country air is going to his head.'

Reeves disentwined the good coat from Mr. Hoggett's head and shoulders, and tottered about the garden in it, practising 'Eh' and 'Aye' in varying tones, more reminiscent of an elderly sheep than of anything else.

'Look at him!' exclaimed Hoggett victoriously. 'He *does* look an old man, a very old man. It might have been anybody inside my coat. Anybody.'

'Aye, anybody,' agreed Macdonald, 'including Mr. Willoughby himself. Thank you for the reconstruction, it has been very helpful and suggestive.'

'There's something in it,' said Mr. Hoggett thoughtfully. 'Now I have an idea about immediate employment for myself. John Staple and Richard Blackthorn are both dipping their sheep at Great Gill to-day — they make a practice of doing it together to economise labour. They ought to be just about through now, and I thought if I went along now it'd be a good chance of a crack with them. Old Moffat'll be there and maybe Gilbert Clafton. If we don't discuss the local problem from every angle I shall be very much surprised.'

'That's very sound,' agreed Macdonald, and Reeves put in:

'I'm not on in this act. If I went too I should cramp everybody's style. If you're going up to see Vintner, Chief, I should like to browse about down here. I've heard about the bogie and the pool and the willow tree and all these fields — dales, you call them, don't you — but I'm not on terms with them. I just want to stare.'

He turned to Giles Hoggett: 'Now then: you've got fishing rights from Chough's Close upstream where the shilla bank is, down to the end of Jacob's Buttery — that's right, isn't it? — and upstream from you it's Mr. Shand's water; downstream from you it's Garthmere water. That right?'

'Aye. Very good.'

'And on the south bank the Carnton anglers fish from Garthmere right along to the shilla bank?'

'That's it.'

'Good. Well, I'm going to have a look-see. Where's that bogie?'

'In the barn. I'll show you,' replied Mr. Hoggett.

'Oh, no, you won't. I'm going to find out. I'm like Ginner, I'm going to spy out the land, and I'm like Vintner. Nobody's going to show me anything. I'm going to find out . . . For two pins I'd wear your coat . . .'

'This,' said Macdonald, 'is where we leave him to it. A Londoner in Lunesdale. Good luck to you.'

A few moments later Macdonald and Hoggett set off up the brow together, leaving Reeves deep in contemplation in the garden of Wenningby Barns.

III

When Mr. Hoggett reached the fold-yard at Great Gill, the air was still full of the cries of sheep who were complaining bitterly about their recent experience. Richard Blackthorn's sheep had been dipped first and they were now in this paddock, half-heartedly attempting to pasture and then raising their heads again to lament. John Staple's sheep were folded in a corner of the yard, standing in an unhappy huddled flock guarded by his dog. The two farmers were lighting their pipes and old Bob Moffat from Garthmere stood leaning on his crook, cogitating contentedly over a strenuous job well done. The sheep had been dipped in a deep stone trough at one side of the fold-yard. Richard Blackthorn had handled the struggling creatures before they entered the dip, gripping them by the forelegs and the loose skin on their necks. Moffat had seen that they were thoroughly immersed, and Staple, with the dogs to assist, had seen that the sheep were folded when they emerged, so that the poisonous dip could drip off their coats before they went back to pasture.

Giles Hoggett had had no dealings with sheep, save when he had tried to give assistance when he found one in danger, such as a sheep on its back, or marooned under the river bank when the water was rising: from this he knew the weight and intractability of a struggling ewe, and he still marvelled at the skill and judgment which enabled the expert to deal with them at dipping time.

'Good-day, Richard,' said Giles Hoggett. 'You're through in good time.'

'Aye, Giles, we managed,' chuckled the farmer. (Mr. Blackthorn had known Giles Hoggett and George Castleby since they gathered blackberries in the last years of Queen Victoria's reign, and Giles and George they had remained to him ever since.)

'That's a job you haven't learnt yet, Mr. Hoggett,' said Staple, and Giles replied:

'I know little enough about my own cattle, Mr. Staple — and nothing at all about sheep.'

'Ah, but you're learning a lot about detection,' chuckled Richard Blackthorn. 'It's a story and no mistake, these doings in the Wenningby dales. Fact is, we nearly drowned those ewes, Giles, with Mr. Staple here telling me the rights of the story when he ought to've been getting they ewes out on their feet again.'

'They ewes is champion,' said old Moffat. 'Happen it's easier to get ewes out o' yon trough than t'sack out o' river.'

'Aye, it's a real story,' said Mr. Staple. 'I told you there was summat amiss when you first told me about the sack and the iron dogs being gone, Mr. Hoggett — and now I'm told they've run in old Reuben Gold. He's an owd varmint, but I'm sorry he's had a hand in this here.'

'But there's nothing *proved* against him, Mr. Staple,' said Hoggett. 'It's true he was taken in charge, but that's because he went for the Chief Inspector and tried to knock him down — and got more than he bargained for.'

'Eh — reckon he did. Yon's an ill man to scrap with,' said Staple, seating himself on the stone bench by the barn-door. 'We've been chewing it over, Mr. Hoggett: aye, we're like a dog with a bone — can't leave it alone. Now then, Bob Moffat, what's this about the big chap you did see in dales just before the weather went back?'

Giles Hoggett sat down too, and pulled out his pipe. This was just what he had hoped for — a good, lengthy, leisurely talk: the farmers had finished their job with the sheep, they were just tired enough to be glad of an 'easy,' and there was a good hour to go before milking time.

'Aye. 'Twas the day after we'd finished carting Mr. Lamb's oats,' said Bob. 'I reckoned the river'd be oop soon, and they ewes is like to get caught under bank. I went down to river past t'ould hull — you'll be minding where I mean — and I walked upstream to Mr. Hoggett's fence. 'Twas Mr. Hoggett I thought I did see, in's big coat, just by they thorns. Ah, I said, he's a fine hefty chap these days, farmin's been t'making of him.'

Bob took a deep breath while the others chuckled.

'Eh, but tha's stouter than tha' were that first summer, Giles,' said Richard. 'Skin and grief tha' was then. Now 'tis skin and muscle, eh, Bob?'

'But I wasn't down by the river that day,' said Giles Hoggett. 'I didn't go down to the dales at all between August 28th and September 15th. Now who could it have been, Bob?'

At this juncture another visitor arrived to swell the committee meeting. Giles Hoggett's reaction to Mr. Shand's appearance was 'Confound him. He'll put old Bob right off his stroke,' but Staple and Blackthorn got to their feet with the courtesy of men seeing a visitor on their own ground.

'Good-day, Mr. Shand. Weather's brighter again,' said Richard Blackthorn.

'Yes. A very pleasant day, Blackthorn. I'd say I'm not far out if I make a guess at what you're all talking about.'

'Aye, can't keep off it,' said John Staple. 'Now maybe you can help, Mr. Shand. Bob here was saying he thought he saw Mr. Hoggett down in the dales at end of harvest, and Mr. Hoggett said he wasn't down by the river that day.'

'Why did you think it was Mr. Hoggett?' enquired Shand, but Bob Moffat was unable to talk with the same ease in the presence of the less familiar and more pretentious land-owner.

'Eh, I thought like t'were Mr. Hoggett,' he mumbled, and Giles took up the story.

'Bob recognised my old coat, Mr. Shand. It's almost an antique — not another like it in the valley.'

'Coat? What sort of coat?' enquired Shand, barking out his queries. 'The fact is that I saw an old chap in an outlandish coat on your land, Hoggett. Big long thing, flapped like a scarecrow. Funny thing, I thought it was you for a moment — but it was a much older man, bent about the shoulders and knock-kneed.'

'Now when would that have been, Mr. Shand?' enquired Richard Blackthorn, but Shand turned and looked closely at Hoggett.

'No. I don't think it could have been Hoggett,' he said. 'Not unless you were fooling for fooling's sake, Hoggett.'

Giles kept the grin from his face — he felt that Mr.

Shand had some justification for his last remark.

'No, Mr. Shand. Not guilty. I haven't worn that coat of mine for a twelve month. My wife wouldn't let me. Now say if you describe the coat you saw.'

'Describe it? You're asking rather a lot, aren't you? It was an old coat . . . any colour or no colour. Long. It looked as though it'd been taken straight off a scarecrow. It flapped in the wind round that old chap's spindle shanks. Now I come to think if it, it *had* got some colour on it somewhere. Coloured lining, maybe, or perhaps it was mended with another colour.'

'Aye, you're quite right,' said Hoggett. 'That coat is lined with coloured material — a sort of faded green tartan. It was a very warm coat. My mother had it specially made for my father when he went abroad one year.'

'Good God!' said Mr. Shand, and then added hastily: 'Yes, I see: a very old-fashioned travelling coat. That'd be it.'

Bob Moffat suddenly spoke up. ''Twere a rare good coat. Aye, and him that wore it had no sort of spindle shanks like. He was a gcy gurt hefty chap. Aye.'

'Have it your own way,' said Shand with a shrug, and turned again to Hoggett. 'I've told you my opinion, and I shan't change it. The chap was a weedy-looking beggar — well, to tell the truth, like that painter you think so well of.'

Bob Moffat moved towards Staple's sheep. 'Happen I'd better be driving of 'em up like. They'll take their time and all,' he mumbled, and the dog which had been sitting watching the sheep sprang to attention, ears cocked, eyes alert. Despite his interest in Mr. Shand's narrative, Giles Hoggett watched the business of getting the sheep moved, because he had never ceased to marvel at the skill of shepherds and dogs: bleating and agitated, the wet draggled flock was guided through the gate, with Bob Moffat apparently making no effort at all — but it was his watchful eye and warning whistle which controlled the dog. Meantime Richard Blackthorn's old dog, knowing this was no part of his business, sat with lolling tongue beside his master. When Giles turned back to concentrate on the conversation, Staple was saying:

'If you could fix a date, or get near it it might help, Mr. Shand. Bob says he saw the old chap at the end of harvest.'

'Hard to say. There was nothing to fix it in my mind,' said Shand, and Blackthorn added:

'Can you remember the weather, Mr. Shand? Was it a fine day? The weather broke on the 15th though the day before was poor-like. Happen the weather might place it.'

'I don't notice the weather like you fellows do,' replied Shand. 'It certainly wasn't wet, though. Now I wasn't here during the first week in September, so it'd have been before then.'

'Aye. You was away at the end of August, too, Mr. Shand. I wanted a word with you so I mind that,' put in Blackthorn.

'Quite right. I remember now. It must have been a day or two before that, about August 26th,' said Shand. 'I'll look up some dates in my diary, but I think I'm right. August 26th.'

'Aye, you think it over,' said Staple, and Shand turned to Blackthorn with the quick speech of a town-dweller who is irritated by the slow speech of countrymen.

'Think it over, eh? It's likely you'll go on thinking about it till kingdom come. Now, Blackthorn. You're tenant of that pasture near the Knabb, the five-acre opposite Lamb's barn. My tenant's been complaining about a broken fence between his pasture and yours. It's in a poor way and it's your business to put it to rights.'

'Aye,' admitted Blackthorn placidly. 'I mind the fence. Maybe I ought to've fettled it up a bit, but mind you, Mr. Shand, 'twas your tenant's horses destroyed that fence. I'll see to it when I'm on the job. Hedging and ditching'll get seen to some time.'

'That's the trouble with all you farmers hereabouts. Some time does,' said Shand. 'No time like the present's a good motto. Good-day to you. Good-day, Hoggett.'

They bade him good-day and Blackthorn chuckled.

'Like father, like son. I mind his father — always in a sweat over summat. Made a pile though, did old Mr. Shand. He weren't that rich as a young 'un.'

"Like father, like son,' Richard. I don't like the sound o' that. Puts me in mind Mr. Shand *has* got a son, and there's not much good said about him,' put in Staple.

'Well, it can't have been Mr. Shand's son wearing Mr. Hoggett's coat,' said Blackthorn. 'He's a nowt. Now I've got a few bits to add, Mr. Hoggett. Your friend Mr. Macdonald walked past the Middle Upfields this morning.'

'Aye. He did. I told him about the path.'

'Reckon he's not the only one that's used that path of late,' went on Blackthorn. 'Tom Profert, he's one that sticks to's own business and don't do much cracking, but I went and had a go at him last night. 'Twere hard work, mind you. Tom's as near dumb as makes no difference — but he sees a thing or two. Reuben Gold was that way during harvest. A funny thing it was. Tom had got some sacks he wanted to be rid of, and he saw Gold on that path one morning — passing t' farm he were, but he'd not got his cart with him. Tom reckoned he'd been out after mushrooms — a powerful price they are now — and he wasn't too pleased. Tom says Gold came from the valley way, like as he'd come up through the woods. Aye, and Tom saw another chap way back — when he was cutting Broad Ash; end of August, that was. I asked Tom to describe him, but he was no hand at that. Called him a watch and chain man and said he minded him of the auctioneer's clerk at the cattle market.'

Giles Hoggett scratched his head. He was certainly acquiring evidence, but he began to fear that his memory would be overburdened. Accustomed all his life to writing things down he took a pencil and diary from his pocket, and Blackthorn laughed heartily.

'Why, it's the dead spit of a policeman you're getting Giles, with your little book and all. You only want the patter and they'll be taking you on in the Force.'

Staple was cogitating deeply. 'See here,' he said. 'Old Bob was main vexed when he went off like that. Mr. Shand's ower sharp like — but I'd as lief put my money on Bob being right as Mr. Shand. I'll go on after him and have another word with him.'

'Aye — and I'll come too,' said Giles Hoggett. 'How'd it be if we persuaded Bob to come down to the dales and have a look at one or two of us in my old coat?'

‘Aye, that’s sense, that is,’ agreed Staple. ‘He’s no talker, old Bob, but he *sees* things — and when he says he’s seen a thing, he’s to be trusted.’

‘Aye. That’s an idea,’ said Giles Hoggett, and he and Staple set out together, leaving Richard Blackthorn sitting on the bench in the sunshine.

14

I

Macdonald got Mr. Hoggett's car out and turned eastwards to reach the road for Thorpe Intak. He passed Mr. Shand by the high barn, and the land-owner favoured him with a sketchy salute. Macdonald realised that Mr. Shand had formed a poor opinion of Scotland Yard off-duty, and reflected that it was as well that Hoggett's and Reeves's wrestling match had had no observers. These north countrymen took a bit of knowing, pondered Macdonald. In the south they had the reputation of being dour, mirthless folk . . .

> 'The men that live in North England,
> I saw them for a day:
> Their hearts are set upon the waste fells,
> Their skies are fast and grey . . .'

Hillaire Belloc's grand lines were running in Macdonald's head: he admired Belloc wholeheartedly — but went on to reflect that he had never laughed more over a case than over this one in which Giles Hoggett was co-operating so actively, and that he had never heard a more mirthful chuckle than that of Richard Blackthorn.

Before he reached Thorpe Intak, Macdonald drew up to speak to one of Inspector Bord's men.

'He's there at home, sir,' reported the constable.

'Given us no trouble at all. He's been out to the local once or twice — sozzling. Brings some liquor back with him, I reckon.'

'Does he?' enquired Macdonald thoughtfully, and drove on pondering. When he last saw Anthony Vintner the man had undoubtedly been hungry and had said that he was penniless. His financial condition must have changed rapidly if he had money to spend on liquor.

Macdonald walked again over the sour grass, duly followed by Belinda and the sad little donkey. This time Macdonald had thought of them in advance, and rather shamefacedly produced some of Mr. Hoggett's carrots from his pocket. The carrots were called 'Red Elephants' and justified their name: they induced in the recipients a sort of incredulous rapture which made Macdonald forget that he had purloined those carrots without either permission or acknowledgment.

He knocked on the kitchen door, which was secured from within, and Vintner came and opened it.

'Hallo, Scotty. Come in. I'm working — come in and look.'

Vintner was undoubtedly somewhat intoxicated; he slurred his words, and he was even untidier and grubbier than he had been before, his reddish hair rumpled up into an eccentric top-knot. Even without seeing Vintner, Macdonald would have known that he had been 'sozzling,' for the place reeked of stale whisky.

Following Vintner into the 'studio,' Macdonald saw a large-sized canvas on the easel and stood and stared. It was a fantastic picture, representing a scene Macdonald himself had witnessed: a thin, lithe figure racing over flooded ground in the moonlight, with a dark crouching figure in the fore-ground. Even in its present unfinished state it was a notable composition: apart from the mastery of the draughtsmanship it had an eerie quality which communicated fear. The running figure conveyed terror, the crouching one, menace. The head of the crouching man was blocked in in charcoal, but clearly it was not Giles Hoggett's head, for the skull was round and the profile thin and mocking.

Macdonald stood and stared, and then turned to the painter.

'Why were you afraid of him?'

'Who?'

'Ginner. That's his head.'

Vintner sat on the corner of the table and fiddled with his palette knife.

'No. It's nobody. Just a picture.'

Macdonald was silent for a moment; then he reached across the table and set upright an empty whisky bottle.

'Last time I was here you told me you were penniless. Whisky costs money.'

'I know that, Scotty. Thirty bob a bottle, damn it. I sold a picture.'

Macdonald looked steadily at him. 'If you were sober you'd have the wits to think of something better than that. You haven't sold a picture. You've been watched all the time.'

'Damn you, it's not your business.'

'It is my business. According to your own admission, Ginner stayed here with you. No one has seen him alive since he left here. Ginner had money with him. Now you have the money. I want to know where you got it from. You can please yourself about answering.'

The trenchant voice had a sobering quality and Vintner stared back, his self-assurance melting away, but he argued back:

'You say you've watched me. If you know I haven't sold a picture, you know I haven't been anywhere to get any money.'

'That's perfectly logical. You had the money all the time.'

Vintner watched the other man, his facial muscles quivering.

'You think I went without food, nearly starved, while I'd got money? I tell you I grubbed up turnips and potatoes from the fields and lived on them.'

Macdonald sat silent, considering a number of things. He was remembering the ashes on the hearth at Wenningby Barns. The ashes, as Mrs. Hoggett had said, were the remains of woollen material, plus some waterproofed fabric. It had been reasonable to assume that someone had burnt Mr. Hoggett's famous coat for reasons of their own — but now the coat had reappeared. Macdonald had another idea about those ashes. He spoke again, sharply:

'When Ginner left here, what topcoat or raincoat was he wearing?'

Vintner nodded wearily, as a man does when he gives up trying. 'Oh, all right. If you know, why worry me?'

'He wore your coat — perhaps to impersonate you — and your hat.'

'He pinched my coat, damn him! He went off with it, with my money in it and my last packet of fags — dirty dog that he was.'

'And he left his own coat behind?'

'He hid it. I only found it yesterday. He'd got some money in it and I took it. He took mine.'

Macdonald watched the pale furtive face with the red-rimmed eyes. He knew that on the evidence he was justified in taking Vintner under arrest and charging him. There was no doubt whatever in Macdonald's mind as to the verdict of the Coroner's jury when they heard the result to date of the investigation in Lunesdale. Motive, Means, Opportunity. It would have been easy to kill Ginner in that cottage — and Anthony Vintner was a good swimmer. Nevertheless, because his conscience was much stronger than his desire to make a quick arrest, Macdonald persisted with his questions.

'Where did Ginner hide his coat?'

'In the chimney of his bedroom. He wrapped it up in an old black-out curtain and shoved it up the chimney.'

'And how did you find it?'

'Because I looked. If you're ever hungry you'll find it sharpens your wits. When I thought he'd just pinched my coat and walked out on me it didn't occur to me he'd left anything behind. He hadn't any luggage — just a rucksack with shaving and sleeping gear and he'd taken that. Then you told me he was dead. He couldn't have expected that, could he?'

Vintner began to laugh, a strained hysterical laugh. 'He didn't expect that. It's funny, damn it if it isn't funny. No one expects to be murdered.'

'Stop that!' snapped Macdonald. 'You're in a mess, Vintner. You can't afford to laugh. Pull yourself together, man, and talk sense.'

'It is sense, isn't it? D'you think he said: 'I'm going to be murdered soon so I shan't want anything'? Of course not — but maybe he said: 'I'll hide my stuff till I want it. That poor bloody fool won't think of looking for it.' I tell you I nearly pulled the walls down. I found his coat in the chimney and a whole wad of notes. I spent some — the rest are in here.'

He pushed a tin towards Macdonald, the self-same cigarette tin which Vintner had taken from Wenningby Barns, and Macdonald's cautious mind said: 'Were those notes in that box all the time, and he took it under my very nose. I didn't open it.'

Steadily as ever, Macdonald asked: 'Where is the coat now?'

'I sold it . . . to those potters you're so fond of talking about.'

'The potters haven't been near this house lately.'

'Who said they had? I wore it when I went to the pub. Walked past your cop in it . . . Ginner's raincoat . . . I wore it and the cop didn't notice. Of course he didn't. One of the potters was at the pub, and I went outside at the back and asked him if he'd like to buy a coat. I didn't want it. I hated Ginner — and I hated his bloody coat.'

Quite a story, meditated Macdonald. He had given a lot of consideration to the matter of Ginner's coat. He had had no raincoat on when his body was found: it looked as though the murderer had overlooked the coat when he put the body in the sack and had found it later and burnt it, together with the rucksack. Macdonald went on:

'What else did you find in the pockets of Ginner's coat?'

'Nothing worth anything. Some bits of paper he'd made some notes on.'

'Where are they now?'

Anthony Vintner shrugged his shoulders in a helpless way. 'I don't know — how should I? I put them back in the pockets.'

'Can you remember anything about what was written on them?'

'They didn't make sense. Sort of lists. A. B. and C. and dates and numbers. Like this: A.250. Sept: 1. Point X. Then something about gold, silver and copper. There was a lot about gold, and more dates or numbers or something. The last bit was about a hand at cards — but it was a sort of gibberish. I tried to make sense of it, because I thought there might be something in it. Baring — or Ginner, or whatever you call him, tried to show me some swindling card tricks while he was here — how to deal the sort of hand you want. I couldn't make anything of it.'

'Can't you remember at all what was written down?'

Vintner looked helpless. 'It was an awful scrawl, almost illegible, and it didn't make any sort of sense. You know the way in bridge problems they call the four hands north, south, east and west. Well, he'd scrawled down the cards in four hands, or some of them — like this.' He took a piece of paper and scribbled hastily, and handed the result over to Macdonald. It ran, 'West's hand K.5.7.1.4.' 'It was something like that,' went on Vintner. 'Anyway, it didn't make sense, and I can't really remember it. I just scrumpled up the bits of paper again and shoved them back in the coat pocket. I know I did that, because I remember feeling the ball of paper in the coat pocket when I had it on.' He started drawing on the sheet of paper as though he had lost all interest in the matter, and Macdonald spoke again sharply:

'You say that you sold the coat to one of the potters. You told me last time I asked that you didn't know anything about the potters.'

'Quite true. I didn't. I heard a chap in the bar say something about one of the potters outside, and how they'd buy anything. I got the idea quite suddenly — get rid of Ginner's coat. It's a beastly coat anyway. I went round to the back and found the bloke — a real tough — and shoved the coat at him and asked him what he'd give me for it. He gave me ten bob — I asked for £I, but he wouldn't go higher than ten bob.'

'What was the potter's name?'

'I don't know. I didn't ask. Big tough with a beard. He just mooched off. What are you going to do now?'

Macdonald had got to his feet, and he replied: 'I'm going to see if there are any other interesting relics of Ginner's among your possessions. You can sit still — and stay sitting still.'

Macdonald spent some time looking swiftly through Anthony Vintner's chaotic possessions, while the painter sat with hunched shoulders and scribbled, on bits of paper, on the back of a canvas, on the deal table top. The drawings were all of Macdonald — profile, full-face, three-quarter; the shape of his skull, the setting of his head, the slope of his shoulders; Vintner drew them all from memory, hardly bothering to glance at the man he was drawing.

Macdonald went upstairs into the bare little bedroom where Ginner had slept on a camp-bed. There was a crumpled black curtain still shoved into the small fireplace, and a quantity of plaster from the chimney had been dragged down and lay about the floor. There was a cupboard in the corner of the room where the shelves had been dragged out and the wallpaper torn off. The whole appearance of the room bore out what Vintner had said about searching — even the floor boards had been lifted. It seemed to Macdonald that a man as lazy as Vintner must have been pretty certain there was something to find before he undertook such a vigorous search; anyway, there was nothing else of interest to be found.

Macdonald went back into the studio again where Vintner was still working at his drawings:

'Look here, Vintner, I'm willing to believe you've got a poor memory for facts, but you can't pretend that you've got a poor visual memory. You told me that you saw an old man by the river wearing Mr. Hoggett's old coat.'

'So I did, it's quite true.'

'And you knew it was Mr. Hoggett's old coat because you'd seen the coat in Wenningby Barns,' went on Macdonald. 'You'd noticed where Mr. Hoggett put the door-key and you'd been in there once or twice. Ginner had been in there, too, because you told him about the place.'

Anthony Vintner sat in glum silence, not bothering to make any disclaimer, and Macdonald went on:

'You say you saw a man in Mr. Hoggett's coat. Other people saw him too. Could it have been Ginner wearing the coat?'

'No. I thought of that,' replied the painter. 'It wasn't Ginner. Not his shape. It was more like Hoggett — but it wasn't him either. I know the way he moves. He couldn't have been as clumsy as that.'

'Could it have been the potter — the man you sold Ginner's coat to?'

Vintner considered, and at length replied: 'Yes. That's more like it. It was about his build . . . heavy and clumsy.'

'Have you ever seen the potters in the valley?'

'No — unless it was that chap in the old coat.'

'When were you painting the view across the valley from the gap in the woods on the Upfield path?'

'After Ginner had left and before the weather broke — the first week in September. The picture's there. I asked Shand to buy it. He offered me a pound-note, damn his eyes!'

'When did Mr. Shand see it — while you were painting it?'

'No. He came to see me here. Wanted to turf me out. He can't — there's rent restriction.'

'I thought you hadn't paid your rent?'

'I haven't. I offered him some pictures instead — including his own portrait. You should have seen his face when he saw it. By the way, you wanted to know when I saw the chap in Hoggett's coat. I've just remembered. It was while I was painting in that gap — I saw him by the river. I thought of putting him into the picture, I remember now. I painted in the evening light, and I stayed on a bit in the twilight — it's a good spot. I saw that queer old figure in the half-light . . . where's that picture? I'll show it to you . . . I believe I did a sketch of that old bloke.'

Vintner got up and rummaged among the canvases stacked by the walls and Macdonald watched him. The Chief Inspector had looked through the canvases on the first occasion he had come to the cottage, but he had seen nothing of that particular view. Vintner stood still and scratched his head.

'Well, that's rum. It's gone . . . I had it here somewhere. Belinda must have eaten it.'

'Perhaps you'll find it later on,' said Macdonald. 'Meantime — a question I've asked you before. Where did you get this piece of rag?'

He produced the paint-stained orange rag from his pocket, and Vintner shook his head.

'I don't know, I just don't remember. I bought a bundle of rags from a junk shop in Kirkby, perhaps it was there. Maybe I picked it up. I believe I did find some bits in the dales, when those kids were playing down there. I'm always looking out for rags. I may live in a muck, but I do look after my brushes.'

'Finally,' said Macdonald, 'which route did you take to that clearing? Down from the Upfields or up from the valley?'

'Up from the valley. I don't know the other way. I walked to the barns just before Netherbeck and went down the bank there, over the fields, and along the river past Wenningby Barns.'

'You've been in the valley at night several times, haven't you? You must have been to have done that flood picture.'

Vintner was silent, and Macdonald went on: 'You were there one night when somebody shouted at you from the shilla bank in Chough Close.'

'No, I wasn't!' Anthony Vintner sounded surprised. 'No one's ever shouted at me down in the dales. I should remember it if they had. It's silent down by the river — silent with the peace of God . . . until *you* came.'

'You mean until Ginner came,' retorted Macdonald, 'and it was you who brought him here. Remember that when you're feeling disposed to self-pity.'

Vintner's face quivered miserably. 'You're self-righteous, like all Scots,' he said bitterly. 'Some pious Victorian poet once wrote a line about 'bound with gold chains about the feet of God.' One is bound all right — by chains, link holding to link. One's never free of the past. Do you think I *wanted* Ginner here, damn you? He was the last thing I wanted. I came here to get away from all that.'

'Do you realise what you're saying?' asked Macdonald. 'If I repeated the substance of that as evidence, what is the conclusion that would be drawn?'

'That I killed him. I know. I'm beginning to wonder if I did. I hated him. Because he knew of things I'd done in the past, he was trying to force me to do his dirty work for him. I was to deliver his beastly letters. I didn't. I told him I'd put the cops on to him and risk the results. That was why he beat it. He was cunning, he knew just how far he could drive anybody.'

'You say that you didn't kill him, Vintner. Then who did?'

'I don't know. I tell you I don't know. If I did, I shouldn't tell you, but I don't know.'

'Where did he want you to deliver his letters?'

'I don't know. I told him I'd see him damned before I did anything of the kind. It was a swindle — he lived on swindles, but I can't tell you what it was about.'

Anthony Vintner peered at Macdonald's face as though he were trying to read his thoughts.

'Are you going to arrest me and hang me for killing Ginner?'

'Not unless I'm satisfied about the probability of your guilt. In any case, my duty is done when I make an arrest. I'm neither judge nor jury.'

'I didn't do it . . . I'm certain I didn't do it. If you'd only leave me alone I could start again here . . . I could clean up those hen-houses and start again, and sell some of these pictures. I've learnt a lot. I *could* start again.'

Macdonald looked at the puffy, unhealthy face

and red-rimmed eyes and got to his feet. He knew that Anthony Vintner had no chance of getting out of the district, and it was for that reason he risked leaving him. There was other evidence to be gathered before any arrest could be made, but Macdonald was conscious of the grimness inherent in a weak man's words. 'I could start again if . . .'

He left Anthony Vintner brooding over his pictures, muttering to himself the while.

II

When Macdonald reached Carnton Police Station, he found Inspector Bord looking cheerful.

'Well, Chief, we've collected a few of the items you wanted. Mrs. Gold has been staying in Slaidburn; that's right over the fells on the other side of the Lune. It's a place that's none too easy to get at from these parts. Mostly folk'd go round by Clapham or you can get there by road from Lancaster. Now Gold didn't choose either of those routes: he seems to have followed the track by the River Roeburn — that's a tributary of our Wenning — and he took his missis up to the top of the fells and she seems to've walked down to Slaidburn by herself — and that's a tidy walk. I reckon Gold took that route because it's so lonely and he thought they wouldn't be noticed — it's pretty desolate fell country up in those hills.'

'That was a mistake on his part,' said Macdonald. 'The lonelier the country, the more likely it is that a traveller will be noticed and remembered.'

'Aye, that's true. There's no actual road the way Gold took — just a track over the fells.'

'Wasn't there a Roman road that came north from Manchester to Castleton over the fells past Slaidburn?' asked Macdonald unexpectedly. 'I walked part of it once, and it's grand fell country — the track still follows the Roman road.'

'Does it, indeed?' enquired Bord. 'Well, you're teaching me something about my own country I didn't know. The track's still there, and that's the way the Golds went with his pony, right up to the top of the fells, and there he must have left his wife and she walked down into Slaidburn. One of our chaps there who's keen on studying birds actually saw them on the fells, and that's how we found her. She's staying in a cottage outside Slaidburn. The other thing you asked me to find out was Mrs. Gold's maiden name. Dr. Castleby was quite right. Mrs. Gold came originally from the Kirkby Stephen country and her maiden name was West. We traced that through the records in Preston.'

'Good work,' said Macdonald. 'You've done your part well, Bord, and done it quickly. I shouldn't have got far without you.'

'Well, it's nice to know we were able to lend a hand, Chief. It's your case, but we like to be able to do our stuff as far as we can. Now you'll be wanting to see Gold? He's as mum as a graven image. We charged him with being in possession of stolen property and assaulting an officer in the execution of his duty — the charge sheet's there. Gold didn't say a word, but I reckon he's had time to think things over a bit by now.'

At this moment a constable came in with a slip of paper, saying that it was a telephone message just sent through by Mr. Giles Hoggett. Macdonald took it and read: 'Profert of Middle Upfield saw Gold passing his farm on foot early one morning during harvest. (Profert harvested between Aug. 28th and Sept. 10th.) Gold was coming away from the river and walking towards the main road.'

Macdonald passed the message to Bord, saying: 'That has come just when it's most useful. I think Gold may decide it's wiser to speak out.'

A small room was given to Macdonald for his interrogation, and Bord said he would come in as witness. When Gold was brought in, Macdonald told him to sit down and began:

'The charge set down against you, which will be heard by the magistrates, is that stolen property was found in your possession and that you assaulted a police officer in the execution of his duty, but I think you should understand that you are suspected of being concerned in a more serious crime. I warn you that anything you say may be taken down and used as evidence.'

Macdonald met the man's surly gaze and after a second or so continued: 'On Sunday last, September 19th, the body of a man was recovered by the police from the River Lune. This body had been tied up in a sack and was chained to the roots of a willow tree in a deep pool known locally as Jacob's Buttery. This pool is a few hundred yards downstream from the cottage called Wenningby Barns, and a short distance upstream from the path through the woods which leads towards the main road between the farms called Middle Upfield. The chain and weights attached to the body were stolen from the chimney at Wenningby Barns. The owner of the cottage reported the thefts to the police, and at the same time reported that he found some fragments or orange curtain material outside the cottage. These fragments were torn from some old curtains which Mrs. Hoggett of Netherbeck Farm gave to your wife some weeks ago.'

Macdonald paused here and studied the man in front of him. Reuben Gold sat motionless, but very rigid, his big fists clenched, his jaw set. His light-coloured eyes stared straight in front of him, unblinking and unafraid. The only sign that he gave that he was in any way affected by the narrative was the tenseness of his muscles. He had not moved his position, but Macdonald knew that the stillness was due to the contraction of his muscles.

'This morning when I saw you on the Carnton road,' went on Macdonald, 'there was a piece of the same orange curtain material in your pocket. Have you anything to say about what you did with the stuff after it was given to you?'

''Twas na given to me. 'Twas given to t' wife. She tore it up likely. 'Twas good for nowt.'

'Very well. In that case your wife can answer the same question. She has not been seen on the road with you for some time, Gold, but you were both seen on the fells above Slaidburn.'

The potter made no reply, and Macdonald went on: 'I asked you this morning what you had been doing in the dales. You replied that you had not been in the dales for two years. Do you still stick to that?'

'Aye.'

'Yet one morning, during harvest, you were seen coming away from the dales. The farmer at Middle Upfield spoke to you, and he can swear that you were walking up from the valley.'

At last the man spoke. 'Mebbe I was on t'road by Middle Upfield, but I wasna' in t'valley. I was out after wild mushrooms.'

Macdonald was interested in the reply, because it showed that Gold was cognisant of the law. The operative word was 'wild.' A farmer can only claim that the mushrooms on his land are his own property if he has planted spawn to raise them. Since mushrooms have risen in price, some farmers have taken to planting a brick of spawn in their fields; if a dispute as to the ownership of the mushrooms arises, the farmer who produces the receipt for the cost of mushroom spawn can claim them as his own property because they are cultivated mushrooms. It is a legal offence to gather cultivated mushrooms but not an offence to gather wild ones. A farmer has the right to order a trespasser off his land, but he cannot claim wild mushrooms as his own property.

Macdonald returned to his statement. 'Very good. You have not been in the valley for two years. How is it that fragments of this orange curtain stuff which was given to your wife were found tied to bushes by the path through the woods which leads from the Middle Upfields to the dales?'

'Some child's trick. Nowt to do with me.'

So far, so good, from Gold's point of view. In the few brief words he had spoken, he had met Macdonald's case, and though Gold's speech might be rough, the answers were skilful enough. His admission about gathering 'wild mushrooms' was skilful — he knew he was quite safe there. Macdonald went on: 'About the same time that Mr. Hoggett of Wenningby Barns reported thefts from his cottage, Mr. Willoughby of Clunterbeck Cottage reported that his fishing hut in Chough Close had been broken into and his waders stolen. Those waders, marked with his initials, were in your cart when it was examined this morning. If you have never been in the dales, how did you get those waders?'

Gold was startled at last. He stared unbelievingly at Macdonald, and sweat broke out on his forehead.

'You haven't got to answer, Gold,' went on Macdonald quietly. 'I have stated my case. You have the wits to know what a jury would think if they heard it. I have given you a chance to explain. If you have no explanation you will have to answer the question when you are charged in court. I have cautioned you, and I am not trying to make you give evidence against yourself.'

'Ah never went near t' fishing hut,' broke out Gold. 'If so be Ah'd done what yo're trying to make oot, would A've been fule enough to keep t' waders in ma cart? Tha's got a maggot in thi brain if tha reckons that. Ah bought t' waders off a chap oop Kirby way.'

'Very good. When did you buy them?'

''Twas weeks ago. Back in August 'twas. A chap on t' road, same's ussen.'

'It won't do, Gold. I know when Mr. Willoughby last saw his waders in the hut.'

Macdonald got up, as though he had heard enough, and his movement startled Gold into speech. Macdonald knew that the potter, rough of speech as he was, had followed every implication in the evidence. He knew exactly what he was up against — a murder charge — and he was frightened at last. He had realised the strength of the chain of evidence.

'Nay, Ah'll tell tha,' he protested. 'Ah never bought t' waders. Ah found them. Throon awa' they was. Shoved into a hole in t' wall roond old park at t' Middle Upfield. 'Twas plain they was throon awa', and I took them, same as I take any old rubbish the farmers don't want. Ah was niver in t' dales. Niver.'

'Did you ask Mr. Profert if he wanted the waders, or if he knew whom they belonged to?'

'Nay, I never named them. 'Twas harvest time, and there was no one about that way.'

Macdonald paused a moment and then continued: 'You know Mr. Vintner, the tenant of Thorpe Intak. He had a visitor staying with him in August. What was your business with him?'

'Ah had no business wi' him.'

'What about the messages he asked you and your wife to take for him?'

Gold hesitated: he had no means of knowing that Macdonald was guessing, but Gold's hesitation told Macdonald that his question wasn't far off the mark. The Chief Inspector went on:

'You generally keep to the roads with your cart, and you don't know the field paths very well. That path through the woods isn't easy to find at any time. The rags were tied on to the bushes to mark the path, and they were rags torn off the stuff which had been given to you. The path marked by the rags leads straight down to the meadows by Jacob's Buttery.'

Gold was sweating freely now, his hands clenching and unclenching, his breathing heavy. Macdonald went on:

'Deceased — the man whose body was found in the river — was seen in the dales at the end of August. He was then fishing without a permit on private water. It is known that he was at one time in Wenningby Barns. He was murdered, and his body was put in a sack and hidden in the river under the roots of the willow tree. Footmarks were observed by a responsible witness in the soft ground by the beck in front of the cottage. These footprints were probably made by a man wearing the big nailed brogues sold to wear over waders.'

Gold burst out into violent speech. 'Tha's saying I murdered him. Why should I ha' murdered him? He was nowt to me.'

Macdonald's voice when he answered seemed all the quieter in contrast to the other's roar.

'I am not accusing you of murder. I am telling you plainly what will be told in court later, and I am giving you the chance to explain the evidence which appears to connect you with the murder. There is one other question which you would be well advised to answer if you are innocent. Why did you take your wife away by that lonely track over the fells? And why was her maiden name found on a paper in the dead man's coat pocket?'

Macdonald sat silent again for a few seconds and then he said: 'You can take your time over answering those questions, Gold — but lies are no good. You've got to make up your mind to tell the truth if you are innocent. I'm not going to press for an answer to those questions now, but there's one point I do want an answer to now. You bought a coat from Anthony Vintner outside the Inn on Monday night. It's fortunate for you that I know how you came by it, for that coat belonged to the man who was murdered. Where is the coat now?'

Reuben Gold's face was a study: his eyes stared, his heavy lips were parted, his cheeks were furrowed.

'T' dirty bastard!' he roared. 'Thissen's his work — that Vintner. Sold me t' coat, did he, a'ter he killed that other. Put it on t' me. Ah'll see he gets what he's earned. Ah'll tell tha, in my own time I'll tell tha!'

'Be careful what you say, Gold. You can be charged as accessory after the fact if you say that you knew who committed a murder.'

'T' hell with tha' and thi lawyers' talk. Ah'll tell in my oon time. Ah've no cause for fear.'

'If you have no cause for fear, you can tell me where to find that coat, Gold. I've been straight with you and I told you that I knew how you came by it. If I had traced it to you without knowing how you got it, it would have gone hard with you.'

Gold studied the other with painful intentness. At last he said: 'Tha was straight ower yon coat. Aye. Ah'll say tha was straight. Yon Vintner sold me t' coat outside t' bar. Said it was his'en, and he wer' broke. Tha'll find yon coat in t' rag shop at Carnton, Bob Traske'll show it tha. As for yon Vintner, it's thi job to get him. Aye, you get him and let me task him. Ah'll mak him crack, aye, in my own time I'll show tha.'

Inspector Bord was surprised that Macdonald took the matter no farther. The Chief Inspector got up and Gold was taken back to his cell.

'Seem's a plain enough case to me, Chief. If Gold didn't do it, he knows who did. You've got on to his trail down to the river valley plain enough. No jury'd be in two minds about a verdict after they'd heard the evidence I heard just now.'

'I don't think they would, if they heard that and nothing else,' agreed Macdonald, 'but I can make out an even plainer case against Anthony Vintner, complete with motive, and a straightforward enough case against Mr. Willoughby of Clunterbeck Cottage in addition.'

'Eh? What's that?' asked Bord, his eyes opening wide.

'Ginner was wanted for stealing clothing coupons and was concerned with some fraud in the wool trade,' said Macdonald. 'Willoughby is the one man in this district who is in the wool trade: he was frequently in the valley, he is an angler and a swimmer — and I found him with Mr. Hoggett's old coat. It's no use, Bord, we're not through yet. We shan't be until I know why Mrs. Gold went and hid in Slaidburn, and what is the connection between Gold and Ginner — because connection there is of some kind. Now I'm off to find Bob Traske. In the meantime, put an extra man on the road beyond Thorpe Intak, and I'll probably put Reeves on duty thereabouts as well. He'll contact your men somewhere, so you'd better tell them he'll be there. The only pity is that we can't let Reuben Gold out to follow his own devices — but I think he'd see through it if we did.'

'Well, you know your own business best,' said Bord, 'but I reckon your Mr. Hoggett was right first guess. He said it was likely the potters — and I still think 'tis likely he's right.'

15

I

Giles Hoggett and John Staple walked together up the hill above Wenningby. It was a beautiful September evening and the sun was warm on their faces as they breasted the rise until they were at the summit and could see westwards, right beyond Lancaster and Morecambe to the glinting waters of the bay; to their right they could see the Lakeland hills, Scafell, the Langdale Pikes, Striding Edge and Helvellyn, blue against the northern sky. Here they paused, in tacit appreciation of that familiar skyline, and at length Staple said:

'Dost reckon it's the potters, Mr. Hoggett? Seems to me they must know more than they should — and that owd chap Bob saw wearing thi coat, why it might ha' been Gold, sure enough. He's rare big shoulders, but he's none so stout about the shanks. Never done any walking whiles he could ride.'

'Aye. I thought of that,' agreed Hoggett, 'but it's hard to say. You passed me on the Chapelton road yesterday, cycling with another chap.'

'Aye, a dark young chap, neat as a bird. Another of these C.I.D. men, eh?'

'That's it. Named Reeves. By the way, Macdonald's found my old coat. At least, Mr. Willoughby found it, and Macdonald came on him with it.'

'Mr. Willoughby? By gum, lad, 'tis wheels within

wheels. Yon Mr. Willoughby, I've not a word to say agin him, but he's in the dales oftener than most. Aye, he's been down fishing after dark, and swimming, too — and he's a sturdy chap for all he's no chicken. I mind I've seen him lifting some rare big branches out o' t' river when the floods have brought stuff down.'

'Aye.' Giles Hoggett sounded glum, because he had always liked the cheerful little Yorkshireman. 'It's a hard nut to crack, Mr. Staple, and all I can do is to try to get the facts straight. About my coat: I put it on Reeves, the other C.I.D. man. You can't imagine how different he looked in it, with George's old tweed cap on his head making him look taller. It's a rum shape, that cap. It's shrunk up until it's conical in shape and makes a man look taller.'

'Aye. I see what you mean — the big coat'd make him look stouter. Well, we'll ask Bob. Bob's got very good eyes, like all these shepherds. He can't see a thing near-to, but at a distance he can see things better than I can — and I've got good eyes for far away.'

They came on Bob Moffat leaning on a gate watching the sheep in one of Staple's pastures. The flock had forgotten their recent troubles and were setting to grazing vigorously, making up for lost time, their backs to the light breeze. Giles Hoggett went and leant against the gate, too.

'They're all right now, Bob. Safe home again.'

'Aye, Mr. 'Oggett. They'll do. None so bad they be this year. I seen worse.'

This was Bob's way of expressing his conviction that the flock was a credit to him, and Staple looked over them, saying:

'Aye. They'll do nicely. You ought to have a few sheep, Mr. Hoggett, they're useful stock, and you've got a bit of rough grazing that's not much use to your cattle. Now see here, Bob. Mr. Hoggett and I, we thought 'twas more likely you'd got a better idea about the chap in Mr. Hoggett's coat than had Mr. Shand. No disrespect meant, Mr. Shand's a townsman before he's a countryman and I'd sooner trust your eyes than his spectacles, Bob.'

'Aye.' Bob spat, strongly, judiciously, and waved a horny fist as he usually did before the effort of formulating a sentence.

''Im? 'E don't even know t' names of 'is own fields. 'E axed me once, tell me t' owd names, 'e said and I towd 'un: Crow Flat, Summer Fold, Whinney Hill, Clerk's Field, New Banks, Ella's Close, Longlands, Fortyfold, Broad Ash, Fat Pig, Lamb's Lot. Could 'e name 'em agen? 'is own fields? Not likely. As for when 'e's doon in t' dales, he does na know thine from hissen. Canna' tell ewes from lambs, stirks fra' heifers, gilts from hogs. Sheep, 'e says. Cows, 'e says, and beasts for 'em all. Aye. 'Im and 'is spectacles.'

Giles Hoggett did not laugh: he listened very intently, because he hoped to repeat this effort verbatim to Kate later. It was seldom that Bob Moffat indulged in speech at such length, and to Giles Hoggett's mind the effort was memorable. Very soon there would be no old men like Bob left to recite the age-old names for the fields.

'Aye, Bob. I like to hear you tell the old names,' said Hoggett, and the old man replied:

'Eh, tha's awreet, Mr. Hoggett. Thi folks lived here, like us. Tha won't forget.'

'Now see here, Bob,' said John Staple. 'You're through for to-day. What about coming down to the river with me and Mr. Hoggett, and telling us just where you saw the owd chap in Mr. Hoggett's coat? Aye, and he'll put the coat on, and maybe I will, and you can tell us just what you think.'

'Ah don't mind if ah do,' rejoined Bob, 'though t'weren't neither of you, that I do know.'

II

The three turned and made their way through the fields until they reached the path through the woods below the Upfields. When they reached the valley flats, Bob took charge and led them to a stretch on the river bank on Garthmere land and turned and pointed upstream.

''Twas there I saw un, close by t'ould willow. Eh, Mr. Hoggett, thi granfer did tend those willows praper like, for baskets: many's the teenel they made from yon willows, but they've been let go and now they're fit for nowt. Aye, 'twas here I saw the owd un, close by yon willow it was.'

It took little persuading to make Bob agree to stay where he was by the river, while Hoggett and Staple hurried back to the cottage and found Reeves, apparently busy loading up the bogie with logs.

'Hi, you can come and help over this,' he called.

'Aye, but first you can help us,' replied Mr. Hoggett. 'We've got old Bob Moffat down by the river, and he saw the chap in my old coat. We want to get an idea of the man he saw.'

'I get you,' replied Reeves. 'You want me to put the coat on and act suspicious-like. Right-o. Here it is . . . If this is what you call a *good* coat, chum, give me utility every time. It weighs a ton to start with . . . and the hat . . . best dustman's model. Got any specs on you? Might as well do the thing in style.'

'I'm afraid I've only got horn-rims, but Mr. Staple might lend you his.'

Mr. Staple was struggling manfully with the mirth that beset him: 'By heck, I wouldn't have believed it,' he said. 'What was't I said? Neat as a bird. Look at him now: He might be old Tim Thorpe over at Highfell. Ninety-two he is. Here's my specs, lad, and no games wi' them, if you please. They do suit me proper . . . I don't like those neat blue trousers of yours with this outfit. Not in the picture like. Leggings he should have. Nay, don't spoil the job by being hasty like. Bob won't mind waiting. Mr. Hoggett, you'll have some old leggings here somewhere?'

'Aye. I won't be a minute. I've got the very thing.'

A moment later Reeves' shanks were being suitably encased, while Staple murmured:

'Spindle-shanks he said. Aye, spindle-shanks. That's true enow. You'll do, lad. Go and do thi part.'

Reeves entered wholeheartedly into the spirit of the game. He walked clumsily out of the garden and made his way towards the river. With every step which took him farther away, Giles Hoggett felt more strongly that it would be impossible ever to swear to the identity of a man in those garments. The figure he saw was no longer Reeves — it was nothing like him. The bulky shapeless coat made him double his own size, the hat concealed his face and altered the character of his head; in short, the figure by the river was unrecognisable.

Staple stood and stared. 'Yon's a rum go,' he said. 'That coat and hat, 'tis champion for a disguise. If so be the villain wore those, reckon nobody could swear to him.'

When Reeves returned, Mr. Hoggett went through the same performance, and finally Mr. Staple went and poked around by the willow tree similarly clad. After this, leaving coat and cap behind, the three men went and joined Bob Moffat.

'Eh . . .' he said, "'twas as good as a play, that was. First, the little chap there. T' coat did reach nigh to's ankles, but I saw his legs when he climbed up a bit to t' bank by t'owd willow. Neat as a donkey's tha legs is, lad — and tha hands right oop t' sleeves, I marked 'un. Then thee, Mr. Hoggett. 'Twas more like, aye, 'twas more like, but tha moved lissom-like, wi' fine long strides, and thi shoulders swung like a man used to hills. Aye, that's it. I seen tha go oop hills easy-like; long strides tha takes, not like Mr. Staple. He's nearer the build, likely, but he sets his feet firm wi' not so much spring. T' chap I saw, he wer stouter and he slipped wi's feet. Not used to muck like.'

'Bravo, Bob! You see a thing or two,' said Mr. Hoggett. 'You're a better detective than I am.'

'Now, Bob. You know the potters — Reuben Gold that comes round with his old nag,' said Staple. 'Could it have been him you saw?'

Bob considered. 'I never saw no beard, but t' chap I saw had collar right oop round 's chin. Gold, he's always in his cart. Ah niver seen 'im step out — but ah reckon 'twas nearer Gold than any of thee. A bit 'unched about the shoulders he were, aye, and stoutish. Ah can't tell for why, that coat's powerful big, but ah did think 'twas a big chap inside un — stout like.'

With that they had to be content, and Mr. Staple and Bob Moffat went home to the comprehensive tea with which the farm world celebrates the end of the main part of the day's toil.

Hoggett and Reeves walked back to the cottage, and Hoggett said: 'What were you doing with the bogie and those logs?'

'Now you're here, I shan't want the logs,' said Reeves. 'You'll do instead. As you probably know, a human body is an awkward thing to lift if you don't know how to do it. I weigh ten stone odd; I guess you weigh nearly thirteen, but probably I could carry you farther than you could carry me because I've been trained to do it.'

Mr. Hoggett looked sceptical; Reeves didn't look much like a weight-lifter — but Hoggett also remembered the ease with which Reeves had reduced him to helplessness in the ju-jitsu demonstration.

'Aye, perhaps you could,' he admitted, and Reeves went on:

'In your original evidence you mentioned the bogie tracks by the small stream there. You saw those tracks after it had been raining for twenty-four hours. Before that the weather had been dry for weeks.'

'Aye. It's like this. The ground as a whole was dry and hard up till September 15th, but the ground by that beck wasn't dry. As the water in the beck fell lower, the ground along its course dried as river silt does dry, going through a stage when it will take an impress and retain it. The tracks I saw were made before the weather broke and had dried hard, so that even after twenty-four hours of rain they were still observable.'

'They had probably been made by a considerable weight. All the same, Hoggett, that bogie's a Heath Robinson contraption — no disrespect meant. I've been trying it out. It's no sense of balance, if you see what I mean.'

'I know,' replied Giles Hoggett. 'I made it myself, long before we lived here. I thought we could haul our suitcases up the brow in one journey. Kate always said it wouldn't work. She was quite right.'

'Well, if you made it, see if you can work it, chum,' replied Reeves cheerfully. 'I'll get in it, so . . . Now you push me as far as the willow trees.'

'I can't,' admitted Giles Hoggett. 'The ground's too soft now; those wheels would sink right in. If the ground were hard I could have done it.'

'Oh, don't give up without trying. The track's fairly hard. Give me a ride as far as the brow.'

With Reeves as cargo, Giles Hoggett manhandled the bogie about fifty yards along the rough path. Then he took an easy and stood panting.

Reeves scrambled out. 'Yes. It sounds easy on paper, but it's not so good in practice. Your turn now; load up.'

With Giles Hoggett's long limbs disposed somehow on the groaning contraption, Reeves set to work to push. He worked manfully, putting his back into it, but the bogie jibbed at a rut and finally capsized, tumbling its burden out.

'That's just what I expected,' said Reeves cheerfully. 'I'm no sort of hand at this here. Stay where you are, chum. I'm going to do a bit of fireman's lift.'

Greatly to Mr. Hoggett's surprise, he found himself draped around Reeves' shoulders while the latter crouched beside him and then the tough little Cockney raised himself until he could walk, and with bent back he carried Hoggett bodily back to the cottage gate, where he released him.

'I bet that's how it was done, chum. He tried the bogie and it worked on level ground, then it capsized.

I tell you one thing — that Vintner lad never did this job. He's not got the physique for it.'

'Do you think two men were involved, one hauling, one pushing?'

'No. If there were two they wouldn't have goated about with that there thing. They'd have lifted between them.' Reeves walked back and collected the despised bogie. 'It's like this. No one with any sense would ever have imagined they could get that thing across to the river with an awkward weight on it. I reckon the chap who did this hadn't much mechanical sense. The fact that you saw the bogie marks proves he tried — but it wouldn't have worked far. Lifting's the only way.'

Mr. Hoggett looked rather depressed. 'We don't seem to have got much further,' he said, but Reeves replied:

'If you knew a little more about our job you wouldn't say that. Here a little and there a little is our motto, and it's quite as important to find out what didn't happen as what did happen. Why, I've sometimes put in a week's hard work and got less out of it than I got out of this evening's little game.'

'Well — I must go and get on with milking,' said Mr. Hoggett. 'My cows will be bawling their heads off.' He paused and then asked: 'Ever milked a cow, Reeves?'

Reeves grinned. 'Never — but I hope to try my hand at it before I leave Lunesdale.'

'Aye. I remember coming across a very good motto once — 'What one fool can do, another fool can do.' I'll go on up now, and I'll ring through to Carnton to leave a message for Macdonald about Profert having seen Gold on the Upfield path.'

'That's right. Good liaison work,' said Reeves.

III

When Macdonald had finished interviewing Gold, he drove back to Wenningby. First he went and saw Giles Hoggett; standing in the shadowy barn, Macdonald leaned on the partition above the shippon, conscious of the pleasant fragrance of hay and cows, and heard an accurate report of the discussion in Richard Blackthorn's fold yard and the subsequent activities by the river. Giles Hoggett was a very good witness on this occasion, using only his excellent memory and not drawing on his intrusive imagination. Macdonald then went down the Brow to the cottage and found Reeves just completing a country tea, in which eggs, tomatoes, honey and rosy apples had all played a part.

Macdonald, aware that he might have a long evening before him, expressed himself in the local idiom: 'Don't mind if I do,' and enjoyed a similar repast. During his meal he exchanged with Reeves all the items of information collected since they had last met. The two detectives examined every shred of evidence, balancing detail against detail. It was a merciless analysis, in which two expert minds built up an edifice of proven fact, side by side with the deductions which could be drawn therefrom. The facts were essential and unalterable, but the deductions, as both knew full well, might have to be modified later.

Finally Macdonald spread out the Ordnance Survey map and saw to it that Reeves was cognisant of the lie of the land around Thorpe Intak. The local men would guard the roads, but it was possible to approach the steading from the rear, and this was to be Reeves' job.

'I may be quite mistaken, in which case you'll only

have the stars for company,' said Macdonald, 'but it's just possible that an effort may be made to throw a spanner in the works. There's more than one adventurer abroad, including the one who removed those orange rags this morning.'

Reeves grinned. 'I get you. I'll do my best, Chief, though the Mile-end Road's more my beat. Still, I've scouted a bit in my time.'

Macdonald chuckled: 'Maybe it is a bit steep to put you on to this, Reeves, but I'd rather have you there than the locals taking it all round. I've a great belief in your survival value, and you're the most suspicious chap I know. Now I'm going over to find Bob Traske at Carnton; if I get through with that fast enough, I'm driving on to Slaidburn. I'll drive back by the road behind Thorpe Intak, and I'll leave the car by the Borwick turning and come down that old bridle-path which is marked here. I shall follow the line of the wall over that rough pasture and then come down by the thorn trees to the beck. I ought to reach the boundary wall there by midnight — but I can't be certain . . .'

'O.K., Chief. I'll wait here until sunset and then go up on that bike to the rear of the premises so to speak . . . Put some of those apples in your pocket. They're champion.'

16

I

It was shortly after seven o'clock that evening that Macdonald reached Bob Traske's 'shop' on the outskirts of Carnton. Traske was another member of the potter's community; he had a cart and a nag, but he also had a store. This latter was a small stone building which had probably been built on farm property long ago. It was now roofed by dilapidated corrugated iron, and various sheds had been put up against it on the lean-to principle. The whole conglomeration of shoddy buildings stood in a yard of which Traske was free-holder, and in this yard were sundry piles of oddments — old metal, old wood, bottles, broken furniture, rags and paper. It was evident that the potters collected what is now called 'salvage' from homesteads too remote for the official salvage collectors.

Macdonald was terse and peremptory with Bob Traske — a dirty fellow of heavy build and uncertain age. The C.I.D. man told his status and business abruptly and stated that he had a search-warrant. The last-mentioned item made a considerable difference to Traske's truculence — it was quite plain that he did not want his premises to be searched. Macdonald told Traske (although certain that he knew already) that Gold had been detained by the police, and then that Gold had stated that he had sold a raincoat to Traske the previous evening. Bob Traske agreed that that was so, and went in search of the raincoat, inviting Macdonald to be seated while the search was made. Macdonald waited, looking around at the miscellaneous junk in the store. By arrangement with Bord, the place was being kept under observation to prevent a get-away, and Macdonald learned later that a boy carrying a sack had been stopped leaving the back of the yard. This sack, filled to the brim with rags and waste paper, was found to contain two dozen eggs, a chicken (plucked) and a salmon. Macdonald left this matter to be dealt with by the Carnton police; what he wanted at the moment was the coat. The latter was produced by Traske — a cheap raincoat bought in Manchester, and in one of its pockets there was still a screwed-up ball of paper.

Macdonald found that he had been right in one of his hunches — when he had argued that Anthony Vintner should have a good visual memory. It was probable that Vintner had studied the scribbled notes eagerly, hoping for information that would be of profit to himself. There were some notes on the paper which probably did deal with card tricks, because the references to certain numbers had roughly scrawled (♥ ♦ ♣ ♠) heart, diamond, club, spade symbols beside them. In addition were the words 'gold, silver, copper' as Vintner had stated, and references to A, B and C, with figures which might have been dates. All the handwriting was illegible to a degree which made it very difficult to decipher, and words and symbols and figures were run together without punctuation and without capital letters. It struck Macdonald that the writer of these notes might have written thus illegibly of intent; there was just enough written down to help a man who could not trust his own memory, but not enough to help any other person to make sense of the scrawl. In addition to the script the paper was heavily scored with 'doodles,' which might have been more interesting to a psychologist than to a detective.

Macdonald, sitting in Giles Hoggett's car, tried to make sense of some of the notes, ignoring those which referred to playing cards. 'goldaptXspt5silverbptoaug31' might be interpreted as Vintner had suggested: 'Gold. A. point X. September 5th' and refer to a meeting with the potters at a prearranged spot. Macdonald wondered if 'point X' could be determined from the 'doodles' at a later date. 'Silver. B. point O. Aug. 31st' seemed a reference of a similar kind. Macdonald felt disposed to believe that his earlier assumption about the potters acting as dispersal agents for Ginner was probably right. Gold himself, plus two associates referred to in the notes as 'Silver and Copper' might well have been commissioned as messengers. Remembering the promptness with which the orange rags had been removed from the woodland path after Gold's arrest, Macdonald had grounds for believing that 'Silver and Copper' were still watching in the locality.

Returning to the study of his scrap of paper, Macdonald concluded that some of the numerals were probably telephone numbers — a matter which could be determined later. Finally were some further hieroglyphics which Vintner had read, quite reasonably, as reminders of card tricks. Macdonald deciphered one line as 'trump card west's hand k5714' and another as 'east's 19k' followed by 'Sx1059.'

Having considered all these scribbles in the light of what he admitted was an imagination akin to Mr. Hoggett's own, Macdonald returned to police headquarters and induced 'Trunks' to connect him with London with quite remarkable promptitude. He then issued certain directions to Inspector Jenkins, C.I.D., and hung up the receiver shortly after 9 o'clock.

Bord was still at the police station, and Macdonald inquired if he would like a drive to Slaidburn.

'What — this evening?' inquired Bord, slightly startled by the Chief Inspector's evident intention of continuing his researches well into the night.

'Aye, this evening,' replied Macdonald. 'From what I've seen, these potters have quite a system of passing on information. Slaidburn's a tidy distance, and I'm hoping to get there before information received causes Mrs. Gold to move on again. We mightn't find it so easy to catch up with her another time. You know her by sight, don't you, Bord?'

'Aye. I can swear to her. I saw her in court when Cobley thought he'd got a plain case and found he hadn't.'

'Right — then off we go. I make it via Hornby and Clapham, and then leave the main road and up over Clapham Moor. That right?'

'That's about it,' agreed Bord. 'I'll just put through a call to the constabulary over there.'

Later, as he and Macdonald set out, Bord said: 'It's a rough road, mind you, and a long pull. The fells on the top of Clapham Moor are on the 1400 feet contour line.'

'There's going to be a good moon, so it ought to be a fine drive,' said Macdonald.

The road to Hornby lay through the farm country Macdonald was beginning to know well; just before Hornby they swung east towards Clapham, slowly mounting from river level. After half an hour's driving they turned right from the main road and began a steep ascent up a secondary road, which soon took them above the last pastures to the open fell. It was dark now, though the sky in front of them was paling towards moonrise, and as they drove Macdonald was aware of the honey-laden scent of heather on the breeze that blew in from the open window. It was a long steep pull and when he reached the summit Macdonald pulled up.

'I'm going to have a look at this — one minute will neither make nor mar us,' he said.

It was a memorable sight on that remote fell-side; the harvest moon, past the full now, was shedding a white light over the rolling moorland, wave beyond wave of heather, bilberry and rough pasture like a sea whitened by the moonlight, with densest shadows etched in the hollows. The stars were brilliant in the cloudless sky, and Macdonald turned to see the Plough in the north-west, the Pole star overhead, and Cassiopeia and Gemini glittering in the north athwart the sky, with Pegasus and Aries to the south. It was moments like that which made up for the more sordid commonplace of detection routine, he meditated, as he got in the driving seat again. It was not given to all men to drive over such a fell-side on a starlit night in the execution of their duty.

Bord was sitting smoking, quite uninterested in the moonlight. 'It's downhill now all the way,' he said. 'One of the local men will be looking out for us at the ford. We don't want to go right into Slaidburn.'

A young constable was waiting for them as Bord had arranged and got into the car to direct them.

'The woman you asked about is staying in a cottage

by Fell Foot Farm,' he said. 'It belongs to a woman named Mrs. Howes — quite a decent body. She's lived there for years and we know nothing against her. There's a lad home on leave from the B.A.O.R. — he only came there to-day. That's the place, along this track away to the right. There's still a light in the kitchen window.'

Macdonald drew the car in to the grass verge and pulled up.

'Stay here and keep your eyes open in case any one tries to get away,' he said to the constable. 'The Inspector and I will go to the house.'

The two men walked quietly up to the cottage; it was a lonely, primitive little building, stone walled with a stone-flagged roof white in the moonlight. Macdonald knocked on the door close by the lighted window and the door was promptly opened while a cheerful voice said:

'Come right in, Stephen lad. Whativer art tha —'

The voice broke off on a note of frightened query, and Macdonald had to hold the door to prevent it being shut in his face.

'Mrs. Howes?' he asked. 'I have come to see Mrs. Gold. I am sorry to come so late in the evening, but I've had a long drive.'

The quiet pleasant voice seemed to reassure the little greyhaired woman at the door, but she still stood firmly by the door.

'What dost tha want?' she demanded. 'Mrs. Gold's my sister and she's none too well.'

'I am afraid I must ask to see her,' persisted Macdonald. 'I am a police officer. Reuben Gold was detained by the police to-day in Carnton.'

A thin voice spoke from the kitchen, bidding 'Lizzie'

to 'let un in.'

Macdonald, with Bord behind him, entered the little lamplit kitchen, and saw a thin, white-haired woman with a frightened face staring up at him. Macdonald remembered that Castleby had mentioned her odd eyes — one blue and one grey.

'Mrs. Gold?'

She nodded and broke out: 'What hast tha done? Reuben's done nowt. Tha's nowt aginst Reuben.'

'I don't want to frighten you, and I'm not asking you to tell me anything which would go against your husband,' rejoined Macdonald. 'No wife can be asked to give evidence against her husband in this country. I want you to answer a question about something which happened a long time ago. I can find out for myself, because all marriage certificates are kept, but if you choose to tell me it will save time and so help the law. I want to know if you were first married in Kendal on the 5th of July, 1914?'

Mrs. Gold stared at him, stared with fear in her eyes, but she refused to answer. Her thin mouth shut in a hard line; she was obstinately silent.

In the distance, somewhere outside in the moonlight, a man's voice was heard singing unmelodiously 'Roll out the barrel.' The sound added to the rigid fear of Mrs. Gold's face, but it seemed to galvanise Mrs. Howes into sudden life.

'That's Stevie. Y'don't want him to hear all this,' she said, and turned to Macdonald. 'Her lad's hoom on leave. Tha's a decent chap; that won't spoil it for him. Coom in here now — Ah'll tell tha what tha wants in two shakes. 'Tis all the same now — but don't tha let Stevie see no p'lice here. Come in t' dairy, do now.'

Bord was again surprised when Macdonald acquiesced and followed Mrs. Howes' urging arm into a little candlelit dairy. Bord followed, and the two big men stood listening.

Mrs. Howes back in the kitchen said:

'Pull thiself together and say good-night to t' lad. He'll be ready for 'is sleep likely. Ah'll see to this here and don't 'e fret luv; 'tis long past now. Here he be.'

They heard the outer door opened and Mrs. Howes saying shrilly: 'Why, Stevie, tha's late, luv. Thi mother's tired like; 'tis a long day. So oop to bed wi' you both — and there'll be eggs for your breakfast coom morning. Up tha goes, lad. I've had enough of t' day and no mistake.'

In the dairy, Macdonald and Bord heard the heavy footsteps mount the shallow stone stairs at the end of the old cottage — Army boots followed by the slip-slap of felt slippers. Mrs. Howes called after them: 'Aye, get in to thi bed and sleep. Ah'll do fine doon here.'

A moment later, the little body opened the dairy door and motioned to Macdonald and Bord to come back into the kitchen. With a finger on her lip she besought them to speak quietly as she whispered:

'Tha'll not spoil his leave now? 'Tis a good lad, and only hoom to-day.' She looked at Macdonald with her bright eyes, a flush on her thin wrinkled cheeks. 'Tha's reet aboot t' marriage. I towd her, they keeps yon registers till doomsday. Tha can't do nowt — but 'twas all that time ago, and if so be she took Sarah's name for t' Government Cards, what matter?'

Bord was puzzled by all this, but Macdonald understood it well enough. He said quietly: 'She used her dead sister's name for her second marriage, and Gold doesn't know about the first marriage?'

Mrs. Howes nodded. ''Tis no use denying a' that. Sarah died in 1916 and Susie took her name an' said none would know — but they keeps those registries, I do know. And see, I had Stevie here since he was a lad, like ma oon he's been and none wiser. Tha'll never goo and tell on that after all this time? Not that's any matter now, wi' Stevie grown and us all gone grey. As for Reuben Gold, I reckon he's done nowt that matters. Not a bad man 'e's been to her, not as men go.'

'And he still doesn't know — about Stevie?'

Mrs. Howes twisted her apron between her fingers:

'A can't tell, not now. She hid it, long eno'. Life was cruel hard to her.'

'The boy's father left her — deserted her?'

'Aye — and her carrying her child, wi' none to help. Not even me she towd till long after. She was afeared of our dad, for he was a hard man and he cast her off. Mebbe he'd reason for anger — but young blood's young blood, an' she toiled right hard for a motherless girl.'

'That was at home, up near Kirkby Stephen?'

'Aye. Tha knows. 'Tis a hard life up yonder. Tha'll not mak trouble for my Susie now, not when she's owd and Stevie a reet good lad?'

'The trouble won't be any of my making, Mrs. Howes. You've done your best for me — and I'll do my best for you.'

'Eh, 'tis t' lad I'm thinkin' on. Ah'd lie right enough for t' lad — but when tha knows, 'tis no use lying.'

She looked at them, her hands folded in her apron, bright eyed and unafraid, and added:

'As for yon Reuben, I don't think all that o' t' potters, but he's not been a bad man to Susie and ah reckon it's not that black what tha has aginst 'im. Will tha go, now? If Stevie came doon, it'd be trouble — and reckon there's trouble enow in t' world without asking for more.'

'Aye, there is,' agreed Macdonald sombrely, and continued: 'Will you promise to try to keep your sister here, in case she's needed? If she runs away, she'd only have the police after her.'

'Mebbe. I tell you straight I can promise nowt — but she won't go away while Stevie's hoom, poor lass.' Arms akimbo she faced Macdonald, independent, fearless. 'Thee men, tha makes trouble enow, tha dost, and 'tis lasses like my Susie bear t' brunt. Ah've no patience with tha, I tell tha straight! Police tha may be, but tha might let ould troubles rest.'

Macdonald found a smile on his face; he liked the gallant little grey-haired woman, fearlessly charging him with trouble-making.

'All right, Mrs. Howes — and thank you for your help. I'll do my best for you — and for your lad. Good-night.'

He turned quietly to the door and Bord followed him without a word.

It was not until they reached the car that Bord burst out: 'Well, I'm damned! She's got a cool cheek, telling us to let old troubles rest.'

Macdonald chuckled. 'I liked her. She's straight and shrewd. She'd got the sense to know it was no use refusing to answer, and I liked the way she turned on us in the end. I could do with a few more women like that. You know I felt more than a bit ashamed of myself, Bord. There's something undignified in two large chaps like you and me setting out to overawe a little old woman like that.'

'If you had some of our routine jobs of keeping even with those same little old women over jobs like pig-killing and disposal of carcases and keeping poultry off the black market, to say nothing of illicit marketing of eggs and butter you might take a different view,' said Bord. 'They'll diddle you every time — and that's a fact. However, the point is — you got what you came for?'

'Aye. I tried out a guess based on a dirty piece of paper I found in the late Ginner's coat pocket,' said Macdonald. 'Here's the paper. Like to try it out yourself — or shall I save you the trouble and tell you?'

'No. By heck you won't,' said Bord. 'If I'm diddled I'll say so, but I'm not giving in without trying.'

They got back in the car and dismissed the attendant constable who would continue to keep an eye on the cottage, and Macdonald turned the car north again to climb the fell road.

Bord lighted his pipe and ruminated. 'It's a case of old sins coming home to roost,' he said, and Macdonald agreed.

'Aye, old sins, coupled to the cupidity of a smart Alec who thought it easy to make money out of his knowledge of them. Ginner took a lot of trouble to avoid bombs, but, for all his smartness, he hadn't enough wits to know that there's other explosive material in the world in addition to what's manufactured for armaments. Tempers up north are said to take more rousing than tempers down south — but when they're roused they're formidable.'

As they mounted the crest of the moor again and saw the vast expanse of heather-covered fell in the moonlight, Macdonald reflected that this untamed moorland had altered little enough in the centuries of man's endeavour — but man himself had altered less than the pundits were wont to claim.

II

It was nearly midnight when Macdonald parted from Bord in Carnton, and the C.I.D. man then set out again driving westward, towards the road which bounded the hills and rough pasture at the back of Thorpe Intak. If Reeves were to have a sleepless night on the chilly hill side, Macdonald was quite game to share it with him. In the Chief Inspector's mind was the thought that Anthony Vintner was given to asking for trouble quite as much as anybody else in the case, because his attitude to other people's problems was the classical reaction of the rogue:

'Anything in this for me?'

Whether Vintner had made his own interpretation of the scrawl he found in Ginner's pocket, Macdonald had no means of knowing at present, but he hazarded a shrewd guess that Vintner had tried to profit by other people's troubles in more ways than one.

Leaving the car safely parked off the road-side, Macdonald set out on foot along a quiet by-road parallel with the Lune. To his right the fields rose gently to the summit of the fells above the valley, to his left the ground fell more steeply and unevenly, the main slope interrupted by hilly ridges with swampy hollows between — this was the poor ground behind Thorpe Intak. Having no depth of soil it had not been worth draining and tilling, and remained — as it was to-day — rough pasture. The road was bordered by low stone walls and to the southwards gave a view right across the valley to the southern fells, but on account of its position on the hill side it also commanded a great expanse of sky. The moon was in the zenith now, shedding a bland white light, and the stars seemed almost to flash in the clear frosty air, some blue, some yellow, some exceedingly white against the void of a dark cloudless sky, with a long train of nebulæ milkily drawn out in faint shining gossamer.

After he had walked some hundred yards, Macdonald stood still and stared and listened. His eyes had accustomed themselves to moon and starlight after having concentrated on the white swathe made by his headlamps as he drove, and his ears caught the sounds of the night. He could smell the soil and with it a fragrance not always analysable, the scent of small herbs in the stubble or pasture, the smell of dung and hay and sometimes the scent of beasts in a walled field. Above all was the tremendous pageant of the heavens . . . 'Canst thou bind the sweet influence of Pleiades or loose the bounds of Orion?' . . . but Orion was still hidden, a constellation of the winter months.

He walked on quietly, looking out for the wall and the row of ancient thorns which marked the bridle-path connecting up this road with the parallel one some half mile below it which ran through to Netherbeck. The track was probably ages old, connecting up with another on the further side of the lower road, but though the paths were marked on the big Ordnance Survey, they had fallen into disuse and only occasional thorn trees marked the path that pack-ponies had once taken down the valley sides.

Climbing a gate whose ancient hinges had long been replaced by twists of rusted wire, Macdonald set out over the rough pasture, downhill at first, and then rising to the ridge above the steading. He moved slowly, pausing to listen and to look around. This was sheep land, and Macdonald knew that it was possible to blunder into a sleeping sheep which would rouse the whole flock with its complaints. As he reached the ridge of the hillock he was able to see right over the intervening land to the steading, and he saw the sheep, too, their fleeces pale, casting black shadows in the moonlight. The thing that interested him was that the flock was on the move; slowly, sleepily, they were coming towards him — an unexpected thing for sheep to do at night. The wind was blowing from the west — from the direction of the sheep to where Macdonald stood — and they had not spotted him yet; they came on slowly, fussily, as though uncertain of what to do. Macdonald guessed that somebody else was over there, across the pasture, standing as he was standing, waiting to hear if the flock would raise their voices. Reeves? Possibly, but he couldn't tell.

A sound suddenly broke the stillness, surprisingly abrupt and loud. An indignant blackbird had woken up and was shouting its alarm call. This decided the sheep; they began to hurry and they came on to within a yard of Macdonald before they were aware of him, and then they broke back, fussily, panicking, as is the nature of sheep. Macdonald promptly sat down and kept very still, anathematising the silly sheep quite unjustly; they might spoil the whole show, he meditated; his show, of course — not the sheep's. After a few minutes, during which the flock fell to grazing on the higher ground, Macdonald moved away from them more to the line of the thorns, and soon found, as he had expected, that he was in the path of a small beck trickling down the slope. Resenting the fact that he had now to squelch through marshy ground, he held on his course until he reached the level and stood on waterlogged ground by the old thorns where he had agreed to meet Reeves.

Reeves, however, was not there and Macdonald stood still and cogitated. Somewhere away to the west on the higher ground above the steading, someone had been moving cautiously. Their movement had been enough to rouse the sheep but not to frighten them into a rush; it had been sufficient to wake a blackbird, and blackbirds commonly roost in shrubs or hedgerows or gorse bushes. Whoever was on the move must thus have traversed part of the grassland where the sheep were resting in a huddled flock and then turned towards the hedgerow or gorse bushes further up the slope. The next thing that Macdonald heard was the rising note of a curlew, and knew that another sentinel had offered him information gratis. The curlew roosts on the ground, preferably on rough grassland — so the other intruder was pretty certainly on the hill side, but not very far away. Standing in the shadow of the thorns, Macdonald could see clearly across the open level ground which lay between him and the low stone wall which divided him from the house. There was nothing in sight, but a moment later he heard a stone dislodged and the sound was clear enough to locate — it came from the stone wall at the back of the house. Macdonald decided to move forward and made his way towards the wall. There was only one door into the house and he decided that he was going to get within sight of that door. He reached the wall without mishap, and crouched beside it to listen, conscious of footsteps beyond.

It was then that the silence was rent by a sound which was almost shattering after the preceding stillness; it startled Macdonald with the sharp impact of the totally unexpected. Just over the wall, the hungry little donkey had scented the presence of one whom its mind connected with fine fat carrots, and it raised its head and hee-hawed with vigour. No one who has not heard a donkey bray at very close quarters in the silence of a moonlit night could realise the weird shrillness and power of that ludicrous sound. Hee-haw! Hee-haw! Hee-haw! she brayed, almost next to Macdonald's ear. The next unexpected sound was that of a human voice.

'Damn you! Shut up!'

It was not only Macdonald who had been startled by the donkey's vocal virtuosity. If the donkey's ears were flapping, so were Macdonald's; it was not Reeves' voice which had thus apostrophised the donkey; neither was it the idiom of the potters. Further than this Macdonald could not decide. Still crouching ludicrously beneath the stone wall, he was aware that the donkey was hopefully nosing in the direction of his own head, but footsteps from the grass-grown yard in front of the house made him realise that someone was on the move there. Feeling strongly akin to Bottom the weaver and using the ass's head as cover, Macdonald raised his head and peered between the long ears of his opposite number and realised with some surprise that a light was still burning in Anthony Vintner's 'studio.' The next moment the unknown in the yard came into collision with an old tin can with an astonishing dividend in the matter of noise. The donkey took to his heels, Belinda bleated querulously, and a moment later the door of the house opened and

Anthony Vintner's voice demanded:

'Who the devil's there and what the hell do you think you're up to?'

His voice indicated that he was well primed with Dutch courage and prepared to have a row with anybody.

The answer came in a quiet propitiatory voice: 'I've brought you that bottle of whisky. I was passing and I saw your light, so I thought I'd come along and leave it. Why the deuce can't you tie that damned donkey up?'

'The donkey's all ri' . . . more sensible than some people I know. Come along in. Got something to show you. Yes. Something to show you.'

The figure close by the house showed in silhouette for a moment against the vaguely lighted door before it entered the house and the door was shut. Macdonald, listening intently, realised with satisfaction that the bolt had not been shot. There was no light in the kitchen either, save that which shone in from the studio door. Anthony Vintner, true to type, had but one lamp and no candles.

Macdonald made short work of climbing the wall, and heard sounds in the paddock beyond which caused his suspicious ears some enquiry before he had analysed the sounds to his satisfaction. The explanation was: (1) Reeves; (2) Donkey; (3) Apples.

Macdonald remembered Reeves' voice saying: 'Put some of those apples in your pocket. They're champion.' Macdonald had done so — and forgotten all about them. Reeves, who claimed later that every Cockney understands donkeys, promptly put his apples to suitable use, thereby giving Macdonald an opportunity to make his way unattended to the kitchen door. He opened the door soundlessly and slipped inside into the stuffy kitchen. The further door was just ajar, allowing a gleam of light to shine in, and Macdonald made his way forward until he was able to see through the wide crack at the hinge into the further room, while he himself remained concealed in the shadows.

Anthony Vintner, swaying a little, was cleaning his palette with a palette knife, working with the clumsiness and absorption of the semi-drunk. His visitor, standing by the table, presented a broad back in silhouette.

Vintner was talking garrulously and persistently. '. . . Tell you I'm fed up. I've had more than enough of this . . . Police all over the bloody place. I didn't want to have anything to do with it, by God, I didn't. 'Snot my fault. I didn't do anything. Serve the dirty dog right — but I'm not going to stay here and be pestered. Got that? . . . Going to clear out. Yes, clear out and start again. I didn't do anything.'

'Have a drink, old chap . . . you'll feel better if you have a drink,' suggested the other.

'Not me . . . Want to make me drunk, do you? I'm damned well not going to get drunk to please *you*. Oh, no. You've made a mistake . . . damn' big mistake, trying to bully me. Won't do. You've got to do what *I* say now. Yes.'

Between his slurred sentences he took strokes with his palette knife, scraping the paint off the palette and then cleaning his knife on the table-top with the solemnity of a drunken man.

'What do you want *me* to do?' enquired the other wearily. 'You said you wanted a bottle of Scotch — well, there it is.'

'Yes. Think that's enough, do you? I don't. You're going to get me out of this. In your car. Police won't stop your car. Oh, no. Police friends of yours. I know. You talked to them in that cottage . . . said I was a bad lot, I know. You poor flat, you're kippered. D'you know that? Kippered.'

'No. I don't know it. You're drunk, man. You're pretending to be important.'

'Pretending, am I? See that envelope? The letter's not inside it any longer. Oh, no. I'm not that drunk. Letter's quite safe. Ginner left his coat here. He must have written you that letter before he was bumped off. He left it. I read it. Got that?'

Still with the same automatic action the painter went on cleaning his palette, while the man in front of him breathed slowly, heavily.

Vintner went on obstinately: 'You're going to get me out of this — to-night. To-morrow won't do. If I'm here to-morrow I'm going to show the police that letter. It's no use killing me — if you do, they'll still get that letter. I thought of that. You're going to get me out of this to-night. I'm fed up.'

'Look here, Vintner, don't be unreasonable. I can't take you anywhere to-night. The police are patrolling all the roads. If you move to-night, you're done for. I'll do my best — obviously I'll do my best — but not to-night. If you're caught bolting to-night you'll be arrested — and once you're arrested you'll have a precious poor chance. Be a sensible fellow and sleep for a bit. I'll stay here with you — come along, have a drink and be sensible.'

There was the sound of a cork being drawn from the whisky bottle and the gurgle of the spirit pouring into the glass. Macdonald still watched and waited.

Vintner suddenly threw his palette down and slumped into a chair and fell to whimpering.

'It's not fair. Always the same. I came here and I tried. God knows, I tried . . . then that beast came and pestered me. Said he'd tell everyone and get me discredited . . . He'd got an I O U of mine and I'd promised to help his beastly swindles. Why couldn't he leave things alone?'

'Why couldn't he leave things alone? Dear God, haven't I asked that? Just leave things alone . . . that was all.' The words burst from the other man as though he couldn't contain them. 'You're complaining . . . That's all you're capable of. Complaining. I stopped his damned blackmail — stopped it once and for all. Pull yourself together, Vintner. You're shaking, man. Have a drink and forget it. I'll get you away to-morrow. I'm a man of my word. He found that out . . . too late. Drink up and forget it!'

The glass was in Vintner's hand before Macdonald moved and opened the door. He took one of the apples from his pocket and threw it, good and true, so that the apple knocked the glass clean out of Vintner's hand. The painter screamed, and as he screamed Macdonald sprang forward and snatched the whisky bottle away from the other man's outstretched hand. With a crash the table went over, the lamp with it, and the report of a pistol barked out. Then came the heavy thud of a falling body as Macdonald snatched the flaming lamp up and flung it out of the window. Reeves' voice called, 'You all right, Chief?' as he bent to smother the burning oil on the floor, and all the time Anthony Vintner went on screaming: 'There wasn't a letter! I tell you there wasn't a letter. Shand believed it all, but there wasn't a letter.'

Reeves took the painter by the shoulders and shook him until his teeth chattered. 'That's enough from you. Be quiet, or I'll shake the teeth out of your head.'

Macdonald, torch lamp in hand, was examining the body on the floor.

'Done the job properly, hasn't he?' enquired Reeves, and Macdonald nodded.

'Yes — right through his brain.'

'Saved the hangman a job — and a good thing too,' said Reeves, while Vintner went on sobbing to himself:

'Shand believed there was a letter, but there wasn't. There never was a letter. I tried it on and he believed it, but there wasn't a letter.'

Reeves suddenly sniffed: 'Potassium cyanide, Chief. I swear I can smell it.'

'Aye, it's in the whisky — for Vintner,' said Macdonald.

'Was that the way of it? Suicide and a forged confession,' said Reeves. 'Well — it's been tried before and doubtless it'll be tried again. They're all optimists.'

And still Vintner whimpered his one refrain: 'You see there never was a letter.'

17

I

It was nearly a fortnight later that Macdonald spent a night at Netherbeck Farm. He had attended the inquest and later the adjourned inquest, where full chapter and verse had been produced to put the verdict beyond doubt. The bodies of Gordon Ginner and Barton Shand had both been buried, and the Lunesdale farmers were busy ploughing. The life of the land was incomparably more important than the deaths of two men who had never realised that man still lives by the land and that its tilling is more fundamental to human needs than the accumulation of money.

The quartet sitting around the good wood fire at Netherbeck was made up of Giles Hoggett and his wife, the imperturbable Dr. Castleby (Macdonald was always to remember him as 'George'), and the Chief Inspector himself. They had just had supper and enjoyed some sea trout which George and Giles had caught with worm, for the river had been up again and made 'a big water.' Now they were waiting to hear Macdonald tell them just how useful their mutual efforts at detection had been.

'You know you had all the data between you,' began Macdonald. 'Speaking as a detective, I have never been so spoon-fed in my life. It is your due that I should acknowledge, here and now, that you are all three first-class witnesses, having accurate memories, a power of detailed observation and a gift of narrative which I have seldom found equalled in the sophisticated south.'

Giles smiled happily; George accepted the bouquet with urbanity; but Mrs. Hoggett spoke trenchantly.

'Yes. We had all the facts and we couldn't make anything of them. We're *not* detectives, none of us. George states his facts and leaves it at that. Giles sees a certain number of things and then uses his imagination to account for them. I notice things accurately — but I'm stumped when it comes to putting the bits of the jig-saw together.'

'Well, let's go back to Hoggett's grand effort at reconstruction,' said Macdonald. 'It was almost classic in style — I've noted it down verbatim, and I shall preserve it as a model of its kind. 'We are considering the death of a man who was murdered in this valley. So far as the evidence goes, he was a stranger here: a man concerned with certain frauds in the industrial Midlands, yet the evidence shows that he met his death at the hands of someone who knew the conditions of this valley and could utilise that knowledge. At the same time the murderer was lacking in a sense of detail and of real understanding of the inhabitants, for it did not occur to him that any intelligent construction would be put on the theft of various trivial objects from the cottage.''

'Yes. I applauded that at the time,' murmured George, and Giles said:

'I see now . . . I was really saying that the murderer was someone who believed that I, personally, was a fool of a farmer.'

'Aye, that's about it,' said Macdonald cheerfully. 'Now let us consider Mrs. Hoggett's contribution, which is more detailed and shows considerable powers of inductive reasoning. She said: 'Have you realised what was the murderer's initial mistake? The thing which really gave him away was interfering with Giles's wood-pile and leaving the logs tumbled about. If it hadn't been for that, Giles would never have gone inside the cottage that day, or even if he had he probably wouldn't have noticed that anything was missing, because he wouldn't have been feeling suspicious. The man who stole the chain and iron dogs was *not* a careless person; he had swept the floor and cleared the hearth, but he didn't know how to clear hearths properly. Finally, he was the sort of person who did not know that small valueless articles would be missed' — and that,' added Macdonald, 'took us a good step further along what we might call the 'general enunciation.' '

'It took you,' murmured Mrs. Hoggett to her knitting. 'It didn't take us.'

'Well, for the Good Lord's sake, allow me some results from nigh on thirty years' concentration on reading evidence,' said Macdonald. 'You can do a lot of things I can't, Mrs. Hoggett, and I don't complain. Every man to his own last. Now let's get on a bit. I judged that I was safe in an original assumption that the murderer was *not* 'a scoundrel from the slums of an industrial city,' as Hoggett's wishful thinking made him conclude. The murderer was much too good at utilising certain features of Wenningby Barns and its surroundings to be a slum product. He knew, for one thing, where to replace the key of the cottage. He knew all about Jacob's Buttery and the recess in the bank and the willow roots; he knew all about the power of the stream and used chains to make the sack fast. He knew how strong salmon line is — though it doesn't look it. No. Not a slum-dweller — *but* a man who regarded the cherished chimney fittings at Wenningby Barns as so much junk; also a man who didn't consider that the person who carried those iron dogs down the brow would value them.'

'Oh, come; he couldn't have *known* I carried them down,' put in Giles.

Macdonald considered. 'I may be being irrelevant, but as a Londoner I'd like to claim the privileges of that status,' he said. 'We have a museum, called the Victoria and Albert. It contains, among many other relics, a completely furnished cottage chimney, with chains and cranes and other adjuncts. I, who have studied it, know that those iron dogs were no part of the original equipment. Any farm or cottage dweller hereabouts would know it, too. Those iron dogs were a personal touch, Hoggett — but they conveyed nothing to one who was unfamiliar with the equipment of an ancient open chimney.'

'Yes,' murmured George to the fire. 'It's a nice point.'

'Having considered the character of the unknown murderer to some extent,' went on Macdonald, 'let us note a few points about the dead man, Ginner. He may have had his good points, but they were not obtrusive. I knew he was a swindler so far as the law was concerned, and I had good reason for believing that he was a swindler in a viler sense — that of obtaining money from elderly women by promising to marry them, but Ginner was not a rogue who used violence; he was one that lived by his wits. Reeves found plenty of evidence that Ginner was a coward, because he ran away from London Civil Defence duties when the bombing began. In other words, Ginner sought profit without the element of personal danger — he was a trickster and confidence man. Now, I have frequently found that that is the type who tries blackmail, and it's worth remembering that a man who is being blackmailed has been known to commit murder to rid himself of his tormentor and the fear of exposure.'

'And that was why George's story of Mrs. Gold's son interested you,' murmured Giles, but Kate put in:

'You're jumping at conclusions. What I want to know is the process of detection in detail, step by step.'

'I'm afraid that it doesn't always work out like that, Mrs. Hoggett,' rejoined Macdonald. 'I try to emulate scientific method. In actual fact I often resemble one of the less methodical birds — say, a starling — who hops about picking up other birds' food and imitating their voices. In a narrative like this, I tend to make the detective method much more orderly than it is in actual fact, because I omit the irrelevant and the unsuccessful gropings. Your husband is quite right in saying that I seized on Dr. Castleby's story with avidity — and that brings us to the potters.'

'Aye, the potters,' said George. 'I never believed that Gold was the murderer — but I couldn't produce any sound reasons for my conviction.'

'Nevertheless, he was such an A 1 suspect he had to be taken seriously,' said Macdonald. 'Points against him: the famous orange curtains, the mention of a 'pottery' and a row in the lorry driver's evidence, the fact of his mobility, and the fact that his wife, who had accompanied him for years, had disappeared. Queries: Could Gold, who had never been seen in the valley, know 'the usual place' where the cottage key was kept? Would he have disturbed a good wood-pile by inexpertly taking logs from the middle instead of from the top? Could he swim? Finally, could he cast a fly, as the old man in the coat was said to have done? In my own judgement, men of the nomad type have their own sort of cunning, but they always use it in their own environment. Unlike Dr. Castleby, I was quite willing to believe that Gold was capable of a crime of violence, but if he had committed one I believed it would have been 'on his own beat,' somewhere on the lonely fell-side where a man's body might be hidden with a minimum of trouble. The river valley is alien territory to Gold, and the river, not an ally, but a fearsome enemy.'

He turned to Giles Hoggett. 'You gave me a very interesting exposition concerning the potters, and you said, 'They each have their own territory which they work on their own like robins, keeping others off it.''

'Aye,' said Giles. 'So I did. I'd no idea I'd been so useful.'

Mrs. Hoggett's exclamation was as near a snort as made no difference.

'Sorry,' shc said apologetically, 'but that's just like Giles and his philosophy. He *does* know things — and that's all there is to it. Wouldn't you like a cup of tea, Mr. Macdonald? I'm sure you need one. I think your patience with us is the most remarkable thing about you.'

'Thank you very much, I should,' replied Macdonald, 'but don't think I undervalue your husband's assistance. He practically solved this case for me and Reeves — but he didn't realise that he'd done so.'

II

Kate brought the tea tray in, and George quelled his low-toned mirth as Macdonald continued:

'Next, there was Vintner. Here was an able artist but a man who had no stability of character at all. He had a motive to commit the murder, because he feared and hated Ginner. He had the necessary knowledge of the locality and he was a good swimmer. Nevertheless, I didn't believe he'd done it for the very reasons Mrs. Hoggett adduced—he is chronically untidy and unmethodical and he hasn't the determination to carry anything through. At the same time, I did believe that if he were arrested and charged he would certainly have been found guilty. The evidence was all circumstantial, but the circumstances were dead against him. That sort of bloke,' added Macdonald meditatively, as he sipped his tea, 'is an absolute menace to a detective. He simply asks to be arrested, and the very fact that he lies, feebly and unconvincingly, annoys one enough to go against one's better judgment and arrest him. My favourite nightmare is that I shall one day produce convincing chapter and verse to charge a man like Anthony Vintner, and that I shall be unable to prove he's innocent before he gets himself hanged.'

George grunted in acquiescence. 'I follow that,' he said. 'My own nightmare is that I shall disregard the moans of an old chronic and that he will die on me before I realise he's really in danger.'

'You're neither of you in the least likely to do anything of the kind,' said Mrs. Hoggett firmly. 'You both of you suffer from excess of conscience, not lack of it. But it's quite true,' she added, turning to Macdonald, 'that I was glad you looked obstinate. Obstinacy is a valuable quality in intelligent people.'

'Aye,' murmured Giles. 'That is. I'll remember that. Go on, Macdonald. What about little Mr. Willoughby?'

'Yes. Mr. Willoughby. He was a fine suspect. He'd got almost every qualification, I found him in *flagrente dilectu* with your old coat, Hoggett, *and* he was in the wool trade. Aye, he was a grand red herring. You see, if he was speaking the truth, he gave me the case complete, but I'd no means of knowing if he were speaking the truth. He told me about how he went on the shilla bed and *saw* Shand, when Shand didn't see him, *and* he saw the man in Hoggett's old coat that very same evening, having seen two men, whom I took to be Vintner and Ginner, the evening before. And the date he gave, quite positively, was the first week in September when Shand claimed he was away in Derbyshire.'

Macdonald paused, and then added: 'That brings us down to brass tacks. The most damning evidence Shand gave against himself was when he told Hoggett in the fold-yard that he (Shand) had seen the old man in the preposterous coat. He said it was before the weather broke, and that he'd been away all the first week in September. Blackthorn reminded him he'd been away for the last four days in August, and Shand agreed and said it was a couple of days before that he saw the old coat — that is, on August 26th.'

There was silence, and Giles Hoggett said: 'Well, why not? He could have —'

'He couldn't!' cried Mrs. Hoggett victoriously. 'At *last* I've seen something for myself. George and the children were staying at the cottage then and the coat was there all the time they were. *No one* could have taken the coat while the children were there, because they'd have noticed if it had gone.'

'Aye. So they would,' agreed Giles amiably. 'Very bright of you, Kate. But you *are* bright,' he added proudly.

III

'Well, having acknowledged in full my debt to the Hoggett-Castleby contingent, I had better put in a word for C.I.D. routine work,' said Macdonald. 'We're a very industrious organisation — Mrs. Hoggett would approve of us in that way. We collected chapter and verse about Ginner and his early life, which led to the successful work done by Reeves and Hoggett in Chapelton-Lonsdale. We learnt that Ginner was probably familiar with the Kendal-Appleby-Chapelton-Lonsdale area, and later we used our searchers in Somerset House to complete the case. Meantime, I followed the trail of the orange rags and proved to my own satisfaction that Gold had something to hide. I felt pretty certain that Gold had acted as go-between for Ginner in communicating with his friends, and that the trail of rags was to guide Ginner to a meeting-place in the dales. Finally came the unexpected incident about Vintner finding Ginner's coat and the paper in the pocket. The chief item on that paper was a scrawl which Vintner interpreted as: 'West's hand. K.5.7.1.4,' preceded by the words 'trump card.' As you can see, there are no capital letters and no stops, the words and numerals being run together. I read it as 'West. Shand. K.5.1.14.' For the K I hazarded Kendal, because I knew Ginner had known the place. It thus read: 'Trump Card. West. Shand. Kendal 5.7.14' — and when I learnt that Mrs. Gold's maiden name had been West I believed I had interpreted Gordon Ginner's trump card. If he *knew* that Shand had married Sarah West on July 5, 1914, and that both parties to the marriage were still alive but married bigamously, it accounted for Shand losing his temper and killing a rogue who was trying to blackmail him, and for Mrs. Gold going into hiding with her sister at Slaidburn.'

'It sounds quite simple when you relate it,' said Giles Hoggett. 'If I'd been more careful I might have thought it out for myself . . . No — I shouldn't have . . . I haven't the application to detail. My routine work is very poor.'

'Your routine work is very good,' said Macdonald, 'but you haven't learnt to co-ordinate your facts yet. Now let us consider all the facts I had gathered about Shand. First, Hoggett met Shand coming up from the dales early on the first day the floods were out. Shand was a fly purist in the matter of fishing, I gather. What Hoggett calls a 'gentlemanly fisherman' — yet there he was, out with his gear, on a day when no trout would notice a fly and the water was too high to cast one. What had he been doing? Inspecting something? I didn't know, neither did Hoggett. Next, Shand came and visited Hoggett at the cottage that evening. One thing was evident — he thought Hoggett was a simple soul who could be instructed and condescended to. Having a suspicious mind I watched him carefully as he thumbed those books. Shand knew that the thefts had been reported to the police, and he knew that even in rural areas the police take fingerprints. Was he supplying an obvious explanation for the presence of his own fingerprints, supposing he *had* been in the cottage on other than lawful occasions? It was a possibility.'

'But you said that nearly all the surfaces in the cottage had been wiped clean of prints,' put in Giles Hoggett, and Kate said:

'Haven't you ever said to yourself: 'Did I really do everything I meant to do before I came away? Did I put out that last cigarette, and lock the windows and lift things off the floor in case of floods?' How often have I gone back again to the cottage to make certain? I can quite see a man saying: 'Did I really rub all my fingerprints off?' '

Macdonald nodded. 'That's the idea. So many men have given themselves away because their nerves gave them no peace until they had gone back to make sure. However, that was only surmise. What was more certain was Shand's insistence that the potters were innocent of the thefts — an odd attitude for a landowner. Why did he want to protect the potters? I hazarded an answer to that when I heard Dr. Castleby's evidence about Mrs. Gold's first marriage. It was sheer guess-work, but I felt that something was needed to account for Shand's championship of the potters. Next, Shand's attitude to Vintner — and there I felt I was on to something. Hoggett, if you wanted to evict an undesirable tenant who doesn't pay his rent, what would you do about it?'

'Put it in the hands of my solicitor,' replied Giles. 'The process of the law is quite straightforward and well known to every landlord.'

'Yes, but I found that Shand, who was a very '*de-haut-en-bas*' type, going to call on Vintner personally to argue with him about evicting him, even preparing to offer to forgo arrears of rent; and Vintner saying that Shand *bullied* him. It all seemed a bit odd to me. Since Vintner had neither paid his rent nor kept his land in order, the matter of eviction was simple, yet here was an intolerant landlord like Shand havering over it. It looked to me as though Vintner had some leverage, some knowledge, which enabled him to sound so certain when he told me that Shand couldn't turn him out because of 'rent restriction'—which was pure rubbish. Well, there it was. Ginner had stayed with Vintner and Vintner seemed to have some sort of hold over Shand, and Shand was busy telling people that Vintner was a rogue. It was plain to any intelligent person that Vintner was an ideal scapegoat. That's why I had the approach to his house watched so carefully. Whoever the murderer happened to be (and I didn't believe it was Vintner) it would be a most satisfactory solution if Vintner committed suicide and left some drunken scrawl acknowledging his guilt.'

'I don't follow one point here,' put in Giles. 'How was it that if Shand felt that Vintner had a hold over him Shand risked accusing Vintner of the thefts when we were talking in the cottage?'

'You must remember that that was before the body was found,' said Macdonald. 'Shand had every reason to believe the body would not be found, and at that time he did not know Scotland Yard was after Ginner. Shand's feeling was that he had successfully disposed of Ginner, and the sooner Vintner was discredited and cleared out the better. I argued that Shand wanted Vintner to be under suspicion in case any enquiry ever arose about Ginner—and having taken up his stand by accusing Vintner, Shand thought it wiser to be consistent.'

IV

'Well, that's a rough outline of my own gropings towards a reconstruction,' said Macdonald. 'The end came while the case was still thoroughly untidy, but Shand made a desperate bid to straighten things out. He was in a miserable position, poor wretch. He had killed a blackmailer and thought he had been successful. Then, because of Hoggett's persistence, Scotland Yard heard of the iron dogs and came and found the body. Shand made another mistake there. He let me know that he had been out on the fell-side watching at eight o'clock on a Sunday morning. He must have used binoculars to see all that he did from that distance — again, a bit odd. Next, Vintner let Shand know that he (Vintner) knew there was some connection between him and Ginner. Vintner is cunning enough. He thought out the idea of pretending he had found a letter from Ginner involving Shand. The only surprising thing to me is that Vintner hasn't got himself murdered long ago for his beastly tricks.'

'I hope he doesn't get murdered in Lunesdale,' said Mrs. Hoggett hastily, and Macdonald replied:

'I can assure you he won't have any opportunity of doing that for a long time to come. He suppressed evidence which he ought to have given, and his last *tour de force* ensured him a reasonable retirement at His Majesty's expense. Now for the final exposition, which includes ascertained facts obtained from Gold, Vintner, Mrs. Gold, Mrs. Soper, and last, but not least, Somerset House.

'Gordon Ginner, when a boy of 15, saw a married pair leaving a Registry Office in Kendal and learned their names out of curiosity, because they looked an odd pair to him. Young Shand, then a lad of no fortune, married Susie West and later deserted her. Some years later, Susie married Reuben Gold, using the name of her dead sister, Sarah West. Susie also sent home a report of her own death, so that when Shand made guarded enquiries he learnt that the girl he had married was dead, and he also married again, being now a prosperous manufacturer. There it might all have rested had not Gordon Ginner, with an uncannily good memory, seen Mrs. Gold at a café by the road-side and by some freak recognised her — and said so. I think the thing which caused him to recognise her is that she has one blue eye and one grey. Then, in August of this year, Ginner came up here to hide and stayed with Vintner and heard about and saw Barton Shand. Then the stage was set. Ginner attempted blackmail, and at the same time busied himself in getting into touch with his swindling associates through the medium of Gold, whom he bribed. When Mrs. Gold saw Ginner again, she persuaded her husband to take her to her sister's in Slaidburn.

'Ginner certainly used the cottage, obtaining information about it from Vintner, who *knew* that Ginner had met Shand there. The rest can be argued from the evidence you know; Shand killed Ginner and hid his body in Jacob's Buttery, trying to use the bogie to transport the body, and finding, as Reeves did, that it was impracticable. Shand made a good many mistakes, none of which would have mattered had his original argument held good — that the body would never be found. After he abandoned the bogie, he left it in the dales, because he forgot it. Gold saw him move it later — and Gold guessed for himself, when he had time to think it over, that it was Shand who stole the waders and the brogues, in order that his own footprints should not be identified, and it was Shand who hid the waders under the wall of Middle Upfield.'

'And it was Mr. Shand who wore my coat,' said Giles, as though that were the most surprising point of all.

'Aye. It was a good idea, mark you. Shand didn't want to be seen on Mr. Hoggett's land, nor yet by Jacob's Buttery, and the disguise was a good one. No one recognised him, though he was seen by a variety of people, and he was enabled to spy out the land and make his plans.'

Mrs. Hoggett sat forward, her elbows on her knees, chin in hands, brooding.

'The most interesting part of it all is that the evidence gave a clear idea of the type of man the murderer must be — and yet we never saw it. We practically told Mr. Macdonald that the murderer was fairly prosperous, that he wasn't used to manual work, that he knew Lunesdale but was not of Lunesdale, that he was careful but slipped up because he didn't know our ways — and even then, we never spotted it.'

'There are two reasons for that,' replied Macdonald. 'One is lack of training in reading evidence. It seems so easy, but it's really an expert job. The other is this: when a person is part of a familiar world, you just accept that person. Mr. Shand? Oh, yes, you laughed at him a little because he was pompous and self-opinionated and thought he was so much superior to the farmer. Hoggett said: 'He's not a bad landlord. I've known worse' — a sort of 'irritated toleration,' to use his own phrase. But someone 'from away,' like myself, sees you all in fresh perspective.'

'I shall put those iron dogs back in the river,' said Giles Hoggett meditatively, and Macdonald put in:

'Then may I send you some more — proper iron dogs such as there are in that chimney at the V and A? It'd be good for you to accept something which came from a London junk shop and yet belonged in the cottage.'

'Thank you very much,' said Mrs. Hoggett. 'We should like you to have them.'

'And what can we give you in return?' asked Giles. 'We should like you to have something to remember us by.'

'I don't think I'm likely to forget you, Hoggett, but since you've made such a kind offer, in addition to all your noble hospitality, would you give me that little English grammar in the Latin tongue which belonged to your grandfather Ramsden?'

'It's here, Macdonald. I've brought it for you,' said Hoggett. 'You see, I saw the way you looked at it and held it, and I was a bookseller once, before I turned farmer.'

Macdonald took the shabby little leather-bound book in his hands and rubbed his fingers appreciatively along the raised sewing bands at the back.

'Thank you, Hoggett. I didn't know my covetousness had shown in my face, but your routine work then, as ever, was excellent.'

Other titles published by Ulverscroft:

MURDER IN THE MILL-RACE

E.C.R. Lorac

When Dr. Raymond Ferens moves to a practice at Milham in the Moor in north Devon, he and his wife Anne are enchanted with the beautiful hill-top village lying so close to moor and sky. At first they see only its charm, but soon they begin to uncover its secrets — envy, hatred and malice.

Everyone says that Sister Monica, warden of the local children's home, is a saint — but is she? A few months after the Ferens' arrival, her body is found drowned in the mill-race. Chief Inspector Macdonald faces one of his most difficult cases in a village determined not to betray its dark secrets to a stranger.

FIRE IN THE THATCH

E.C.R. Lorac

The Second World War is drawing to a close. Nicholas Vaughan, invalided out of the Royal Navy, takes refuge in Devon, renting Little Thatch in the beautiful countryside at Mallory Fitzjohn. Hard work and rural peace make it a happy bachelor life for him.

At Manor Thatch lives the bored, flirtatious June St Cyres, an exile from London, staying with her father-in-law while her husband Denis is being held prisoner in Burma. She resents the fact that Vaughan was granted the tenancy of Little Thatch over her friend Tommy Gressingham, an entrepreneur whose ambition is to build a country club in the area.

When Little Thatch is destroyed in a blaze, all Vaughan's work goes up in smoke — and Chief Inspector Macdonald is drafted in to uncover a motive for murder . . .

BATS IN THE BELFRY

E.C.R. Lorac

Bruce Attleton dazzled London's literary scene with his first two novels, but his early promise did not bear fruit. His wife Sybilla is a glittering actress, unforgiving of Bruce's failure, and the couple lead separate lives in their house at Regent's Park. When Bruce is called away on a sudden trip to Paris, he vanishes completely — until his suitcase and passport are found in a sinister artist's studio, the Belfry, in a crumbling house in Notting Hill. Now Chief Inspector Macdonald must uncover Bruce's secrets . . .